'I am used to having people speak of me,' she said. **'They must speak of someone, so why not me? I have laughed the loudest. Life is a grand jest.'**

Then she reached up, pushing an escaped curl towards her bun but feeling the wisp spring back into place.

'Perhaps.' He stepped forward and with his left hand captured the curl. His fingers brushed her skin as he slipped the errant lock behind her ear. 'But, Lady Riverton, there is more to you than words in a scandal sheet.'

She put her hand on his sleeve. 'You don't understand the vipers of the world. They wish to bite, not cuddle. I cannot turn them into lambs.'

'No…'

His voice quietened, but it didn't lose the rumble, the masculine richness that pulled her like a vine twining towards the sun.

'I can help you, though. We can create a new world around you. One in which you glitter as you should. This blunder tonight could be fortunate. It can be the moment you begin painting the world around you in the colours you wish.'

'You are daft. No one has a brush that can do as you suggest.'

'What is the harm in trying?'

Author Note

Hand me a romance novel with a tortured hero, brooding in his mansion, rescued from his solitude by the love of a beautiful woman, and I'm hooked. But I wanted to add a different perspective to the old tale of a beauty and her brutish hero. I thought of a heroine wanting to hide in her art studio, and a hero hoping to rescue her from her scandals.

After viewing James Gillray's caricatures, and some of the less acceptable drawings his contemporaries created, I realised that an unfavourable portrait circulating in the early 1800s in London might have been similar in consequence for the subject as having a picture posted on the internet would be today. The term 'scandal sheet' is relatively modern, but I wanted to use it as a vehicle to illustrate the concept of news travelling fast.

With that in mind, Beatrice and Andrew's story began—and I embraced writing it. I hope the characters curl into your heart as they did mine.

THE NOTORIOUS COUNTESS

Liz Tyner

First published in Great Britain 2016
By Mills & Boon, an imprint of HarperCollins*Publishers*
1 London Bridge Street, London, SE1 9GF

Large Print edition 2016

© 2016 Elizabeth Tyner

ISBN: 978-0-263-26301-5

Our policy is to use papers that are natural, renewable and recyclable
products and made from wood grown in sustainable forests.
The logging and manufacturing processes conform to the legal
environmental regulations of the country of origin.

Printed and bound in Great Britain
by CPI Antony Rowe, Chippenham, Wiltshire

34759204

Liz Tyner lives with her husband on an Oklahoma acreage she imagines is similar to the ones in the children's book *Where the Wild Things Are*. Her lifestyle is a blend of old and new, and is sometimes comparable to the way people lived long ago. Liz is a member of various writing groups and has been writing since childhood. For more about her visit liztyner.com.

Books by Liz Tyner

Mills & Boon Historical Romance

English Rogues and Grecian Goddesses

Safe in the Earl's Arms
A Captain and a Rogue
Forbidden to the Duke

Stand-Alone Novel

The Notorious Countess

Visit the Author Profile page
at millsandboon.co.uk.

Chapter One

Andrew Robson felt a burning urge to smash in his cousin Foxworthy's nose. One more story about Lady So-and-So's eyes or Lady This-and-That's breasts or Lady Whoever's whatever and he would punch Fox right in that ugly face of his that women swooned over.

Brandy in hand, Fox leaned sideways, catching his balance to keep from falling off the desk. 'You're a virgin.' He sloshed liquid on his frock coat, but it hardly showed against the dark wool.

Andrew gripped the ledger. If it had been any other book, Fox would have felt the weight of the volume right between the eyes. 'My life is not your concern.'

'How many times have I invited you along on my encounters and you have declined?' Fox finished his brandy and then stared at the empty glass, yawning. 'I'm thirsty,' he grumbled, and reached for the pull to summon a servant. He missed and almost lost his balance again.

'Reach the decanter yourself,' Andrew snapped.

Fox yawned, refilled his glass and pinned a glance on Andrew. 'Who have you done?'

Andrew picked up his brandy, swirled the liquid and downed it. 'A gentleman doesn't speak of such things to another man.'

'Neither does a virgin. And I've told you of every skirt I've lifted since I discovered what I had behind my buttons.'

'I suppose less than half of those tales are true and less than half of those occurred as you recounted them.'

Fox grimaced, patting the stopper on the decanter. 'I do not do numbers, my friend. Quality—not quantity—always my rule.' Fox frowned. 'You're my cousin. My blood. And you've no notion of the true pleasures of life. You stand there so—' He twirled his finger. 'Sombre, dressed like a man in mourning… Or dressed like the man already buried. And you've reason to look grim, I suppose. No woman to put a smile on your face.'

'I have to hide you from enough husbands and beaus that I don't relish doing it for myself.' That was the only thing he truly hated about Fox. His cousin did not understand how his actions could affect others.

'I told you,' Fox murmured. 'They jump to conclusions. Because I am such a stallion, a man cannot bear to see me even talking with his wife without assuming I have ulterior motives.'

'You do.'

'But you do not. You ever tup that Hannah woman you spoke so poetic about?'

'Most certainly not. She was quality. An innocent. One does not despoil innocents.'

'She wasn't when she was in my bed last summer.'

Fury pumped into Andrew's body. 'You did not defile Hannah.' He slapped a palm on to the book on his desk. 'Even you could not have taken an innocent.'

Fox shrugged and held up the glass. 'We were in love. You should try it.' He gave the lopsided grin which made skirts flutter. 'You'd be a lot happier if you'd just drop your trousers more.'

Andrew's hand clenched the book. He stepped towards his cousin, the tome held firm. He might not throw the book at him, but he could use it to knock him to the ground. 'You dared ruin an innocent? Unforgivable!'

Fox saw something in Andrew's eyes, because he stepped quickly behind the desk. 'She really wasn't a loss, Andrew. Trust me. Just another butterfly for my nectar.'

'I will kill you.'

'Andrew.' Fox put the glass on the table and held up both hands, backing away. 'Innocent cousin. You only feel this way because you have not been able to put your little sceptre in the proper hands.'

'You are going to die—' Andrew slammed the book down, almost hitting the inkwell, and knocking a vase of roses to the carpet. He skirted around the desk. Fox sidestepped.

'My funeral,' Fox muttered, head high, 'will be attended by many distraught ladies.'

'—a slow death. A particularly slow death.' Andrew stepped forward, crunching glass and crushing a bloom under his foot, bringing the scent of roses into the fray.

'And move into eternity with a smile on my face for ever.' Fox's words wavered into a chuckle.

Andrew realised Fox was sliding closer to the door. Andrew dived across the corner of the desk, grabbing Fox's coat-tails, pulling him back and slamming them both to the floor. Fox grunted as Andrew landed on his cousin's back.

Fox scrambled, trying to crawl from Andrew's grasp. The cur would take his punishment. He would learn respect for women.

Andrew secured Fox's wrist, stopping his escape, but Fox kicked out, delivering a bruising blow to the shin. Andrew shifted forward, grabbing the neck of Fox's coat and digging his fingers into the back of the cravat, pulling it tight.

Fox coughed and sputtered.

Andrew gave another lunge, pinning his cousin to the floor. The cravat worked to hold the bounder still.

'I'll forgive you for killing me, but do not hurt my face,' Fox growled. 'I'll get you a woman. Let me go. The passions you do not release are turning you into a savage.'

Andrew gave a twist of the cloth. 'If you dare ruin another woman, you will not live to regret it.'

'You're…choking me…' Fox's voice wavered.

Andrew applied more pressure and then let up slightly. 'You will propose to Hannah.'

'I cannot,' Fox said, arms flailing. 'She is in love with Lord Arvin. I allowed her to call me by his name and we were both pleased.'

Andrew paused. 'I find that more than a little odd.' He released the cravat, twisted his body up and slapped his hand across the back of Fox's head with a satisfying pop. Fox's hair briefly splayed before falling back into a tousled look Andrew could not even accomplish with a valet's help.

Andrew perched back so Fox could rise.

'You would,' Fox said, sitting and arranging his cravat. 'You do not have the first notion of passion. You need someone like Sophia Swift to teach you'

Andrew stood and dusted his knees. 'I will not get within a furlong of that crazed woman.' He straightened his lapel and spoke softly. 'She bit me.'

Fox stilled. 'Women sometimes bite. It's all in play.' He took in hearty breaths and pushed himself to his feet. 'I'll explain once I have another drink.'

Moving quickly, Andrew pulled off his coat and slung the garment on the desk. Then he undid the buttons of his waistcoat and dropped the silk to the floor. He pulled his white linen shirt from his trousers and raised the garment from his skin. He pointed to the scar on his chest.

'She. Bit. Me.' His teeth clamped on the last word.

Fox leaned forward, staring, eyes wide. 'Made a lasting mark.' He peered closer for a few seconds. 'She does have well-spaced teeth.'

'I am sure she will be happy to bite you. I will even suggest it to her. But I cannot remain enthusiastic when a woman draws blood and it is smeared on her cheek. I cannot.'

That had been in his sixteenth year. His father had suggested that Andrew must partake of a woman's favours or he would never be able to use good judgement in finding a wife. He gave Andrew instructions he said he wished his own father had given him. He'd even made sure Andrew could stay the whole night at Mrs Smith's establishment.

Sophia was only a few years older than Andrew and she'd promised to show him all he would ever need to know. They'd had a grand time initially, but that had not lasted long past the first kiss. She was all he could have wanted—and then her passion had overcome her.

'Hellish.' Fox stared at the skin. His voice rose. 'And she was willing?'

'She was. I was *not*—any longer.' Andrew threw down the tail of his shirt. 'Some day a wife will see these marks.'

Fox straightened. He squinted and said, 'Do not concern yourself. While saving a lady—an invalid grandmother—from a cutpurse, the thief bit you. He was taken to Newgate and sentenced to death.' Then his eyes twinkled. 'Or maybe just tell the truth.' His voice turned poetic, he took in a breath and put a palm to his chest. 'A woman driven mad by passion.'

'She is just mad.' Andrew shook his head. 'Fingernails like talons and…three mirrors.' The sight of the dishevelled woman begging his pardon from three angles had been rather like a bad dream.

'I might take you up on the offer to meet her.' Fox looked the ceiling. 'To see if you tell the truth.'

'Oh, by all means, please do. The two of you should get on quite well together.' He shook his head. That night he'd felt he'd been in a room with a marauding animal. In the beginning, Sophia's vigour had grown with his own, but then he'd had to calm her when she'd realised what she'd done to him. He'd spent an hour reassuring her that it did not hurt—all the while it *did* hurt. He'd not wanted a repeat of such an encounter. The one time he had let himself be swept away by passion, it had turned on him. His father had been right that the encounter with Sophia would make Andrew a man. He'd felt one from that night forward, though perhaps not in the way his father had intended.

'You really must learn to experience life.' Foxworthy's throat rumbled with a fluttery burst of smug disapproval.

'Ha,' Andrew grumbled, pulling his coat from the desktop and hooking a hand over the back of a chair. He slid the seat to the front of the desk. He sat, and both hands gripped his coat, but he didn't don it. 'I see you dancing on clouds one moment. The next you are wallowing on the floor in a drunken heap because of the fickle nature of your heart. You think to be in love and say she is the one for you for ever, and then she falls into your arms and you can't bear her. Next you distance yourself and hurt her. Or she returns to her husband and forgets you—in which case you cannot get her name off your lips.'

'It's all worth it.' Fox sniffed.

Andrew snorted. 'The next time you are knocking on my door at midnight wanting to hide due to a jealous husband or you're gasping tears of despair because this month's one and only true love has not fallen at your feet, I will remind you, *But it's all worth it*, and kick you out on your arse.'

Fox straightened tall, his chin up. 'I visit your house because I wish to play cards with you. Sometimes I am a bit melancholy due to the fickleness of women. Or sometimes I may have had a misadventure. But I am not hiding.'

'You wish to sleep without worry of someone bursting into your house to kill you. You learned nothing from your father.'

Fox's eyes narrowed. 'And you learned nothing from yours.'

A cannon blast of thoughts plunged into Andrew's head and mixed with a powder keg of emotion. Andrew clenched his fist, tightened his stance and locked eyes with Fox. Neither moved.

'I beg your pardon,' Fox said, raising hands, palms out. 'You know I meant nothing by that.'

Slowly, with the precision of climbing backwards from a cliff edge, Andrew calmed himself. He would not let anger overtake him. Even when he had throttled Fox, Andrew knew he'd not really been in a fury, but acting in the only manner Fox listened to.

Andrew squelched the emotion and controlled

himself. Fox did not consider his actions or his speech before doing either. His cousin never saw the rashness of any behaviour. He likely would have been killed long before if not for Andrew's intervention.

'Fox. Tread softly.' Andrew spoke in a controlled voice.

Fox examined Andrew's eyes, and then stepped back, raising a palm. 'I meant nothing by it. You know that. So your father had one little misstep in life.' He shrugged. 'He was better to us than my father ever was. I did not mean to speak ill of him. I have mourned him more than I would my own father.'

The familiar pang of grief touched Andrew's chest, but anger tempered it. He wasn't furious at his father any longer, but Fox was another matter. He continued to cause disruption in other people's lives by acting on his desires. Constantly, Fox either broke someone's heart or his own, and he always landed on Andrew's doorstep. But within a few days, his cousin's melancholy would fade and he'd be in love again, for what it was worth.

Fox sighed, but then his eyes sparked and his

lips turned up. 'It saddens me to see you dying on the vine.'

Andrew blinked. 'Dying on the vine? No. If I need to see the rightness of my actions I only have to look at you. You're the one landing in an overripe mess on the ground.'

'Sadly, I think you may have a point.' Fox turned his back. 'I may have erred. Caused irretrievable damage to a young woman.'

'You've done that countless times.'

'But this time...' His shoulders heaved from the breath he took. 'I fear she was of too gentle a nature. Too delicate. And I worry that she will not recover.' Fox turned to Andrew. 'I have received a post from her friend telling me of the woman's deep sadness. I fear... I fear she might take her life.'

'You cannot be serious.'

'I am, very.'

'Then you must inform her family so they can take care she is not overwrought too extremely.' He moved forward. He would make sure Fox did not shirk his duty.

'I can't. She does not live with them. She's a pathetic little thing. Companion. Survives in her lady's shadow. Never gets to go about. The other women jest about her. Call her a spinster. I thought to show her some compassion and make her realise how beautiful she is on the inside. Instead, she became quite infatuated with me. When I told her I did not love her, I thought she understood. But it's said she is quite despondent. I fear seeing her again. It will only increase her misery.'

'Seeing you does increase mine. But you must make sure she does not do something even more foolish than she already has.'

'If I promise—' Fox put a hand across his heart '—that I will take more care in the future, will you please check on her to see that she is recovering? Ascertain she will get over me. Just give her one of those same talks you give me about what a disaster I am.'

'I cannot visit a lady's residence in such a way. It is unthinkable.'

Fox regained his easy posture. 'You can with Tilly. She's a companion and her mistress will be away tonight. I can send her a note asking her to be at the servants' entrance for a private message from me. She will do it.'

Andrew shook his head. 'I cannot let the poor

woman expect someone she loves and then tell her you will not be there.'

'If anyone can convince her that I am a waste of her tears, it is you. You've recited the words to me so many times that you should certainly be able to recall them again.'

'You must do this yourself.'

'No. It will only increase her agony,' he pleaded. 'She will believe someone else telling her that I am not the one to lose her heart over. I have tried. She did not listen. And you can make certain she will not do something foolish like take her own life.'

'We will find someone else to do it.'

'You are the only one. There is no one else. If word were to get out and her reputation tarnished while she is so fragile, it would be too much. You must help me this one time. And I promise, I will mend my ways.'

Beatrice moved from the carriage on to the town house steps, then to the threshold. The door opened before her and she glided inside—until her dress stopped moving, jerking her to a stop. Turning, she snapped the silken hem of her skirt loose from the edge of the open door and heard the rip.

'I would have corrected that for you,' her brother's butler intoned with a voice that could have rasped from a long-dead ghost. If one looked closer, most of Arthur's appearance would have done well on a spirit, except for his height and posture.

'I cannot wait all day,' Beatrice grumbled to Arthur, but she stayed at the doorway, and dared him with her face.

'I must beg pardon. It's my age, you see. I'm slow.' His face revealed no expression. 'Forgetful. It is hard to remember how a person should act.'

'Nonsense,' she muttered. Then she appraised him. 'How old are you?'

'One hundred and three—in butler years.'

The maid stopped behind them, carrying Beatrice's reticule, her book and her favourite woollen wrap that she only used in the carriage, because it was quite tattered, but so comforting.

'And what is that in people years?' Beatrice asked the butler.

'I cannot remember.'

'Arthur—'

'It's Arturo.'

'No, it isn't.'

He raised his nose, and spoke with the same air as King George. 'I am quite sure, madam. I was there.'

'It's Arthur.' Arthur's father had been the old duke's butler, and to lessen the confusion when both men were servants in the same household, Arthur had been called by his given name.

He gave a rumble from behind closed lips and then spoke. 'Whatever Lady Riverton wishes. But Lady Riverton could take better care of her garments. Mrs Standen complains when you're careless and she has to do extra mending.'

Beatrice smiled. 'Listening to a wife is a husband's duty, Arthur.'

'Arturo.'

'Arthur,' she commanded. Shaking her head, she moved to the front door, using both hands to lift the dress so the torn hem didn't drag. She stopped at the base of the stairs, turning back to see the butler's eyes on her.

She gave him her best snarl, and even though his eyes were focused on nothing his lip edged into a smile.

She moved up the stairs and the maid followed along.

'Dash it,' Beatrice grumbled to herself, examining her feet. 'I do not know what I was thinking when I chose these slippers to wear to Aunt's house.'

Taking painful steps, Beatrice scrambled upwards, pleased to be spending time at her brother's London town house instead of her country estate. 'Go to the kitchen and have Cook prepare something delicious,' she instructed her maid.

When Beatrice reached her room, she sailed past and moved on, stopping at her companion's door. Without knocking, she pushed it open, speaking as she entered. 'Tilly. I could not believe...' She paused, staring at her companion. Tilly dropped the comb in her hand.

Tilly wore the amethysts. The amethysts Riverton had given her before they married. And—she gasped—*Beatrice's own dress.* She'd recognise the capped sleeves with lace hearts anywhere. And the bodice. Fortunately, Tilly didn't fill it out quite as well as Beatrice. She needed a few stitches to take in the gaping top.

True, Tilly was a cousin and deserved some leeway, but not the dress.

'Cousin, dearest...' Beatrice kept her voice sweet—overly kind '...when you took ill and couldn't go with me to your mother's, I under-stood. Now I wonder what kind of illness requires amethysts.' She walked closer, examining Tilly, noting the redness of her face. 'In case you hadn't guessed, I didn't stay at your mother's as long as planned. Returned early to make sure you were feeling better.' She frowned, taking a step closer, noting again the colour of Tilly's face and not all of it belonged to emotions. Beatrice sensed a hint of rouge on her companion's lips and some face powder. 'I believe your megrim has quite faded. Am I right, Tilly?'

'Yes,' Tilly mumbled, eyes not quite subservi-ent.

'Tilly.' Beatrice stopped. 'You will personally launder the dress this moment and return it to my room. You know full well it is The Terrible Dress.'

'Yes.' Tilly dropped her head. 'I know you never wear it, so I thought—'

'I never wear it because it is the one I had made for— And I had it on the day that…' She crossed her arms.

'But he's dead now.' Tilly's chin jutted. 'Died in another woman's arms, I heard.'

'Fine, Tilly.' Beatrice took a step forward. 'You may have the dress. Keep it. I will have your things sent after you. Go tell the groom you'll be leaving as soon as they've eaten. Tell them to take you to my house to work with the housekeeper.'

'I refuse. I am sick of the smell of your paints and I am sick of not going to soirées and I am mostly sick of you.' Tilly reached behind her neck and unclasped the amethysts, and thrust the necklace into Beatrice's hand. 'You truly are a beast.' She pulled at the pearl earrings, removing them, and putting them in Beatrice's grasp as well. 'But thank you for the dress. I look better in it than you anyway.'

Tilly reached into the wardrobe and took out a satchel, and thrust a few folded things into it. Then, leaving the wardrobe door open, she sauntered to the dressing table. She placed her brushes and scents into her case. 'Do send my things to my mother's house.' She strolled across the room, Beatrice's imported lavender perfume wafting behind her. The special blend.

Looking over her shoulder, Tilly stopped at the door. 'And by the way, the night you threw the vase at your husband...' her voice lowered to a throaty whisper '...I made it all better for him on the library sofa.' The door clicked shut.

Beatrice shut her eyes. Riverton. The piece of

tripe had been dead over two years and she still didn't have him properly buried. He kept laughing at her from the grave.

She'd moved from the house and stayed with her brother to get Riverton's memory to fade, but nothing worked.

Love. The biggest jest on earth. Marriage. A spiderweb of gigantic proportions to trap hearts and suck them dry.

She kept the jewellery in her left hand, then went to the wardrobe and looked inside. A stack of linens. She picked up a pair of gloves she remembered purchasing, but wasn't certain she'd given Tilly. She slammed them back into the wardrobe. Tilly could have them with good wishes.

Beatrice shuffled through more things belonging to her companion, then she sat on Tilly's bed. Looking around the room, she noticed the faded curtains. Those had once been in the sitting room and they'd been cut down. And the counterpane on the bed, it had once belonged— She supposed it had been on her bed, then later someone had altered it to make it smaller.

So Tilly thought she had a right to the discards—even Beatrice's husband. She held up the amethysts. But these were not tossed out. She doubted she'd ever wear them again. She'd visit the jewellers and see if he might reset them into something more cheerful.

A tepid knock sounded at the door.

She supposed it was Tilly, wanting to beg for forgiveness—or a chance at the pearl earrings.

'Enter.'

The maid opened the door, then took a step back. 'My apologies, Lady Riverton. I came to tell Miss Tilly a note had arrived.'

Beatrice clenched the jewellery in one hand, and then held out the other, unfurling it forward, palm up.

The maid's eyes showed her realisation that she had no choice. Slowly, she put the paper in Beatrice's hand.

Beatrice gave a light nod, both thanking and dismissing the servant.

When the door closed, Beatrice sat alone with the amethysts, the memories, and the note. She'd worn the lace-sleeved dress on her wedding trip. She'd also worn it the day she'd pried Riverton from the screaming maid. Then she'd had to grasp scissors from his shaving kit to keep him from her own throat. It was a wonder he didn't get blood on the cloth, but she'd only grazed him.

The nickname she'd received had infuriated her brother, the architect. Enraged him. No one dared mention it around him and he insisted she repair it. Although in truth, he was more likely to snap someone in two than she ever was.

The irony of it did not escape her. She was called the Beast and yet he was the one with the temper.

Her brother had hated Riverton's indiscretions more than she had. Wilson had raged, feeling the need to protect his sister. She'd not wanted even more scandal, so she'd worked hard at keeping a happy, uncaring facade. She suspected her brother had thought of having Riverton killed, but neither of them had wanted to risk such tales getting about. She didn't mind the stories about her family, as long as they were adventure-filled and showed her relatives in a dashing light. Except, she hadn't done so well in keeping the *on dits* adventurous with the scissor incident. Memories of that day returned. Her husband would have strangled the servant—and the girl's crime had been in not realising he was at home and taking the cleaned bedclothes into the room. He'd thought the maid some kind of burglar.

Riverton. Might he rest in pieces. Small ones. With jagged edges.

She opened the note.

Tilly,

I have procured the amethyst earrings you so desire. They can be in your hands on the morrow if you can convince Lord Andrew you are a retiring sort and deeply distressed because I have tossed you aside. But mostly you must be able to get him to console you and overcome his reluctance to enjoy all the treasures a man can have at his fingertips. Sadly, he has refrained from such joys in the past.

He will arrive at the servants' entrance as the clock strikes midnight. If he stays until morning and you put a smile on his face, I'll have the amethysts to you by next nightfall.
Sincerely,
F.

Chapter Two

Beatrice flipped the paper over, saw no other markings, and then read it again.

A virgin? Lord Andrew? The name was familiar. Perhaps she'd heard it from her brother, but if so that meant he was the duke's brother.

She folded the paper and tapped the edge against her bottom lip, a scent of masculine spice touching her nose. But he was too old, surely, to be a virgin.

Sniffing the paper, Beatrice remembered the curling warmth she'd first experienced in Riverton's arms and how precious she'd felt. She grimaced. Those feelings had changed. Riverton had a gift for saying anything a woman wanted to hear, up to and including a marriage proposal.

When he'd told her that her lack of height made her even more beautiful, she'd not minded wearing the slippers with no heels. He'd even complimented the bit of imperfection of her nose being longish and the way her brown hair always curled and curled. He'd sworn sirens must have looked exactly the same to have been able to entrance so many men. Riverton knew exactly what she'd been unsure of and he'd fanned the insecurity away, pulling her into his web.

She'd never again be so daft. But no matter how much she wished otherwise, she'd loved the feeling of being cherished. Of course, she later discovered she'd have been better off falling in love with a maggot-infested rotting carcase. She was hard-pressed to tell the difference.

Now she was left with the memory of betrayal, and how much a man's caresses could soothe and deceive. And the utter aloneness of being utterly alone. A man could visit a brothel and heads turned the other way, pretending to see nothing. Women, however, had no such meeting place.

She had no wish to court, or do anything to risk another marriage, but she longed to be held. Most widows could be free with their affections—but ones with the notoriety she had didn't get many requests for late-night waltzes. She hadn't really been aiming for Riverton's private parts after he'd released the maid and turned on her instead, but he'd spread that tale from Seven Dials to Bond Street. He'd even claimed to have been asleep at the time.

What man would court a woman who might trim his anatomy while he slept?

To be held again would be nice... But for him to have to *pay* Tilly? She shut her eyes and shook her head. One could not imagine how ghastly he must look. She shuddered, imagining the popping waistcoat buttons and a scalp with little white flecks outnumbering the strands of hair. Perhaps his nose was longish, too. She gazed in the mirror, turned her head sideways and sighed. Her mother's nose.

She crumpled the paper slowly. Even for the most dazzling earrings Tilly was terrible to do such a thing.

Or maybe Tilly was lonely. Incredibly lonely. Beatrice wrapped her arms around herself. Snuffed candles could do wonders for a man's bad complexion. And wine. A lot of wine.

And a duke's younger brother. She wasn't sure which duke—most of them were so advanced in years she'd paid more attention to their grandsons than younger brothers or even sons. Surely this one would appreciate a little less than what Tilly would have offered. A virgin could be cuddled and coddled, and would leave thinking he'd been given a quite wonderful treat. She could even give him the little love nibbles that had always sent Riverton into those spasms of bad poetry.

And she would not let his age diminish him in her sight.

The lord might appreciate the care of a sensitive woman. Small niceties. She believed strongly in helping those less fortunate. The needy. The terribly, terribly lonely. Perhaps he was just very shy.

She walked to Tilly's mirror and reached up, releasing her brown hair to flow around her shoulders. Then she grasped the strands, jerked the hair into a severe knot to capture the curls and jabbed the pins in. Not her best look, she realised, noticing how the bun listed to one side. She'd have to cover her hair anyway.

But if Tilly could wear Beatrice's clothes, and her perfume, then perhaps Beatrice could wear a mob cap with ties under the chin and take Tilly's room. And the housekeeper, Mrs Standen, had some hideous frocks stored. A pair of spectacles she used when mending. Even if Beatrice happened to meet the lord later, she doubted he'd recognise her.

Beatrice hoped Mrs Standen wouldn't mind parting with some of her perfume, too. Beatrice swore the old woman mixed vanilla and cinnamon—because she always smelled as though she'd been rolled in confectioneries. A perfect scent to entice a mature virgin. She'd see if she could turn a sow's ear into a delightful diversion—and give the poor old man a memory to take to his grave.

He'd never know she was Lady Riverton, or— she snorted—according to the scandal sheets, Beatrice the Beast.

Andrew ignored the view of the town houses out the carriage window, thinking back to Fox's words. This was just another example of uncontrolled emotions destroying someone's life. This woman had let her heart lead her and now that same heart was on the verge of destroying her.

This would not be the first time he'd seen a woman distressed over a man's perfidy and had to calm her. Fox knew. Andrew had confided in Fox years ago.

But that was the past. Life went on—usually.

He'd taken great pains with his appearance,

knowing the importance of creating a look of assurance and authority. Fawsett, his valet, had practically hummed his approval. The white cravat lay just so and the black frock coat accentuated Andrew's lean form, and fit him with the same precision a suit of armour might. His chin burned from the close shave and the careful application of the shaving soap which reminded him of the mild scent of freshly sawn wood. He inhaled deeply.

He'd been pleased at the maid's quick appraisal before she skittered away when he'd been leaving his home. He'd seen a certain glint behind her eyes.

The boots, new. The clothing—impeccable. Hair freshly trimmed and he'd had to stop Fawsett to keep him from combing the dark locks into waves.

He stepped down from the conveyance and paused. He recognised the house. He'd not heard the address or he would have known. This was the architect's house. The one he'd hired to make drawings for the renovations he'd had done. A brute of a man who would have been entirely too tiresome except he was better than Nash. Only his reputation for throttling people who disagreed with his quest for perfection kept him from being the most sought-after architect in England.

But, perhaps a mistake had been made.

He looked to the driver. 'Are you sure this is the residence Fox mentioned?'

The man nodded. 'Yes. Foxworthy told me to see you to the servants' entrance.'

Andrew felt little hiccoughs of despair in his midsection. He hoped this woman was not someone he'd seen before or would be seeing again. He did not want to meet her and feel her embarrassment later when she recalled their conversation.

He trekked the steps which led to the tradesmen's entrance almost directly under the main door and was one level lower than the street.

He'd barely knocked when the latch opened. A shadowed face stared at him.

Blazes. This was Fox's amour?

She wore one of the little caps like his grandmother had worn and spectacles, and her hair escaped from under the cap and straggled around her face. The tiny candle she held gave her shadows he supposed he should be thankful for, and the dress—long-sleeved with hanging things and loopy frizzles around her neck. His grandmother would never have worn anything so frightfully odd looking.

Surely she wasn't—? 'Tilly?' he asked.

She raised the candle up, then down, then up again. He'd never seen a candle follow the gaze so.

'Dash it,' she muttered and took a step forward, nearly singeing him with the flames. He stepped away from the tiny wick.

'Tilly?' he repeated, knowing without any hesitation she was Tilly.

Andrew looked at the spinster, clamped his jaw and then opened his mouth, choosing his words delicately.

She let out a whoosh of air, nearly putting the candle out. He stepped backwards and she lunged, grabbing his sleeve. 'Inside. Quick.'

He hardly had a choice—she was about to burn him with the flame. He puffed the candle out.

Dragging him into the house by his arm, she muttered, 'Dark. Pardon. Follow me. I know the way.'

He kept his steps guarded, hoping not to trip over her skirts.

'Oh, my,' she muttered, moving towards a narrow band of stairs, pulling him along behind her.

He planted his feet firmly at the base of the

stairway used by the servants. 'Fox is deeply distressed—'

She turned to him, still gripping his sleeve. 'Shh,' she whispered. 'We can talk in...' she paused '...upstairs.'

'Very well.' He must accept that she had to guard her reputation.

She opened the door to a cramped room with a small bed, not big enough for his length. A wardrobe hulked over the space in the corner. A rather unappealing chamber, although it was hard to tell with only an insignificant candle lit—far from the bed. The room had cooled from the day's heat.

She lit a lamp and placed it beside the candle. Then she pulled the chair closer to the bed, pointing him towards the seat of it. She sat on the bed and held out her arm, indicating he sit. Next, she clasped both hands on her knees.

This was not the shy, grief-stricken woman he'd expected. He sat. 'You appear to be forgetting about my cousin rather well.'

'Your cousin?' She firmed her lips. 'I am deeply distressed. Very sad.'

'I thought you might be dejected by his loss of affection.'

'Yesterday, I was,' she said, 'but this morning I woke up all afresh.'

He stood. 'I am pleased to hear that. I must be leaving—'

She also rose, and then took his hand.

'I am so desolate.' Her shoulders slumped. 'Beyond despair.'

He stared at her and she smiled. 'If it means a chance to keep you here longer,' she added. 'Once I saw you standing at the doorway, I completely recovered.'

He examined her face. 'So you have not really been sorrowful over the loss of Fox in your life.'

'Fox? Lord Foxworthy?' She leaned forward. 'In truth, I danced with him once.'

Andrew didn't speak.

'He's a bit over-fond of himself, if you ask me,' she said. 'And wears those indigo waistcoats to make his eyes look bluer. Plus, he flutters his lashes too much when he's talking.'

'His mother buys those waistcoats for him and he wears them to please her. Underneath all that nonsense he spouts, he's not a bad person. Though he has been complimented on his eyes about one hundred times too much for his own good.'

'Personally...' she leaned forward '...I like a

nice brown in eye colour.' She appraised him. 'Though it's hard to tell in this light.'

'I think there's been some mistake,' he said.

'No mistake,' she said. 'And you do not have to, um…' She shrugged. 'The earrings. Fox may keep them. I don't want them. Meeting you is all the reward I need.'

He took in a breath, his thoughts exploded and everything became very clear. 'I am…so relieved.' Fox! Andrew would let him choose what clothing he wished to be buried in, and then Andrew would assist with the final arrangement of his cousin's body.

She put a hand near her face and fanned as she stared at him. 'I could see you as a knight, or a conqueror. Something majestic. But I am sure you hear that all the time.'

He needed to make sure she knew this was not a transaction. Nor was it to be an adventure such as in the sordid tales Fox told. 'I think you might have formed a wrong conclusion.'

'Yes.' In the dimly lit room her teeth flashed. 'I thought you might be rather…um, unsightly. Rather old.'

'Speaking of age…' He stepped into the middle of the room. 'How old are you?' he asked.

She moved farther from him. Her mouth opened, but she didn't speak.

'Age?' he repeated.

'Twenty-six. Barely.'

'You jest.' Maybe ten years ago.

'I assure you,' she plucked the spectacles from her face and leaned closer. Then she paused and her eyes remained on him, but her head turned to the side. Her voice softened. 'You did not think I could be twenty-six?'

Without the eyepiece, he could tell she was younger than he'd first thought. His courtesies did not desert him, although his honesty did. 'I cannot believe you a day over twenty-three.'

She placed the spectacles on the nightstand, then gave a pleased tilt of her head, smiling. 'And your age?'

'Two years older than you.'

'Perfect,' she said, touching a hand to her face.

A spot of red darkness showed on her knuckles. Surely this lady had not injured herself over Fox? He could not pull his eyes away. 'What is that?'

She raised her hand, looking at the back. 'Vermilion.' She shrugged. 'I painted this morning. Just a miniature I am working on. I have a few supplies here.'

He breathed again.

Her fingers reached out and clasped his.

For a moment they both stood motionless, the room soundless.

'I expected—' She seemed to have trouble with her words. 'I didn't expect you to be so… Well, I thought you'd be more— You're not—'

At her appraisal, pleasure sparked in his body.

She exhaled a breath that came out as a sigh. 'Oh, my.' She peered at him. 'You've legs like a racehorse—only more my speed.'

He tipped his head in recognition of her compliment. Women did not comment on a man's legs, but he was quite willing to let her continue.

'And shoulders.' Her hand still held his, but the free one patted along the top of his coat. 'Hard to believe.'

He concealed his smile. 'Thank you.'

'A reward. For me.' She chuckled and released his fingers. She clasped her hands at her chest, almost bubbling her words out. 'I am so very grateful. I did not expect a man anything like you.'

'You'll get the earrings,' he said. 'But they will be from me. Not my cousin Foxworthy. And simply a gift of friendship. Nothing else.'

She tiptoed up and spoke, her lips almost against

his ear, and the wine scent of her breath touched his nose. 'I will treasure the gift. A memento of a wonderful meeting. Between friends.' Her hands patted down his arms, then moved to his chest and gave little brushes. 'Lord Andrew, I would have found time to get away from my painting had I realised men like you were about.'

She leaned closer. She smelled of—not some jarring scent which spoke of illicit pleasures, but wholesomeness. Of home and hearth.

She wobbled a bit and he steadied her, both hands on her waist. She must have had a considerable amount of wine.

'I should leave,' he said, still holding her. The garment bunched under his touch. She felt like a wraith under her clothing. The dress did not fit her at all.

'Yes, you should. But not just now.' She melted against him with a satisfied, 'Ah…' that he could feel from his chest to his heels. 'Let me enjoy this moment. It has been a very long time since—' she had her arms around his waist '—never.'

'Never?'

'Well, never like you. You're all sturdy. And you smell a bit like a tree. I've never been near a man who smells like a forest.'

Rivers of warmth flowed in his body and he moved carefully, trying to keep her clothing from gathering under his hands and letting the shape of the woman underneath wisp into his mind. She had a nicely rounded *derrière*. Perfect, in fact.

But that didn't matter. He needed to leave. Now.

He stepped back as he moved to extricate her hands, but she stumbled. He steadied her.

'Did you drink an awful lot?' he asked.

'No,' she said. 'I was rather enjoying being close to you and wanted to continue. If you would just stand there a moment longer. Small price to pay. Much less expensive than earrings and, from my perspective, better than any jewellery.'

The door seemed to be getting further away.

With the delicacy of handling an eggshell, but the firmness of his strength, he took her arms and held her erect while he moved back. 'I must be going. I have a cousin to throttle.'

She gasped. Her smile evaporated. 'Well, that was a slap across my face.'

He didn't move. 'I would never—'

She interlaced her fingers. 'I would have preferred you to have said something along the lines of, *I must go now. I wish to thank Foxworthy for the chance to meet you.*' She slid her hands apart and her fingers splayed, before she waved him away. 'Never mind.'

'Miss Tilly, I did not mean any offence.'

She took in a breath so big he was surprised any air remained for him to breathe.

'Ohhhh. Never mind. Truly. Never mind.' Her hands flared out at the sides of her body. 'What you said reminded me of quite a few very unpleasant things.'

He took her hands, not saying a word until her fingers relaxed. 'I would not wish to remind you of anything bad. And I am not the least upset at Fox for engineering the chance to meet you. I am only displeased that he tricked me.'

'I would not really rate that as high on the betrayal scale as some things a cousin could do. And I suspect my cousin has been quite the little vindictive wench in my life. She always has been so sweet to my face. So kind, and yet, now that I look back, I suspect on those moments she was kindest, she was really most cruel.' She bit her lip for a second. 'I just realised that I have been befriended for years by someone who possibly delighted in every bit of misfortune I have had.'

She turned, folding her arms across her chest,

and looking to the wall. 'Perhaps you should go now. I have a cousin to throttle.'

She shivered. He didn't know why, but the movement reminded him of a little bird who'd fallen from the nest. He couldn't very well leave and not put her back on firm footing.

Placing his hands on her shoulders, he rubbed softly, soothing the tremors. He leaned down, lips close to her ear. Voice soothing, he said, 'Simple fix, really. I'll introduce your cousin to mine. It will all work out. They'll take care of themselves for us.'

'Oh,' she said, leaning back against him, moving so her face was only inches from his. 'I suspect they have already met…'

'Then we must make certain they see more of each other.'

'You're perfect. Handsome and vengeful all in one.'

He wrapped her in his arms. He had no choice. 'Not normally. Handsome, that is.'

'Modest, too.'

'Extremely.' They stood so close, comfortable, as if they'd been friends for years. She caused the most satisfying warmth in his body. 'But I really must go. And I am pleased Fox provided me this opportunity.'

The door didn't get closer. Wasn't really his fault. And this was an innocent encounter. The mob cap reminded him to take care. A woman in a cap did not incite any desires in his body— much. He brushed his face against the cloth and his hands clasped at her waist. The fabric of her gown bunched under his fingers. He smoothed it gently.

'Are you by chance in search of a mistress?' she asked. 'I would like to apply for the post. Temporarily only.'

'No. I want no entanglements.'

She squeaked.

She pulled away, her warmth leaving his body, but she turned and, even in their closeness, threw herself against him, holding him with all her might. 'No entanglements. Vengeful, and legs to spare. This is too perfect. I am dreaming.' She relaxed away from him, put her hand up, feeling his jawline, running her hand up until her fingers nestled in his hair. She chuckled. 'You can be in my dreams any time.'

'I would be honoured. But...' he placed a kiss

on her nose, surprising them both '...I must arise early in the morning.'

'I completely understand.' Her breath touched his lips.

'Goodbye.' At the end of the word, their lips met. Nothing mattered but holding her. Their kiss ended, but only barely.

'It was nice to meet you,' she whispered against his skin.

Andrew let his fingers drop over the hooks at the back of her gown, amazed at how easily the clasps slipped open. 'Likewise.'

She pressed against him, causing his desire to rampage. The pulses of heat in his body could have melted carriage wheels.

One of her slender fingers traced down, stopping at the knot of his cravat. 'I do not understand how you men wear such things. They look so stifling.'

'I hadn't noticed it before. But you're right. It's decidedly warm.'

'And it will be much—cooler in here if you remove it.'

Reason entered his thoughts. He could not risk the morass of passion.

But then azure eyes flickered at him and lips

parted, and he was looking down into a perfect face. He cupped his hands to her cheeks just to hold her for a moment. Tilting her head back, he pressed his mouth against hers. Nothing in the world mattered, but Tilly.

Her body pressed into his arousal. She shivered and kicked her shoes away.

Then she snuggled close again and he reached down, tilting her chin up so he could see her lips. Luscious red, full, shaped with promise for a man's gaze.

A promise they delivered on. No other woman had kissed him with the innocent abandon she had.

This woman was worth waiting for. But he didn't want to wait. He'd waited a damn lifetime and a half. He could wait—later. The last hooks fell away at his fingertips and this time when she stumbled, he fell with her on to the bed, cushioning their fall with his hands. They were half on the bed, half off.

Putting a knee on the bed, he slid her to its centre, looking into the most the angelic form he'd ever seen.

She half-sat. Her hand stopped just before she reached her lips. She moistened her fingertip with her tongue. Then rubbed her finger at the fullest part of her bottom lip. Placing a kiss on her finger, she blew it in his direction.

She reached down, slowly, bringing her dress up the length of her legs. The creamy whiteness contrasted with the room. She lifted her skirt higher, and higher, and he could not move. She stopped, just before unveiling herself completely, and he was frozen, awake but dreaming.

Her knees moved apart, the fabric of her gown sliding down, covering the valley between her legs. 'I want to be the first thing you think of when you wake tomorrow.'

He regained the use of his voice. 'I can assure you, you will be the first and only woman I think of tomorrow.'

He reached for the cravat at the same time as he heard a muted irate voice, and footsteps outside the door. And he was too far from the candles to snuff them.

'—and then she threw me out bodily and told me she would send my things to Mother's, but I want my clothing now—' The screeching voice stopped and a strange woman stepped inside, followed by a man he knew.

The pair became immobile. The architect took up the entire doorway.

'Pardon me,' Andrew said, giving a light bow.

'Oh, my,' the woman with the lamp said, then she smiled and looked up at the man beside her. She turned her eyes back to the bed. *'For shame.'* She snickered.

'Tilly. Leave.' The man's voice sliced the air into slivers.

Andrew looked to the bed. Tilly didn't move. The woman with the lamp, however, put her hand on the door facing. 'I guess you may as well send my things. I don't need them as badly as I thought. I need to have a few words with Mother. And she thinks I'm— Ha!' She waved. 'Farewell.'

She flounced out.

Andrew looked on the bed at Tilly and saw that her skirts had managed to slip down to demurely cover her knees, and she reached up to push the shoulder of her dress correct, but it didn't stay.

'Wilson,' he inserted, moving a step towards the bed, shielding Tilly's body from view. 'I understand your wish for decorum in your household and I regret the display, but I do believe Tilly's mistress is away and she is not needed, and we were just leaving.'

'Get. Away. From. Her.' Wilson's fists clenched and his eyes had a cold stare.

The woman pushed herself up and she stared at the architect. 'Don't you have somewhere else to be?' she asked.

Andrew looked to the bed. A companion should not speak so to the master of the house. 'Tilly?'

Andrew dodged the fist. Heard the woman scream 'No' behind him, and then next thing he knew, she'd thrown herself between them.

Just as deftly Andrew moved her aside. He stood ready to flatten the other man.

'Will,' she snapped out from behind Andrew. 'You shouldn't be in Tilly's room.'

'My house!' Wilson growled. 'Lord Andrew, I do not know how you convinced my sister to dress in such attire to satisfy some strange craving you might have. I would never have thought you leaned that direction.'

Hell, Andrew thought as another realisation erupted inside him. He had erred. Just like his father. But he was not wed and he would not disgrace Tilly. 'This woman and I,' Andrew said, 'are extremely fond of each other and are considering marriage.'

'As if I'd let you marry her—' Wilson exploded.

'She's old enough to decide for herself,' Andrew said, his fists ready. 'She's on the shelf.'

'She's a widow,' Wilson said.

Andrew lowered his hands and looked at her. Wilson had called her his sister. A widow. He'd heard of her. Thoughts pounded in his ears. This woman was not Tilly. 'Beatrice the—?'

'I would not continue that sentence,' the woman on the bed told him, standing and smoothing down her skirt. Her mouth had a feral twist. 'Else you will see what a beast I can truly be.'

The only sound since Andrew and Wilson entered the library had been the pouring and sloshing of liquid. The room couldn't have been much wider than the length of two carriages, yet Andrew wagered his brother's ducal town house lacked the same refinement. The filigree pattern of the gold had been subtly recreated in the weave of the curtains. Even the door panels had matching designs. Only the painting by the sconces jarred the room's decor—an odd scene of a woodland frenzy with a growling bear, a badger-type animal and a dragon poised for combat.

The cabinet set back into the wall where the decanters rested wasn't only to store things, but to display beautiful glass. Andrew stood at one edge of it, the architect at the other.

Andrew waited for Beatrice to join them. Wilson had insisted she change from what he'd referred to as her costume.

Beatrice the Beast. He'd nearly pounced on Beatrice the Beast. Not surprising, really. He'd let down his guard.

'A marriage will be forthcoming,' Andrew said. 'I will not tarnish a gentlewoman's reputation. It is unforgivable.'

'I suppose she could do worse.' Wilson broke the silence. 'She has, in fact. Riverton. Thought an earl would do better by her than he did. Sad he died so. First, he waited too long after the wedding. When he did fall ill, he didn't suffer enough. The bumble berry didn't even appreciate good design when he saw it. If not for the generous marriage settlement on Beatrice and the provisions in his will... Still, I didn't see how much of a scoundrel he'd become or I'd never have let him near Beatrice. Would have cracked him like a chestnut.' He thumped his glass on to the wood and stared at Andrew. Wilson's eyes reflected the sheen of brandy.

Andrew quirked his lips. 'I certainly hope for

Beatrice's sake you could tackle something larger than a chestnut.'

'I'm sure I could.'

Andrew moved, reaching for the decanter to pour more brandy into Wilson's glass. He let his brandied breath reach the architect's face. 'If you need any help defending your sister, let me know. I will certainly be able to crack any chestnuts.'

Wilson's brows acknowledged the statement. 'Only reason I agreed to draw plans for you,' Wilson said, 'was because you appreciate a good design.' His brows snapped together. 'Look how you've repaid me. I created a masterpiece for you and you—'

'I made an error, but I will correct it. I thought she was—someone else.' He paused. 'She is a fascinating woman.' Andrew put the glass to his lips, let the brandy rest in his mouth, and then swallowed. 'Even with the cap, she does burst into a person's notice.'

'You're the first man I know of she's shown any interest in since Riverton courted her, wed her and finally did the one decent thing of his life and died. Beatrice has such a sense of honour that she made me swear not to kill him.' He chuckled, shaking his head in disbelief. 'My trusting sister.

If I were capable of murdering Riverton, I could certainly lie about it.'

The architect lifted the decanter. He poured more liquid, then thumped the container against the table top. 'And you must know of the nickname she's gathered in the papers because of the unfortunate incident with the scissors. It didn't help when not too long after she hit Riverton's carriage with a parasol because the lightskirt he'd loaned it to made such a spectacle of showing up at the house. Beatrice's home.' He swallowed a drink. 'My sister's actions catch every eye.'

'With the scissors, she near cut her husband's— leg off.'

Wilson shook his head. 'Exaggeration. He healed. And he deserved it. At the time I was disappointed in her for not doing more damage.' The architect's eyes focused on Andrew and his voice burned into the air. 'I dare say Beatrice would have little reason to dismember you. You keep your cards well hidden.'

Andrew nodded. He preferred to live his own life and not let others live it vicariously through the scandal sheets. He'd seen enough suffering because of their sharp-edged ink.

The architect shrugged. 'You can't be as bad

as Riverton, or whatever else she might pull out from under a dustbin. I admit, Riverton presented well and I thought he would make a better husband than he did.'

The door crashed back and Beatrice swayed in, perched on slippers which would topple a lesser woman.

She waved an arm, 'I hope you two have settled your differences. I must get a letter written to Mother so when she reads of this, she'll not feel the need to interfere.'

She had a dazzling smile, chin out, and just the whisper of what might have been tears at her eyes.

'Your brother and I have discussed this, Lady Riverton, and I would like to talk with you alone.'

Andrew knew he'd lost control in the bedchamber and she would not suffer for it. He would not repeat his father's mistakes. Although he harboured no animosity towards his father, he retained the rage of how innocents could be hurt because someone else traipsed through mud and sloshed it in all directions. He would not cause anyone pain or embarrassment because of his actions.

'No need.' She raised her hand, fingers splayed, and rotated her wrist. 'The scandal sheets need to fill their papers. People must have something to talk about. Better me than their neighbours.' She moved her head, then stilled a moment as if posing for a drawing. 'And I do make for a good tale.'

Chapter Three

Andrew stared at Beatrice. Mob cap gone. No henna mishap. Her hair did slip out of her bun into curls around her face, which he rather liked. Blue eyes radiant without spectacles and a— He blinked. No loopy things or hanging things. He blinked again. This was not the time to be noticing her round parts. He needed to look at the sharp parts. Lady Riverton was not a wallflower by any stretch of the imagination.

Beatrice raised her arms higher, fingers outstretched, a performance. 'This is what I get for doing a good turn.'

'Even I do not believe that was your motivation, Beatrice.' Her brother's voice bit the air.

She shrugged. 'Suit yourself. He is a—' She looked at Andrew. 'He's not especially hideous looking, I admit.' Then she squinted and regarded him. 'I do not really understand your predicament.'

'Deuce take it, Beatrice...' the architect huffed '...he's male. You're not. That's all the reason he needs for trying what he did. The situation was not proper. I cannot have this behaviour under my roof. Nor can I countenance your total disregard for the family's reputation. Think of it, Beatrice. You cannot like to be known as Beatrice the Beast. Now it will be Beatrice the Brazen Beast. By now the tale is halfway to India. I was too shocked to silence Tilly.'

'I do not think you could have,' Beatrice said. 'She is not the cousin I thought she was.'

Andrew watched. Her eyes blinked more when she spoke a dramatic word, emphasising, putting a point to it. The room was her stage at the moment.

She groaned and her head fell back. 'If only Mother had named me something else. Honour. Patience. Prudence.'

Wilson spoke. 'We were lucky not to be named after plagues. Once Mother hears of tonight, she will say I cannot control you and she will insist on more influence in your life. Think of it.' He whispered his last words. 'Mother. On a righteous tear. You must find a way to convince her you are behaving properly, Bea. Lie all you must. Cover your tracks. Keep out of the papers.'

Beatrice shut her eyes, then opened them and looked at Andrew. 'If you'd been as I imagined, none of this would have happened. But you stood there...' She took in a breath as if smelling a delicate rose. 'I simply cannot blame myself.'

Andrew saw her, down to the barest freckle she had just below her eye at the outside corner. 'Marry me.' His words held no inflection and he didn't turn from her gaze. 'Wilson can draft a note for the scandal sheets, hinting a betrothal is forthcoming. He and I can discuss the details of the marriage while you pen a letter informing your mother.'

Her mouth opened. Her arms fell to the side. *'Lord Andrew?'* she gasped. 'You have not even *waltzed* with me.' She shivered and speared him in another way. 'Absolutely not. No. Not now. Not ever. Not even— *No.*'

Andrew didn't move, but watched the muscles in her face and they could not be still.

The architect strode to the door. 'I'll give you some privacy to come to a respectable conclusion, Beatrice, while I...pen a letter to Mother telling her how I have things well in hand. I'll dispatch it tonight so she will see it when she wakes.' He touched the door. 'I will close this. Please do not do anything to disgrace yourselves.' He put a hand to his cheek. 'Oh, too late.'

The door closed decidedly.

'Thank you for the delicate reply.' He leaned against the wall, arms crossed. 'Since all my limbs are unharmed, I will take it that you are considering it.'

'Oh, most certainly,' she said. 'I so wish to return to one circle Dante forgot to mention—the unexplored tenth level of hell.'

He realised his first marriage proposal was taking the same turn as their earlier romantic encounter. But she had no scissors.

'Perhaps you misunderstood the question I neglected to ask properly. Lady Riverton, will you marry me?' He had no wish to be like Foxworthy, always in a race to abandon a woman so he could find another one to desert.

'You could not have misunderstood my answer.'

'I understood.'

'The only reason you ask is because Tilly discovered us and spread the news.' She shook her head. 'My refusal meant that I am declining.'

He moved away from the wall and stood so

close he could touch her. 'But, Beatrice, a be-trothal would certainly—'

'It would *nothing*.' She turned away from him. Her tapered fingers tapped her forehead. 'Now I will have another mark against me. What is one more?' She lowered her hand and looked at him. 'Cousin Tilly will have the enjoyment of dispar-aging me over this. I am to be the Beast for ever and I find I am quite used to it.' She laughed, but the sound had a hollow ring to his ears.

'You do not have to wed me. We merely need to give the idea we are betrothed.'

'No. I do not even want to be seen as consider-ing marriage.'

'You could be viewed as a changed woman. My name has not once appeared in print. I am the younger brother of a duke. My brother next in line has three sons. I'm not an heir to the title, so you will not be viewed as angling to be a duchess. Not even close. We are not a family to appear in the scandal sheets, except for my cousin Foxworthy, but we are connected through our mothers—so his actions don't reflect on the family name. My reputation can certainly weather this little men-tion and you can change the way the world sees you. We could manage this.'

'Andrew.' She spoke slowly. 'Do you even read those papers?'

'I prefer not to.' He moved forward and reached to take her hands in his. He looked down. 'What do you have to lose?'

'I've had a lie of a marriage. I see no reason for a lie of a betrothal. I made myself a promise never to wed again. The first time cured me of any notions in that regard. My husband—he didn't improve with age, drink or distance. I was lucky he had a taste for poppies and managed to do himself in before too many years passed.'

'I have heard that many wives do appreciate a husband who dies early on in the marriage.'

Her mouth turned up at one side, but her gaze speared him. 'Saves on the cost of carriage repair.'

Then her shoulders drooped. 'You tempt me, but it is only a momentary spasm and it passes.' She sighed. 'At the end of my time with Riverton—' her voice lowered '—and we really should not call it a marriage—I only cared because Riverton couldn't be discreet. The marriage itself was neither here nor there because I hadn't spent time with him in several years. But I always had the feeling people knew more about him than I did and I didn't like being... By then he wasn't even someone I would have wanted to speak of at a soirée. So having him as a husband was rather unfortunate.'

'I assure you, I would not disgrace my wife so.'

She gave a tilt of her head. 'Oh, you say that now. But in five years? Ten?'

'Lady Riverton. I do not make a habit of such.'

She shook her head with a wobble, making the movement sarcastic. She turned away, walked to a sconce and stared at it. 'Yes. You are behind. But once you get started, what's to stop you from making up for lost time?'

'I would say it's unlikely that I would be so inclined,' he admitted. 'At this point in my life, I realise I should take even more care than I have in the past. Tonight, for example. You can see how unrestrained behaviour led to both of us being in the wrong bedchamber at the wrong time.' He spoke softly. 'I do not regret holding you close. But I now see quite plainly that it is good for me to be working in the late hours of the night. In the past, when I have wished for a woman's attentions, I have forced myself to work, either with pen in hand or hammer.' He smiled. 'You may note that I have quite the list of completed projects behind me—too numerous to mention.

I have easily surpassed every person of my years in accomplishments.'

Without his celibacy, he would not have been able to increase his small inheritance. The town houses he had purchased and directed to be re-modelled had taken vast efforts of economy to re-pair with so little capital. At the beginning, he'd feared he was going to lose everything with small rent coming in and so much being swallowed by delays and unexpected costs. He'd worked around the clock, planning and researching and oversee-ing every aspect he could. He'd hired Wilson to design more structures and, when those were completed, things changed quickly. He'd had funds to call upon and reinvest with each suc-cessive venture.

On several occasions recently he'd taken a pause from the work and had ridden by his properties, knowing they had been nothing until he imagined them. A contentment had filled him. Now they would be a part of the landscape for long after he'd left the world. How much better that was than the complications he'd found when desires raged within him and he attempted to appease them.

She examined him again. 'You. No one has ever

mentioned you with any talk but of…work. Wilson says you're such a stick, I thought you quite, quite aged.'

He smoothed down the front of his coat. 'I am extremely responsible. I have not had much time for soirées or frivolity in my life.'

She still smelled of baked goods, which disturbed him. He wondered if he would ever be able to eat a cake again without thinking of unrequited lust.

She looked at him. 'I will never marry again. It doesn't agree with my voice. Makes it rise to a shrill note. It seems to not do well for my husband, either. I do appreciate the offer of helping me. I am grateful for your consideration of my reputation.' She ducked her chin, and smiled at him. 'Very grateful.'

Truly, Andrew didn't think his own reputation would be damaged to be associated with Beatrice for a short while.

A few days earlier, Andrew had overheard his valet and one of the maids muttering behind a door. He'd been described in exemplary terms, then he'd heard the last words, added almost as one might curse. 'Dull as ditch water.'

He'd turned and left, not retrieving the drawings he'd left in the chamber—pleased. He'd worked hard to resist temptations of all sorts. He'd not let himself be idle for long periods, drink too much with Fox, or spend funds extravagantly.

He imagined they would hear of tonight's indiscretion, but it would not be a concern. One small blot that hurt no one. He would make sure it did not tarnish Beatrice.

Helping Beatrice would be a pleasant diversion from the hours and hours of instruction he directed to his man of affairs and the restless moments which spurred him to complete his vision of his home. Whenever a room was finished, he had immediately noticed the shabbiness of another area and had begun a new renovation. The carriage house would soon be completed and his entire home and grounds would be as they should be.

Beatrice's movements returned his thoughts to her and caused the warmth that had settled in his chest to strengthen.

Her nose crinkled and the challenge faded from her eyes. 'I'm quite used to not being portrayed well. I am not fond of it. I don't like it, but it's… unpleasant only. I don't lose any sleep over it. Tilly might not even mention…' She waved her fingers. 'No. I know she will mention it, but our encounter might not appear in print.'

'I would not wager silver on that.'

She crossed her arms 'I will survive with a smile on my face.' Her nose wrinkled again. Sighing, she uncrossed her arms. 'Once a beast, always a beast. Perception is everything. Perception is reality. What people believe to be the truth is their truth. I'm used to them getting the facts wrong and changing the details. Besides, Beatrice the Benevolent will not sell the papers.'

'It could.'

Her tone lowered. Her lips turned up at one edge. 'No.' That snort again. 'Read the print. I'm sure you could dig up a copy somewhere.'

'What harm is there in trying? We can work together. One small act on your part will not change any perception of you, but if it is taken as part of a journey, the views of you can be changed. A house is not built with a single stone. Think how many years of your life you have left. Do you wish to be a beast when you truly wear the spectacles and cap?'

Beatrice paused, considering. The man stood before her in the same stance of a warrior who might have stepped from a painting and she wasn't sure if he looked at her as a friend or foe. His eyes had narrowed a bit and she would wager he examined her more deeply than anyone else ever had.

The silence in the room oppressed her. 'Just leave,' she said. 'I am used to the nonsense said of me. I have been notorious my whole life.'

That was true. Her bosom had not developed overly large, but it had matured well before the other girls her age. The stable boys had noticed and smirked. The children all acted as if she'd grown her breasts on purpose. Her mother had thought them blessings and insisted the modiste make Beatrice's gowns show more flesh than Beatrice had preferred. Her mother had forbidden Beatrice to wear a shawl, saying the family must always keep up appearances and one could not wear such a lowly garment.

Her friends and their mothers had thought Beatrice brazen even then. She'd endured it with a smile, laughed it away, jested and pretended her figure was all a woman could wish for. And all men could wish for. On that, she didn't think she'd been entirely wrong. Riverton had certainly been aware of her shape, wanting her to continue in the same gowns her mother had chosen. Within a month of marriage, she'd visited a modiste and ordered all new gowns in a cut she preferred.

She'd thought to gain respect as a countess, but then the whispers had reached her ears. Riverton admired all shapes and sizes, except—hers.

'I am used to having people speak of me,' she said. 'They must speak of someone, so why not me? I have laughed the loudest. Life is a grand jest.' Then she reached up, pushing an escaped curl towards her bun, but feeling the wisp spring back into place.

'Perhaps.' He stepped forward and, with his left hand, captured the curl. His fingers brushed her skin as he slipped the errant lock behind her ear. 'But, Lady Riverton, there is more to you than words in a scandal sheet. I believe your brother once told me that his sister took to art the way some mothers take to their children. He said you hired several men to create figures on the ceiling and you sat in the room with the workmen, entranced, at your easel and canvas, trying to reproduce the scene of the men painting.'

'I may have.' She wrinkled her nose. 'Art is taking something from the air and putting it in front of you so others can see what you see—with a splash of your imagination added.'

'Why do you not do that with your own image?'

She shook her head. 'I don't know what you mean.'

'You draw attention and it has been turned against you. Use it to your advantage.'

She sighed. He had no idea how many times her name had been mentioned in print. No idea how many stories about her husband had been whispered. How many times she'd been about and pretended not to know when she was being discussed, even if sometimes the words had been whispered so loudly she wondered why they were not just said to her face.

Her stomach churned, remembering the marriage. The foul smell of Riverton when he would return home after weeks. She'd hated the servants seeing him. Hated the knowledge that the footmen had had to treat him almost like a child who could not be reprimanded, but had to be cajoled.

She put her hand on his sleeve. 'You don't understand the vipers of the world. They wish to bite, not cuddle. I cannot turn them into lambs.'

'No.' His voice quietened, but it didn't lose the

rumble, the masculine richness that pulled her like a vine twining towards the sun. 'I can help you, though. We can create a new world around you. One in which you glitter as you should. This blunder tonight could be fortunate. It can be the moment you begin painting the world around you in the colours you wish.'

'You are daft. No one has a brush that can do as you suggest.'

'What is the harm in trying?'

She didn't answer, with words, but her lips turned up. 'You have lost your senses.'

'I can help you.'

She examined his face. No laughter lurked. Brown eyes with the tiniest flecks of green studied her. In all her marriage—all her life—she'd never felt another person could see into her as deeply as he did.

She took a quick step back, breaking the connection—giving the world a chance to start moving again. 'You really don't know what you say.'

'I will let you consider it, tonight,' he said. 'Tomorrow we will take a ride in the park. We can discuss it further then. You'll have a chance to decide if you'd like to rebuild your reputation.'

He moved closer, leaning in, lips almost against

her cheek. 'Let that be the first thing you think of when you wake tomorrow.'

After he left, she wasn't quite certain if he'd kissed her cheek or not, but she was certain her heart was beating.

Chapter Four

When Andrew returned to Wilson's home the next day, the door opened one small creak at a time and the butler came into view. Andrew noted the crevasses of age on the man's face. Wilson should have considered the man's health. Ire spiked in Andrew's body at the architect's oversight. The frail servant should have been pensioned off years ago.

'Please let Lady Riverton know that Lord Andrew awaits the moment when he might again be in her presence,' Andrew said.

An infant could have taken a nap in the time it took for the man to nod. But the butler's eyes now had nothing slow about them and he examined Andrew in much the same way a woman's father might assess a suitor.

In the sitting room, Beatrice didn't keep him

waiting. She whooshed into the room within seconds of the door opening, beaming a greeting. She wore a dress the colour of a calm sky and the garment clung above the underlying corset, moving with each step. Even if he turned his back, he would have been aware of her.

She immediately asked if his carriage was ready and was at the door before he finished an answer.

When he assisted her into the curricle and her skirts swished by his hand, he wondered what he'd been thinking to take her for a ride in the park. At the time he only considered it a necessary means to increase the appearance of an established relationship between him and Beatrice. He hadn't thought of the narrowness of the seats in the small open carriage and how close their bodies would press.

As the carriage turned into the park, a breeze wafted, cooling the air and bringing the floral perfume of Beatrice against his face. He didn't miss the smell of baked goods. He much preferred the lavender.

Sitting shoulder to shoulder, aware of every one of her curves, he forced himself to think of plans for Beatrice's reintroduction to society.

She turned her face to him. From the gentle

brushes of movement at his side, he knew he need move only the barest amount and she would be in his arms.

'I don't think your sleep agreed with you,' she mumbled. 'You look quite grim.'

He nodded, aware of her fluid movements, confined by the seat, and yet she didn't still. Her body moved constantly, checking its boundaries.

She coughed and lost all seriousness. 'Did you, um, think of me last night?'

His thoughts jumped from her body to her words. 'Of course.'

Her shoulders wobbled and she managed to squeeze so close to him he braced himself not to be pushed out of the other side of the conveyance. Tickles of warmth moved from the place she touched to flood his entire body. Wide eyes blinked up at him in feigned innocence. 'I do have a place in the country…' Then she grimaced. 'Except it's rather crowded. My mother's there.'

'I was trying to think of ways you might impress the *ton*.'

'I did not think of that once after you left.' She moved closer to her side of the curricle. 'They cannot be impressed by me. I assure you. They've spent too many teatimes murmuring about what has happened in my past.'

Andrew slowed the horse.

'Past. Present. The future. You must only consider the future now. I don't believe anyone is really aware of the events of the night yet,' Andrew mused, 'so I want us to be noted today. A preemptive move for when Tilly's words are spread about.'

He ignored the scepticism on her face. 'Also, you might adopt a worthy cause and pour yourself into it. A cause which shows your heart. With your ability to draw attention you'll gather print. At first people will be unimpressed, but over time you'll gain acceptance. People are fascinated when others change from what is expected. Think reformed rakes. Ordinary people into war heroes. Women who sacrifice for others. Those gather a lot of discussion.'

'So you think to tame the Beast.'

'I think for you to tame her,' he said. 'Things have been exaggerated in your past and now you will merely control what is noticed and embellished.'

She gave a distinctive grimace and touched the blue at her sleeve. 'Not the carriage incident.'

'You must also refrain from rolling your eyes in public, I suppose. And smirking. And using scissors.'

'Is this better?' She brushed her shoulder against his again, kept her chin down and looked up at him. Her lips parted. 'This is my *entranced gaze.*'

'You do that very well.' Too well. He could become quite lost in it. But that would never do. Her volatile nature caught his attention, but concerned him at the same time. He could help her become less explosive in public. True, she didn't deserve all the bad reports. Those did not concern him in the least.

But the bursts of energy—the disorder of her spirit—those concerned him. She'd dressed in a mob cap and impersonated her companion. He smiled at the thought. His friends sometimes did outlandish things. Harris had once worn a bonnet and cape—nearly scaring Waters into an early grave. They'd all laughed for months over that. But friendship was one thing. A romance something else. And someone like Beatrice was best kept at a distance. He could not let himself become close to her. She was too much like wildfire and the night before he'd been closer to being dry tinder than steel.

There was a definite discreet nudge of her elbow to his side. She kept her eyes forward, but her head tilted in his direction. 'You're not terribly unpleasant to look at either, Andrew. Have you had your portrait done before?'

'As a child. I hated it beyond belief. I had to stand still for hours while the artist scowled at me from head to toe.'

'Trust me, I would not frown if I painted you.'

The lilt in her voice caused a similar response inside him. 'It will not hurt for us to be seen about together. We can use the abruptness of it to your advantage and to add interest. We can both attend my older brother's soirée and then, a few days later, the theatre. This will bring everyone's attention to you afresh. You'll have a chance to attract the right kind of notice.'

She did need some guidance concerning how her actions were interpreted by others and he could assist with that.

Her lips thinned. She sniffed in and then expelled the air with more force. 'They may be wondering at what moment I will begin to attack you. The suspense of it all.'

'Let that work in your favour now.'

'It sounds like acting a part. A grand performance. I might like it a lot. Though you are sure your brother will not mind my presence?'

'He will be delighted.' Not really, but it didn't matter. He'd be too refined to show even the flick of an eyebrow to anyone but Andrew.

She smiled and he could see the remains of the boisterous child she must have been. And something he didn't think would ever be tamed. And some sort of planning of her own.

'Beatrice,' he said, firmly, reprimand in his words. 'Think *demure*.'

With a little smirk of agreement, she blinked away her thoughts. 'Very well,' she said. 'I'd like to be seen differently. With my brother being such a bear, and me being a beast, it would be wonderful to be invited—anywhere. My mother doesn't know it, but she reminds me of a dragon.'

Now the portrait above the mantel in her brother's house made sense.

Two public meetings with her should be enough. Perhaps three. He'd make sure some of the more retiring men noted her. Women were not the only wallflowers. Lord Simpson could hardly raise his eyes to anyone and he lived an exemplary life. Palmer was rough at every edge, yet he'd been faithfully married until his wife passed. Either of those men would be suitable for an adventurous woman such as Beatrice.

'I understand. When Riverton and I courted, his past was seen as a youthful indiscretion. Older women smiled at us as if remembering how it felt. Young women looked enviously at me... Then, reality.'

Coldness replaced the warmth in her voice. 'I was blissful—blissfully unaware of what a pit I was dancing into. Trust me. Marriage is a lovely thought, but a bad reality. If murder were not frowned upon so much, few marriages would last beyond two years.'

'Your opinion is harsh.'

'That opinion wasn't pulled out of the air. It is based upon careful study, my marriage and eavesdropping.'

'But my plans work on the premise that you are correct in how research is done by others. Now we must assume everyone is also taking careful study and eavesdropping. That will be to your advantage.'

'It's not been a boon in the past.'

'It will now.' He would guide her. She wasn't the only one involved in this pretence, but his role in it would be short.

'I would love to attend the duke's soirée—if you are certain your brother will not toss me out—and I will act quite the perfect lady.' She stretched her arm forward, fluttered a gloved hand at a passer-by and smiled warmly.

Without looking his way and in an undertone, she said, 'I feel no one wishes to see me, but everyone wishes to watch me. But I will attend the soirée.'

He paused, reminded again of a baby bird fallen from its nest. He did not want Beatrice to feel alone in the world.

Chapter Five

Beatrice looked across the room and her stomach churned. Everyone in the ducal residence seemed too full of gaiety, except when she stood near. The scandal sheet had not been kind. Wilson had grumbled, but the plan to escort her to the duke's soirée had pleased him. She imagined everyone wondering if she'd truly been invited.

If Andrew had seen the scandal sheet, he might have decided to call the whole thing off. He would be wise to do so. He'd not even been mentioned. Apparently Tilly hadn't recognised him and the servants probably had not even known who he was.

Chattering voices, smiling faces and a sea of glasses going bottoms up, and the feeling that everyone in the room was speculating about her private life—as if she'd had one since she married.

So much like when her glittering world as Riverton's countess had crashed.

Had she known how events would unfold, she still would have stopped Riverton when he attacked the maid, but she wouldn't have kept quiet and let his version of what happened become labelled as fact. And she would have found another way to convince his mistress that she wasn't welcome.

She looked to the doorway, wondering if Andrew would arrive. She tamped down those thoughts. At least she could be certain if he did arrive he would not be sotted. Long ago she'd learned it was better not to coerce a man into attending an event where he didn't wish to be.

Then two men entered the grand doorway and Beatrice knew who they were just from their outline.

Since the unfortunate encounter, she'd discovered all she could of Andrew and his family. She'd already known of Foxworthy. Every woman in the *ton* knew of Foxworthy. Andrew she'd only known of from her brother. Wilson had made him sound so tedious. He'd complained that Andrew often asked for the near impossible to be designed, and Wilson had made Andrew sound meticulously stuffy.

Seeing the cousins side by side, though, one didn't doubt their bloodlines. If they hadn't already been written up in *Debrett's*, then she supposed the regent would take one look at them, consider it an oversight and rush to correct the error. No woman in the country would even think of questioning a decision like that. The mothers of unmarried daughters would merely rub gloved palms together—thankful of a boon for the marriage mart.

Dressed in black evening wear, the men appeared to be bookends of each other, but her eyes never really made it to their faces. Both stood tall enough to clear a regular-sized door, but only just. Framed by the entrance, they appeared as works of art.

She tried to imagine how she'd missed Andrew before. Possibly because Riverton had taken so much of her and she hadn't been about in society much since then.

She'd been very young and entranced with Riverton when he'd approached her father and brother with a dream for a new mansion. She'd been too much in love and too green to have any idea what he would be like. His family had flatly forbidden the union, which she knew now had earned her a proposal and a special licence. Riverton had been doted on far too much to believe he didn't have a right to his every wish and he'd been one toddle away from falling into a tangle of his own excesses. Perhaps he'd thought she could save him. Or perhaps he'd known she couldn't.

Watching, she could tell when the men's presence became noticed. Women began to flutter around Foxworthy. One would have thought the sun had just risen. And Fox was clucking to the cluster, gathering them, letting them fluff and preen, while he crowed and postured.

Andrew excused himself and moved aside. Women tried to catch his eye, but he never noticed, intent on stepping away, eyes searching. She knew the very instant he became aware of her, because he stilled.

Her thoughts exploded with possibilities. Her breathing quickened. Strong jaw. Yes. Nose. Yes. Pleasant skin. Brows. All the normal male attributes, arranged in just the right proportions. What she wouldn't give to pull that white cravat aside and see his Adam's apple. She could almost feel it under her hand. Little bristles from shaving.

Masculine mixed with softness of skin. Her mind instantly took care of the excess clothing for her, letting her imagination see him as if no barrier existed.

Beatrice kept her face serene. His body would be perfect for art. It was much like his thoughts if the dearth of information about him was to be believed. Pristine. Cautious. Wilson said Lord Andrew had refused to accept less than perfection from any of the craftsmen he'd hired to work on his properties. A man who did not tolerate flaws well.

He walked to her, moving among the other guests with a quick word here and there, but with little detour. She watched his movements more closely than she'd ever studied another man. Other needs had been foremost in her mind on the night they'd met, but now she could see him with shadows flowing over his face. This was the man she'd been looking for, if not all her life, then at least for a year. If she could convince him to let his hair become a bit unkempt. His jaw could use a bit of darkness on it, too. The valet would have to spare the razor perhaps. She could paint him as a knight, a rogue, a rake for any century.

Yes, the man was exactly what she needed for

inspiration. Already she could imagine him, standing bold, sunlight flowing haphazardly over him. The contrast of light and shadows emphasising the nature of a person, good and bad. If he held a sword, tip into the ground beneath him, perhaps a sheen of moisture on his face, hair in damp spikes on his forehead, framing his eyes. Standing as if he'd been awakened from another century, and risen, ready to do battle with whatever the fates thrust his way.

She might well send Tilly the amethysts with a lovely note. Not any time soon, though.

When he stopped in front of her, she looked up into the depths of dark eyes. Her words crumbled at his feet even before they were spoken. His jawline was firm, but not too long to detract from the beauty of his face. It only made him seem stronger. And she knew, if he were to gain weight as years passed, the thinness of his cheeks would fill and he would only become better to view.

She imagined all the ravages of life she could think of on his face. Andrew would not disappoint in later years. His bone structure was that of society's world, but her brother had said he'd dressed in workman's clothing at the back of his home where repairs were being done. Wilson claimed

Andrew had selected the men who worked on his repairs, inspected their work and directed them. Looking at Andrew, she could imagine him bounding up a ladder, scampering along the frame of a roof, or carrying lumber on his shoulder. Her fingers burned to return to her brushes. She could not speak.

The night she'd first met him would have been so different if she'd known. He would have walked into a room lit by a thousand candles and her eyes wouldn't have blinked.

'Lady Riverton,' he spoke courteously, but nothing soothed her in his countenance. She suspected he didn't enjoy the attention turned his way.

Watching his expression, she flicked a finger against the back of the amethyst earrings he'd sent. They'd arrived that morning. His eyes flashed a glint of a smile and his lips firmed, but he appeared to struggle to keep them that way.

'Lord Andrew.' She waited half a breath. The moment passed and it almost felt as if they were strangers. The man in public did not seem quite the same as in private. But that was for the best. It would not do to become close to him.

But she wanted to paint him. Certain risks came

with that. She had never been able to distance herself from a model completely.

'This is my entranced look for today,' she said, covering for the fact that she knew she gazed at him too strongly .

His nod would have been imperceptible to anyone standing near.

'I thought you might wish to change our—your plans after the sheet was printed. You weren't named,' she said. She didn't want him trapped in any mire. He would not take well to it.

He leaned in slowly, his voice strong, assured and moving over her like a warm fog enveloping a valley. 'The plans have not changed, Beatrice.'

In response, he took her gloved hand and tucked it around his arm. 'The only reason I did not approach the man who printed that trash and thrash him is because he will be quite useful.'

His breath brushed past her ears. Her heart beat in her chest, her knees and her toes. He had to know every eye in the room was on them.

Her mind recovered first and then she gasped. Yes, he knew everyone watched. She could not let herself be fooled.

His eyes tightened. 'Are you choked? Do you need a glass of lemonade?'

'Only the glass. Perhaps with something else inside it.' She had to get herself out of the crush of people. To think. 'Later.' Those same butterflies in the brain feeling from before. Oh, she could not let herself fall into that chasm.

She must talk to him privately. It would look as if they were moving away to be alone because they were besotted. He might not react well, but so be it.

The scent of shaving soap bathed her, but then she realised the aroma might not be shaving soap, but laundered wool, mixed with leather and something she couldn't quite place. Then she remembered. When the carriage house had been expanded, that gentle scent had wafted through the air mixed with the sound of hammers. She shivered inside. He really did smell a bit like a forest.

If she could translate this man into a portrait, it would be her masterpiece.

She leaned closer as they walked. 'I must paint you,' she whispered.

His feet stopped abruptly, causing her shoulder to bump into his, her opposing foot swinging wide. He steadied her.

He raised a brow as he moved forward with her. 'No.' He proceeded on, leading her through another doorway and to the entrance of the duke's gardens. They stood on the steps, the doors behind them. In front, light shone to the open grounds. Several people lingered about, but far enough away to ensure privacy for Beatrice's words.

'No?' she said. 'I'm quite experienced. I assure you. I'm naturally talented.'

'I am certain.' He pulled his arm from hers, but he remained close, his words low. 'I do not have time to be painted. I have too many irons in the fire as it is. I have no time for it.'

Someone chattered, moving closer. She smiled while tightening her arm.

Voice low, she whispered, 'You should make time for art.'

For a moment, neither spoke, moving aside for a couple to return inside. Once the door snapped shut behind them, he gave her a rueful smile.

'I admit, I do appreciate that likenesses are captured for the family to view after a person is gone. But that is about the extent of my tolerance for such things.'

'Art is my reason for life.' What spirit possessed her, she didn't know or care—it always remained nearby. She wondered if she wanted to push him away.

He was a man who could not even allow himself flaws. His clothes fit him to perfection and he was as comfortable at the soirée as if he were the duke himself. She felt like a scullery maid trying to be a countess. She always had to some extent, but then she had not been born into such a life. No matter how much she spent on clothing, her corset always chafed, or the pins in her hair fought to loosen, or her shoes tightened on her feet. She pretended to brush her glove over her shoulder, making sure her chemise had not slipped from under her dress. Luckily, her stockings remained in place. So far they had not tried to bunch at her ankles.

She'd like to be someone other than herself for one night, she supposed. Now she just wanted to leave. To get back to the studio and paint. To close herself into her world and forget about the words that might be printed about her. She did not belong at a soirée—she belonged at a studio.

When she opened her mouth to speak, he stepped away.

A memory surfaced—Riverton leaving while she begged him to stay and left her with the knowledge he was going to another woman. For a moment, a familiar emotion surfaced and stilled the blood in her veins. She took a breath, and reminded herself that Lord Andrew meant nothing and had promised nothing. Fate had brought them together, or Tilly, or a mistake, or whatever it could be called. He didn't owe her anything, truly, and yet he'd agreed to help her. She *would* paint him. The art would be a gift to him. A thank-you for trying to retrieve her reputation. She could already imagine showing him a life-sized mirror image of himself.

'Lady Riverton. We should perhaps return to the others and waltz.' His voice barely reached her ears.

She considered her goal and then thought of him. 'Andrew. If you don't dance with me, you might not be connected to me. Let us part now.'

She hadn't called him Lord Andrew, but he had not seemed to notice, which she appreciated. Riverton would have shot her a killing glare.

'No. I am desperate for a waltz with you.' His lips didn't smile, but happy crinkles appeared at his eyes and his voice was just a touch more resounding, possibly able to carry to others. 'A waltz, Beatrice?'

She kept her words for his ears only. 'Don't say you were not warned.'

'Is your dancing that bad?' His face tipped near hers, words soft.

She raised her chin. 'It's quite grand.'

He clasped his hand over her gloved fist and pulled it to his lips for a quick brush, then opened the door for her. 'Then I will not give you an opportunity to refuse.'

When she stepped into his arms for the waltz, she did not care what was said about her, even in the past. It had led to this moment and this dance, and she looked into the eyes of her muse.

'Andrew. You must pose for me. We did get along quite well the other night and we do now.'

'I cannot be blamed for that. You looked so lovely in the spectacles and mob cap. I was overcome with madness,' he whispered, but his eyes sparked humour. 'And the name…I've always had a penchant for women named Tilly. Sadly, I was misled.'

'Right to the bedchamber.'

'Tilly's bedchamber.' He leaned so close she could see the light flecks in his eyes again.

'Soon we'll attend the theatre together,' Andrew said. 'You must be consistent and appear a new woman. The widow who has put the past behind her and is embarking on a sedate journey.'

The music wafted over her and she had no trouble looking adoringly at Andrew. But her shoes still hurt, her stockings wanted to bunch and she prayed her chemise did not show. It was hard to glide in his arms when she felt the barbs at her back and feared she would somehow embarrass him again.

Chapter Six

Andrew perused the papers, pleased. It seemed their waltz had garnered just the right amount of attention. The engraving wasn't flattering to either of them, but the words did not embellish much beyond the truth.

He'd perused the paper twice that day, considering his plans and how far he should continue with them. He carried the print to his bedchamber to read the story a third time before he prepared for their outing.

The engraving had some merit. They'd actually been able to capture the shape of her lips in the likeness. The over-sized eyes were vile, staring so hungrily at him, but overall the face was hers. It stirred his memory of holding her while they danced.

Beatrice was quite the actress. She had given

him such looks of adoration that even he would have believed them if he'd not known. He'd actually enjoyed the role himself. His hand had slid down her back as they'd parted from the waltz and he'd been aware of each hook on her gown. The dance had ended much too soon, but he could recall every moment of it.

He had not been able to stop thinking of how those blasted hooks had felt and how easy they would fall aside. Corset ties next. A chemise. Bare skin. Tickling laughter.

Blast. Blast. He kept thinking of her skin and then his mind would switch to the sight of her touching her lips in her bedchamber and telling him she wanted him to remember her. He wished to stop thinking of that moment, but he had not been able to.

He must stop such nonsense.

But he'd be seeing her tonight. A perfectly innocent outing with her brother in tow. He'd insisted Wilson go with them to add to the image of the new Beatrice. Andrew had explained twice how it would help with the creation of the demure Lady Riverton. A chaperon would be greatly beneficial in another way. He did not think it wise to be alone with her. Not if he kept thinking of her musical laughter.

Fawsett's perturbed huff as he poured steaming water into the washbasin caught Andrew's attention. Fawsett was boiling, too, but the man had earned the right to a bit of complaint. Andrew had been trying to work away his excess thoughts of Beatrice and the efforts were frazzling Fawsett.

Fawsett sniffed, slapped the pitcher on to the table and turned to Andrew. 'I resign.'

Andrew stood. 'No.'

Fawsett strode forward. 'That is not the way fingernails should look. No amount of care can correct that damage. It will have to grow out and hopefully I am not scarred for life.' He thrust out his opened hand. Then he flipped his hand over, palm up. 'Calluses. Calluses. Disgraceful. Hammers are for ruffians. And scaffolding is for hangmen, not valets. I have decided to find employment elsewhere.'

'Fawsett.' Andrew threw a note of caution into his voice.

'I am not really who you think I am,' the valet grumbled, raising his chin in challenge. 'I am not Thomason Fawsett, but Robbie Fawsett. Thomason is my father. I used his references. I am not a valet.'

'Oh.' Andrew widened his eyes. 'I am so shocked.'

Andrew moved to the washbasin and splashed water on to his face, and looked across to his valet, still grimacing at the sight of his hand.

Last evening's work had not gone well. Andrew had tried and tried to get Beatrice from his thoughts, but no amount of activity had helped. He really shouldn't have kept Fawsett busy after the others had left, but the lanterns lit fairly well. The night air had been the problem. He supposed the sole of Fawsett's boot had got dew on it and caused the accident.

Andrew reached for a cloth, then pushed the flannel to his hairline and slowly slid the fabric downwards. 'If that is true, then it would certainly explain why I have had to purchase twelve new cravats because I refuse to wear the ones with a brown spot from a too-hot iron. And it could also mean you are the son Thomason apprenticed to a carpenter and who ran away after stealing a horse. By the way, Miss Sarah's father never did find the young man who'd romanced his daughter. The man he plans to kill on sight if he ever finds him. Miss Sarah's father, who often goes to the Four Swans Tavern on Bishopsgate Street.'

'Don't worry yourself, sir. My leg hardly hurts

at all.' The valet's miffed words jabbed into the air. 'I always wanted to fall from scaffolding. Prove my loyalty to my employer. Follow him wherever he wishes and hide from my friends the fact that I don ruffian's clothes so I can hold boards for my master. *Boards.*'

'You're paid well.'

'Not well enough,' the man grumbled, starting into the wardrobe. 'My hands should be preserved to fold cravats. Not run to and fro, handling construction equipment like a common carpenter. You could hire labourers for such tasks.'

'I told you when I hired you that you would often be required to do out-of-the-ordinary duties. Lift heavy objects.'

Fawsett gritted his teeth. 'I thought it might mean bringing you a woman, or hiding you from a husband. Or picking up your sotted corpse from the stews. *That* is what I am comfortable with.' He sniffed. 'I did not lie and practise signatures to forge my way into a post where I would have to work harder than shining a boot, or brushing a hat. Questionable activities should better oneself, *never* lead to honest work!'

'This house needed remodelling and I could not find enough workmen with the skills I needed and who could work at my schedule. I very much regret you stumbled. You suffered a minor injury. Happens.'

Andrew studied Fawsett's unlined face and fit form. The man could make a hammer sing and measure with flawless accuracy. Andrew shook his head. He'd never understand why Fawsett preferred taking care of another man's clothing. Except Fawsett did have considerable free time to spend with maids. Andrew frowned, wondering how much truth the valet told when he hinted at his exploits. Probably all true. The maids did flutter around him.

Fawsett could accomplish so much more if he did not let himself be distracted by women. But Andrew could understand, it was not easy.

Fawsett complained, 'You look a sight. Overtiring yourself with work. It is a disgrace. Even my special mixtures will not take the effects of the sun from your face. I have heard that a woman is now on your horizon and I fear you are not considering all the happiness available if one remains unmarried.'

'Stubble it.'

'I am only concerned for you.' Fawsett picked up the pot he had specially mixed at the apothecary.

Something he assured would keep bothersome bugs at bay when out of doors, and attract interesting creatures indoors. It smelled of a wooded glen, so Andrew allowed it. 'The papers are hinting that the Be—lovely Lady Riverton is on the prowl for new prey. Although I am quite certain she is a delightful lady, I would not wish to see you step into a snare of any sort.'

Pulses of anger flashed in Andrew's body. Idle chatter. How that could damage a family. He forced his muscles to remain relaxed. He wadded the cloth and let it drop to the side of the basin. 'I will be going to the theatre tonight, your Haughtiness, and I suggest you keep to your own life and not mine. Show her complete respect.' Andrew raised a brow.

Memories of walking in on his own father weeping flashed in Andrew's mind. The first and only time he'd seen his father cry. He had seen what lack of control could do. The servants. He'd known, even when they walked by without looking directly at anyone, their movements had changed. They all knew what had happened in the household.

He thrust those thoughts aside. Beatrice had taken the cane to the carriage on one occasion and attacked her husband with scissors on another. She was impulsive and she would always be so, but she could re-invent her image enough so the scandal sheets would not pick her bones into pieces. Some day, she would be thankful she'd done it. He wished someone had warned his father. Not that he would have listened.

Andrew looked in the mirror. He resembled exactly the portrait of his father that graced the sitting room. Family history told how his mother had wanted it as a present for her first wedding anniversary. His father had been older., and in his thirtieth year. The man had been a duke first and foremost, except in the evenings when he'd sat with his wife in the library and their contented murmurs had wafted through the room. Those had been the warmest moments of Andrew's life. But then his father had changed. He'd just changed. Andrew hadn't realised how much until the newspapers explained it to him.

'I blame her for my accident,' the valet continued. 'You would not have taken it into your mind to work so long if you had not been thinking of her.'

Andrew shook his head and picked up the razor. The valet was in too much of a tizzy to be shaving near a throat or an ear. Fawsett was not controlling his own impulsive nature. 'Stubble it or you will be working quite late again tonight.'

No sounds answered except for the pouring of water. Fawsett's lips pressed into non-existence.

Andrew reflected on Fawsett's comments. Beatrice had disrupted the order of his life—if only in the fact that he was having to listen to Fawsett talk of this. This was a minor disruption but still, a bobble in the calmness of the household.

Already he had told Palmer and Lord Simpson she had mentioned them favourably.

Fawsett took the pot with scented mixture to hand Andrew as he finished shaving.

Andrew stood in front of the mirror and daubed a smear of the apothecary mixture on to his neck and cheeks. 'You really should not concern yourself about my life.'

'Your life is of extreme importance to me.' His words caught. 'I would hate for you to suffer injury—as I did last night.' Fawsett's chin dipped.

'I had ascertained you would recover. A man who is truly dying does not scream so prettily.' Andrew smiled. 'Can you also do the little hop again?'

Fawsett kept his gaze on the cloth he retrieved for Andrew. 'As you have refused to accept my resignation, might I say that you could not saw a straight line if your life depended on it—and it is not that difficult.'

'That is why I have you.'

'Oh, and one more thing—I did notice you received a well-sealed message from your brother, the duke.' Fawsett's tone turned innocent. 'I'm sure he wishes you the best in your romance.'

'Of course.'

Fawsett's little throat rumble indicated he recognised the falsehood.

Andrew interrupted the smugness. 'But you did not tell me about the note from Lady Riverton.'

'No need. I saw it crumpled on the grates.' The valet stopped, turned back. 'I assure you, if a woman sent me that invitation, I'd not be thinking of boards.'

Andrew shot a glare at Fawsett. 'Do not read my correspondence.'

'I was burning it and it fell open right in front of me.' He shook his head. 'You felt replacing windows more important than viewing her personal artwork.' He snorted. Then he raised his chin. 'Of course, I did not read the note from the duke.'

'Because I burned it myself.'

The duke had numbered thirty-seven more appropriate women for Andrew to associate with, including Mary Bonney, and he assured Andrew that her transportation to Australia could be halted if Andrew would but make the request.

Chapter Seven

The carriage rumbled them along to the theatre. The energy Beatrice exuded bounced from the vehicle walls and permeated Andrew's resolve not to have an awareness of her.

Wilson sat, arms crossed, head down, little snores occasionally snorting into the air.

Andrew kept his face to the window, but followed every move Beatrice made.

She had adjusted the tops of her sleeves three times, frowned out the window, tapped her foot, and once pulled at the edge of her bodice when he didn't think she'd even been aware of it.

'The print was most unkind,' she said. 'The engraver did not know one end of his burin from the other. He would not know a beast if it bit him.'

'Lady Riverton, it takes time to change an opinion.'

'Opinions do not matter to me as much as that engraving did. The person who did that has no idea of how to shape a line. Why? Why must I have the hairy ears?'

'Just a drawing. It means nothing. It will take more than a fortnight to change something like this. Besides, I thought the tufts at the top of the ears rather—pleasant.'

'You did not wish to march down to the print shop,' she asked, 'and pound on their door?'

He shook his head. 'I told you. It will just cause more upset for you. You are supposed to be dousing the flames, not fanning them. Think demure.'

'I am,' she said. 'I did not go to the print shop.'

'You will agree the reports of our exchange at the soirée were the best we could have hoped for,' he said. 'The print hinted at a romance, nothing more. It also commented on your waltz with Palmer and Lord Simpson.' In fact, it had mentioned Palmer and Lord Simpson as being in rivalry with Andrew for her affections.

Andrew's perturbed, half-muttered jealous comments to others had somehow found their way around the soirée. He smiled. It had been so easy.

She nodded. 'I did rather like the notice better than I have before.' She smiled. 'Just as you planned.'

'You will always gather a certain amount of attention in public. Always. It is just a matter of making it the kind you wish for. We are looking for something which is truthful and accurate. Before long you'll do a few good works, people will take note. The world loves turning heroes into villains and villains to heroes—in their minds. We will give them opportunity and they will play into your hands. You must merely remember you are the star of the performance.'

'Thank you, Andrew, for such a generous gesture on your part.' She shivered in such a way as to make the little puffs of her sleeves quake as if a wind blew though the carriage. She leaned forward, bringing a scent of—not baked goods. Something from a woman's bedchamber. A scent of cleanness and a spring morning in the country. Lavender and wildflowers. He didn't know such a scent could rampage through a man's body.

But it wasn't just the perfume she wore.

Her corset and bodice moulded her to perfection. His eyes tricked him, making the cloth no hurdle to his imagination. He locked his gaze on her face, because if he moved it one drop lower, he would move even lower, and then he would be staring at her breasts and that would not be good.

'You must let me paint your portrait.' She leaned back, taking her delicacies with her. 'I insist. I am quite good.'

Andrew shook his head. 'No. I fear the time taken to pose would necessitate my working all night to make up for it.' To burn off the feelings that kept rising when he was near her.

'Nonsense,' she said. 'I'm quite quick with a brush.'

He would like to visit her home. The tales of its beauty were as widespread as the *on dits* of Beatrice's nature.

'I will consider posing for you.' Andrew spoke with the same respectful, polite smoothness he used when telling his brother the duke to go jump off a cliff.

Both understood he had considered and dismissed it. Her expression changed. Sunlight in her eyes dissipated, but only for a moment, and then the sparkle that took her whole face appeared again. And he understood she had totally discarded his refusal.

He caught her eye and gave the tiniest shake of his head.

She raised her brows.

He tilted his head minutely and raised just one brow as he frowned.

Her shoulders sagged.

He smiled.

'I have a painting on display at Somerset House,' she said. 'If you view it, I think you will agree that I do have talent.'

'I have no doubt of that. But I cannot spare the time to pose.'

She sighed the most drawn-out exhalation of dismay he'd ever heard. He studied her face, seeing if she made the noise for his benefit. He didn't think so. Her eyes had wandered to thoughts he couldn't decipher and she was lost to them—unaware of him.

Her glove had slipped to rest at her elbow. One curl tickled her chin. She brushed it aside and then opened her fan. Not to fan herself, but to examine it. He didn't think she truly saw it, but was following reminiscences only she could see.

He puffed out a breath, just enough to flutter the curl at her jawline. Shock plunged into his body. He'd never done such a thing in his life. And she was a countess.

He turned away and saw Wilson watching

him, jaw locked. Wilson had seen the behaviour. Beatrice wasn't even aware, but Wilson stared.

Andrew did not flinch. On the outside.

The street in front of the theatre bustled with vehicles. Their carriage rolled to a stop and Beatrice alighted, Andrew at her side.

As soon as he stepped from the carriage, her brother spotted an acquaintance. The man called out. In seconds the two were involved in an intense discussion concerning the man's plans for a country estate and Wilson had excused himself to sit with the man in his box. Wilson could not countenance the poor man ruining a perfectly good parcel of land by putting a crate on it.

Beatrice realised Andrew had stopped moving. She glanced at him. His eyes studied her and his arm was held out. He waited for her to grasp it. She placed her gloved fingers against the sleeve of his coat and let him escort her to the ducal box. Out of the corner of her eye, she didn't note any heads turning her way, except perhaps one.

Demure was not her strong point. How much easier it was to sashay into the theatre, head forward and unaware of others' hurtful words.

'I really did not like the engraving of me,' she repeated, searching her mind for words to distract her from the march to her seat.

Agatha Crump stood near the doorway, eyeing Beatrice, smirking.

'I didn't like the caricature either, but none the less it's done,' he said. 'Over. The object is to make the next one more to your liking.'

She walked slowly, each step precise. 'The last time I was at the theatre was one year to the day after Riverton died. It seemed everyone watched me. The words I read later: *The Beast is Unleashed Again.* How mistaken I'd been at the end of the evening in thinking it had been a success. I'd thought my dress appropriate. My hair correct. My voice a proper level. My mother and brother the best chaperons. The only thing I'd been concerned about was that Mother had snapped at someone who'd looked askance at me. Everything written was a splash of truth with a kettle of exaggeration.'

'That's the past. Forget that time. Today we want them to watch you. We want them to see your gentle, caring side.' He looked down at her. 'You are the actress tonight, Beatrice. Show them how endearing you can be. Think prim. Think governess. Think vicar's wife.'

She nodded in agreement. Her eyes lingered on him. 'Andrew, could you ever say anything I do not find enchanting?' Her words were of the right tone to zip through the air like an arrow. Then, she spoke low, turning her words into a roughened purr. 'I am good at the pretence of being in love. After all, I have been married.'

That was true. But she had not only pretended. How like a dream to have Riverton dote on her. He was older and wiser, she'd thought. The eldest son of an earl. Wealthy.

Inside the box, she watched as he sat beside her. Again the stoic look to the audience, with just the right amounts of arrogance and humility. If she kicked his ankle, she doubted he would do more than give her the merest glance.

'So what is it that keeps you so busy?' she asked, hoping for a semblance of conversation to keep her mind occupied.

He turned his head away from the stage and lowered his voice. 'Work, sleep. I get up early so I may take care of the paperwork awaiting me before the men arrive to work on the house and confound me with all the hammering.'

'Hammering.' Nodding, her eyebrows bumping up for a moment, then she settled back into her chair, using the fan to block visibility of her words.

She slid back and opened the fan to circulate the air at her face, causing wisps of hair to flutter. She was being rejected, again. He did not care to talk with her in the least. Oh, well, she was attending the theatre and surely something would amuse her.

She stared at his face. His shoulders were turned slightly her way. His smile appeared genuine, but something at his eyes told her he looked at her no differently than he might a bit of produce. She was not a turnip.

'Demure,' he said softly, a reminder. Something changed behind his eyes, but she could not fathom it.

'Oh, yes,' she said, fluttering her fan in front of her face. 'The D word. That ugly word that doesn't suit me either. But the D word is better than the B word, I suppose.'

'It will take some time. Don't concern yourself.'

'Time. That means it will be slow.' She wrinkled her nose. 'I am not a tortoise.' But the night was progressing at the same speed as one. Everything seemed normal enough, except Agatha settled directly in Beatrice's line of vision. Agatha, with a sneer on her lips. She did not see how she was going to sit through a whole evening with Agatha watching every twitch of the fan.

'Patience is vital to success,' he said.

'I suppose...'

Beatrice pushed back a curl and shifted backwards in the seat, brushing a hand over her stomach. Something she ate had not agreed with her, or perhaps it was the way she was being examined.

Andrew's legs were relaxed in front of him, the toe of one boot tapping softly. 'Not a large crowd tonight,' he said. 'But I hear the play is quite entertaining.'

He had put her on display and she had agreed, but she had not realised this was all a pretence to him. Or that Agatha would be present. Agatha had been present the last time Beatrice had been at the theatre. Beatrice took in a breath, leaning in his direction so closely she brushed against his shoulder. 'Could we perhaps leave early and discuss your portrait, at my country house?'

He gave the barest shake of his head.

She opened her fan, noting the scent of her own perfume on it. Fluttering the object, she made sure the air brushed both their faces. 'Such a warm night,' she mused.

'I was thinking. If you created some endearing portraits of children, the papers would take note of it.' His voice rolled across her.

'But I would rather paint you. As we are friends.' He had changed the subject. How polite. Although she was not quite sure she spoke the truth in saying they were friends.

'You sincerely do paint?' he asked.

She nodded her head. 'Painting is my one true and only love and I never will love another. Though I might like someone very intensely. Someone with intense eyes, an amazing jawline… eyebrows. You must pose for me.'

Stones. His eyes were like brown stones. If a rock could examine the turnip, that would be the expression it used.

'We have covered this subject before,' he said.

They were hardly even acquaintances and he was making an appearance with her simply to improve her reputation in the press. He probably had not liked the mention of himself and now he was pretending an affection so he would not be portrayed so badly.

Well, she could not fault him. She pulled the

fan so it only fluttered at her face. The room felt as if the sun glared on her and everyone else was in shadows.

'You are deeply wounding me as I wish to return the good turn you are doing me and give you a portrait. I am a good artist,' she said, grasping at the only thing she could think of to speak about. 'As I said, one of my pieces is on view at Somerset House. I think it is my best work to date.'

'I am certain you are talented.'

'You say that out of courtesy. But I am skilled with brushes and I must show you. Art is much like architecture.' Her fan kept moving, concealing her face from the others in the theatre as best she could. She fanned more quickly, trying to get the heat from her. 'Creations. A craftsman making something to display.'

His eyes changed flashing a bit of concern. 'Beatrice,' he whispered. 'Are you feeling well?'

'Just the temperature is a bit intense.' She continued fanning and speaking. 'Wilson told me you are greatly fond of architecture. It is just another form of art, if done well. Think how you and Wilson immerse yourselves in the plans. How you want the homes to be just so. The little details.

The shapes. How you stand back and inspect the finished product. How it makes you feel.'

'I do see architecture as an art form.'

He was more structure than man, she assumed, no wonder he liked buildings. She slowed her fan. But he was still male. She was quite certain of that.

With her free hand, she nudged her reticule his direction. It fell to the floor at his feet. He leaned to retrieve it at the same moment she leaned into him. 'Pardon me,' she said in her most demure voice, the fingers of her left hand brushing his thigh as she reached for her reticule.

'Beatrice,' he cautioned softly.

'You may call me Countess,' she said, putting the reticule at her side away from him. She could not bear being on display another moment. Sitting beside him. Wondering what he truly thought of her.

'Beatrice. What is wrong?'

'Nothing. All is going just as you wished,' she said. 'Just as I want. And I must keep an appearance of the utmost propriety now. I see that. I agree completely. No one will think less of you.'

'Beatrice.'

'We both have a care for art. Something in common. We have a lot—well, one other thing in common as well. I am practically a virgin as well.'

He didn't respond, but the stone chipped a bit.

'It's true,' she continued quickly. 'Riverton was sotted almost constantly after we married, or had his head in a haze of smoke. He could barely even *stand* erect. Much less remain alert when he was lying down. It doesn't make one feel desirable. Or quiet.'

'You're very desirable.' Measured, clipped words.

She snapped her fan closed. Her gaze locked with his. She moved the fan like a wand, letting the tip of it briefly brush against the top of her breast before she reached to shove the accessory into her reticule. 'I'm sure I'm desirable for all the right reasons.'

She moved to rise.

'Beatrice.' His voice a low, cautioning growl. 'Wait.'

She tilted towards him. 'I don't give a rat's claw what they say about me in the next publishing. I'm leaving. I am not pretending to be someone I'm not. I am *not* acting in this dreadful farce.' Her chin jutted out.

He put his arm at the back of her seat, moving

in, fingertips burning just above the neck of her gown. His face leaned forward, blocking her view of everyone else.

'I'll pose for you if you'll just sit. Pretend. Just this one night. I saw Agatha Crump look at you. Just do this to spite her.'

Her face did not change. 'I would very much like to leave.'

'I was hoping to stay,' he said. His breath brushed her ear. 'You might drop your reticule again.'

He leaned back in his chair, kept his eyes straight ahead, but concentrated on every movement in the seat beside him. He set his foot to tapping again,

Her lashes fluttered. One or two of her feathers fluffed again and she looked at the light fixture. Her chin softened. 'Do you know what the play is?'

'No. Don't care.'

'Are we truly friends?'

He blinked his gaze halfway towards her. 'One cannot have too many friends and it would be an honour to have a friend such as you who can rise above difficulties and not just land on her feet, but manage it in a pair of unstable slippers.'

She glanced down. 'They were supposed to be

comfortable.' Raising her eyes, she said. 'Do you like them?'

'I would not be caught dead in them.' He smiled at her.

'Do you like anything at all about me?' she asked. 'Other than, well, the particular woman parts. I know you have no complaint of my curves,' she said, moving just enough so that her chest quivered.

'You seem boundless, limitless. You sparkle. Like a jewel. In the drawing, I thought the tufts on your ears endearing. I thought the beast looked— sweet. Rather like you.'

She shrugged his words away, but her shoulders relaxed. 'I suppose I can stay. If I left now I would be angry with myself later.' She paused. 'I did not realise it before, but often I do not like being unseen. But notoriety can get a little tiresome, though.'

'Everything does.'

'Even perfection?'

He looked at her. 'I would not know.'

'I would not either.' She took out her fan again and picked at it, pulling something from it he could not see. 'After the mishap with Riverton I no longer wanted to be near my husband. I moved to my brother's home. The maid Riverton attacked was the butler's niece—though I doubt Riverton ever knew it.'

She nodded almost to herself. 'The servants changed in their regard for me after the attack. They were the same, but not at all the same. Arthur was the perfect butler until I took the scissors to Riverton, then he became different. I once said to him that he hopped so fast to my needs that I was reminded of a frog. He looked at me gravely and a sound whished from his lips that sounded exactly like a noise one might hear outside on a warm summer's night. That was the first laugh I had had in a long time.' She swallowed. 'I think he and Mrs Standen would die for me and I for them. So I suppose I owe Riverton some thanks. He increased the size of my family. He decreased the size of my art collection, though. When he left the house after being injured, three of my favourite paintings had been slashed. So I started keeping some of my favourites in my studio in case he returned.'

She looked sideways at Andrew, smiling. 'I will never be the D word. Demure! It sounds like death to me.'

He did not doubt that for one second.

Her cheeks were still flushed. But she was bearing up well. He wanted to leave with her and hold her in his arms and tell her that this was foolishness. That all would be fine and not to concern herself with the Agatha Crumps of the world.

But that would be a lie. The Agatha Crumps carried a lot of sway. He did not quite understand why, but he knew it was the truth. They would always be about. Armed to the hilt with their cruel tongues.

She tapped the back of his hand with her fan. 'In the past, I didn't want the talk of my husband to reach my ears and I suppose I preferred that they talked of me rather than him. That, at least, I had some control over. And if my ways caused reports of him to fall by the wayside faster, all the better. Though really—' She tightened her lips and did not continue her sentence.

She spoke the truth. She could never be hidden. She would always need the eyes and notice of others. 'Why don't we try to turn you into Beatrice the Beloved?'

'I think we have a better chance of sprouting wings.'

'You are a better person than all the scandalmongers combined on their best day.'

Wilson joined them and Andrew did not think Beatrice said another word the entire evening, but it did not mean she was quiet or still.

She smiled and waved at every person who caught her eye, and her fan never stopped. He'd never be able to smell lavender again without feeling an imagined breeze against his skin and remembering a night at the theatre, and a longing to kiss that tiny freckle at the side of her eye.

Agatha's smirk rested on him and he met her gaze until she turned away. He really didn't care what she said about him.

He didn't.

He wasn't his father, no matter how much he sounded like him or looked like him. And nothing would have made Andrew feel better than to have his father in the ducal box with them—the father he'd grown up with, the one who'd wanted to be at home with his family, or at least made the pretence quite well. Not the man his father had become in later years.

Andrew would never be like his father. Ever. And yet, he knew, his father once had thought his family above all others. His father had told him so. Told him how it had changed. Said he wished to leave them and go to the Americas. It was just there was nothing for him there.

Chapter Eight

The frame for the addition to the carriage house stood completed and the rafters of the roof topped the structure. He'd hired men to assist with the roof supports, but now he and Fawsett could work alone.

'You were awake early this morning,' Fawsett said, pounding a nail in. 'I did not wish to wake early—however, I was quite pleased to do so for you.'

'You took your time getting ready.' Andrew frowned. The scent of the wood didn't ease into his senses and remove his cares as it usually did. He kept thinking of Beatrice's discussion of her curves. And his imagination kept lengthening the discussion and he wasn't thinking of sonnets.

'I had to tell the maid goodbye.' Fawsett's hammer paused mid-air. His words became shrouded in a mist of his memories. 'A delicate and tender goodbye. Well, not terribly delicate and she doesn't like it tender.'

At Fawsett's words, the hammer slipped and Andrew hit his thumb. He threw the hammer, cursing.

'That hurt?' Fawsett asked.

Andrew did not move, the pain throbbing through his finger and lancing his whole body. When he could finally speak, he looked at Fawsett. 'Didn't hurt at all.'

'A man in love should feel no pain—at least until after the rope around the neck is tight. Enjoy your last precious moments of freedom before you are pulled into a whirlwind that grasps you and—' he waved the hammer head '—and gobbles you into oblivion.'

'I see that the maids of this household do not have to be impressed with wit.' Andrew stood and nimbly stepped from beam to beam. Then, he moved down the ladder and picked up his hammer from the floorboards, before climbing back to the rafters. He could feel his blasted thumb with every heartbeat.

'If I did not know better,' Fawsett said, 'I would

assume you have not recently got your ashes properly hauled.'

'Silence is required when your employer has a hammer in his hand.' He began working again.

Fawsett snorted. 'You will not kill me or hurt me. I can saw a straight line. And, I have yet to miss the head of a nail.'

'But you cannot be quiet.'

'No. Nor can the maids and they talk among themselves. They tell how the high-born ladies try to catch your attentions. You only have to crook a finger.' He shrugged, then scratched the front of his waistcoat, having left his coat on a rafter. 'I am the same.' He yawned. 'It is a delicate line we walk. Keeping the ladies happy and not over-tiring ourselves.' His lips pressed together for a moment. 'You and I both could be finding other ways to amuse ourselves right now. Better ways.'

A slowing rumble from the street caused all Andrew's senses to lock on to the noise.

They could see the top of the town coach easily from their perch. Andrew stared, his hammer stopping in mid-air.

Muffled sounds reached his ears. The coachman calling out. The carriage creaking to a standstill.

The door opening. Voices. Foxworthy. Blast. The duke. Damn. His mother…

Andrew looked at Fawsett, his voice a direct but controlled question. 'Did you happen to get the newspaper?'

'There is no mention of anything to concern you in the last one. And they have not had time to mention the theatre yet, though it could be out soon. I have a man posted, waiting, for the print. You've seen all that pertains to you and many of the stories from the past that refer to the countess.'

The voices disappeared into the house.

'They did not see you working like a tradesman,' Fawsett said. 'That is in your favour.'

Andrew put down his hammer, noting that his hand still pained him. He nodded and stood, motioning for Fawsett to follow him to the servants' entrance. 'I have been expecting a visit from the duke. And Mother. I just did not expect Fox as well.'

Andrew walked into the sitting room to be greeted by three pairs of eyes. One pair smiling with almost more mirth than they could contain. One pair with a clenched jaw close by. The last laced with concern.

His mother sat in one of the large overstuffed chairs facing the window. The sunlight reflected in her tired eyes and softened the hues in her clothing—only nothing could help with the monstrous matching earrings. His mother—he never understood what she saw in the earrings, but they always matched her dress.

She stared at the stone in her ring and adjusted the band. Then she twisted the rings on her other hand into place.

She stood, reaching her arm out. Fox put newsprint in her outstretched fingers, his glance at Andrew laced with undisguised whimsy. The duke, standing at Fox's side, tried to put a hundred words of censure into his stare.

His mother's grey curls were bobbing as she held out the print. 'Foxworthy picked this up for us on the way here.'

Foxworthy's voice held the innocence of a well-practised liar. 'A friend was at the theatre. I knew you would want your family to know before the paper was officially in print.' He smiled. 'You can count on me.'

Andrew forced his lips into a smile. 'You always are thinking of your cousin and you can be sure I will return the favour.'

The duke's voice boomed. 'Have you read what is said?'

Andrew stared at his older brother and remembered that their mother was present.

'If it is about the performance at Drury Lane, I was there. I do not need to read a review of it.'

His mother took another step, standing directly in front of Andrew. The scent of the same medicinal hair tonic she always used wafted to him.

She pointed to the part she had folded open. 'It says this woman spent the night fanning your face. That the two of you whispered and could not take your eyes from each other.' She touched his shoulder, her eyes filling with worry. 'Andrew, are you infatuated with this woman?'

'No, Mother. This paper...' he took it gently from her hands, and looked at the large engraving, not reacting '...is not reliable.'

Beatrice was the central figure. He was hardly discernible, yet they certainly had his cravat drawn right.

'But, Andrew,' his mother continued, facing him, 'you even saw to it she was invited to your brother's soirée. The duke thought it because of your business with the architect. But it's the woman, isn't it?'

Fox made an exaggerated movement of patting over his heart while looking off into the distance as if he imagined love.

'Mother—I did take the countess to the theatre. We had a lovely but quiet evening of no note. You've said you wished I would work less and I have been.' He glanced at Fox. Andrew held the paper with one hand so his mother could not see the gesture he made beside it which was directed at Fox.

Fox widened his eyes, pretending shock. Then touched his chest, at the approximate place of Andrew's scar, and snapped his teeth.

'They always refer to her as the Beast,' his mother said. 'That cannot be good. And I seem to remember that she may have tried to kill her husband.'

'I'm sure she did not, Mother. Sometimes her spirit isn't understood.' He grimaced. 'It's never understood in the papers.'

'Oh,' Fox inserted, his voice matching the blandness in his eyes. 'Has Lady Riverton been in the scandal sheets before?' He could have been at Drury Lane trying to prompt another actor.

'Truly, Andrew,' his mother said, 'what is this woman like?'

'Mother. She has a kind heart. The engraving is nonsensical. I am certain the person who created it was not there.'

'A kind heart?' His mother's brows rose. 'Andrew, are you absolutely sure you wish to be connected to this family?'

'The architect is really a decent sort. Most days. Lady Riverton is quite entertaining. I have a fondness for her.'

'I'm not so worried about him. I did not want to say this because it is idle talk, but Fox told us that she may have been seen not long ago with a man—' she lowered her voice '—in her bedchamber.'

'Well, I would certainly hope my cousin would pass no judgement on that, glass houses, as they say.'

She moved her head so she could see Fox. 'Well, we all realise Fox does need to be reprimanded on occasion.' She turned to Andrew again. 'But I know how some women, they get a hook in a man and pull him in slowly, and he is getting cooked in the marriage pot before he even knows the fire is lit.'

'Lady Riverton has no wish to marry.'

'Andrew.' She raised her arm, the scent of her

doeskin glove surrounding him as she tapped his cheek in the same way she had when he was a child. 'Anyone can see what a caring husband you'd make. I always knew when my boys were growing up that they would be a treasure for the right woman.' She shook her head. She smiled, reaching for the paper. 'I will dispose of this trash. But you take care around this woman.'

'I do.'

The duke smiled—his mouth moving into the same upturn one wolf would have shown another before the pounce. 'Foxworthy, why don't you show Mother the magnificent work Andrew has been doing on the exterior of the house?'

'Only if you are certain the two of you will not come to blows.' She directed her gaze at her sons before she held out her hand to take Fox's arm.

The duke raised a brow. 'Mother. That is a remark unbefitting of you.'

'But perfectly befitting my sons,' she said.

'Those sheets are often incorrect, Aunt Ida.' Fox tucked her hand over his arm. 'I've been written about—' he held up his fingers 'three—no, four times, if you count being the unknown man who took Lord Baldwin from the hazard tables and being one of the seconds for Beany Beaumont. And the time I was mentioned with Lady Wilmont—' He stood proud. 'It was an untruth. Grossly exaggerated.'

'I do not want Andrew linked with a woman who is not right for him.'

'I agree with you that he must take care.' His eyes met Andrew's as he left and his voice became ominous. 'Because no woman dares poach the Beast's game.'

His mother's response was a mix between a gasp and a mewl. The duke's stare darkened more.

Taking her arm, Foxworthy led his aunt from the room.

Before the duke could speak, Andrew turned to his brother. 'I know what you're going to say. You know I am not going to listen, so if you speak of it, I will know it is only for the chance to pontificate.'

'Then should I wish you all the best?' The duke moved to the unlit fireplace. 'With this woman who once stabbed her husband?'

'Lady Riverton is also a countess.'

'An accident caused by marriage to a man who wished to spite his family.' He paused. 'And, Andrew, that clackety-clackety-clack...' He tapped the mantel three times. 'The way she walks perched on those shoes. Surely you cannot…?'

'I find it endearing.' Andrew stared at his brother. Truthfully, she had good balance and it was quite pleasant to watch her walk.

'I do not care what you do, who you do it with, or how, as long as you are discreet. You must keep it out of the papers. Mother does not deserve any disgrace. Not again. We are a proud family. I understand that a man needs a woman's charms. But do not embarrass us with this countess-carriage-thrashing woman.'

Andrew took a step towards his brother. 'She is a gentle sort at heart and does not deserve the refuse printed about her. Within the next few months, I assure you the papers will not be telling such tales about her.'

'You cannot be certain of that. You are not yourself. This is not like you. I think you must have a serious fondness for her.'

'I am fond of her.'

'She is not right for you. She is not. You must have things planned out for your life and I do not think she is quite the same. You could not bear it if I did not march my toy soldiers correctly. You drew up battle plans. And we could not just fight a simple war.'

Andrew grumbled, 'You never quite understood the importance of supply lines either. A battle can be won or lost based on the ammunition and tools provided to soldiers. Not to mention food.'

'Pardon me,' his brother said. 'I forgot. The supply lines. You had to plan those the night before.'

'I do like to bring order to things,' Andrew said.

'Ah…' The tension left the duke's glare, melting away as he examined his brother's face. 'Yes. I see… This aberration of your nature makes sense now. I beg your pardon for being concerned. Foxworthy took us by surprise when he showed up at the door, insisting you were deeply besotted by this woman. I should have known, Fox is hardly a reliable source. And you have always wanted to correct— How many properties have you redone now?'

Andrew knew the connection his brother was making. 'She is perfect as she is. A bit high-spirited, but that is a refreshing change in my life. I am not trying to remake her. I am merely trying to help others see her as she is.'

The words he said reverberated in his head. He was not trying to help others see her as she was.

How untrue. But as he wished her to be. She had sensed that at the theatre, he was certain. And how unfair, to try to change her. What a disrespect to Beatrice.

It would be best for her if he left her to her own devices. To try to change someone only led to resentment. His father had wanted Andrew to accept his devotion to his mistress. Andrew could not. He could not accept the betrayal to his mother.

But he would have to see Beatrice again and not only because of his agreement to let her paint him. He could not walk from her life without telling her goodbye.

His brother nodded. 'I see.' Then he raised his hand to the painting hanging above the mantel—a peaceful reproduction of a meandering stream in a forest—and with his fingertip, he nudged the corner a bit. Then he appraised Andrew and smiled. The painting was now askew.

Andrew did not move. Irritation flowed into him and his brother was well aware.

The duke nodded. 'I suppose I should collect Mother and Fox. I have a lot of work waiting on me and did not plan on traipsing about, but Fox spoke with Mother first and convinced her that we must save you from the clutches of this woman.'

Andrew raised a brow. 'Did he do so in that way of seeming to be all concern and family heartiness?'

'Most certainly.'

'Some day, someone is going to rearrange that face of his into a series of black-and-blue knots. It will break my heart to see such a thing. I will have to close my eyes while I do it.'

'You'd best hurry if you wish to be first to throttle him.' The duke laughed. 'But don't concern yourself with our dear cousin. That Fox has been in too many chicken pens to remain unscathed for ever.'

'We should not leave him alone with Mother too long,' Andrew said. 'He's sure to remember something we don't wish for her to know.'

'In the carriage, he talked Mother into a trip to Somerset House as well. He thinks viewing the paintings will be good for Mother's vision. He's always spreading some tripe.'

Andrew paused. 'Fox wants Mother to view the art? At Somerset House?'

'Yes, I discouraged it.' The duke turned to leave the room. 'But she thought it a grand plan for us to have a family outing.'

A fuse sputtered alight in Andrew's head. Andrew remembered Beatrice's mention of a painting on display.

The duke grimaced. 'I have better things to do than viewing artwork. But Fox said we cannot miss it.'

'Of course, I shall go with you,' Andrew said.

'Let's collect Mother and Fox and we'll be on our way.' The duke left.

Andrew took a huge stride to the landscape above the mantel, straightened it and strode to the door. He could not let them travel to Somerset House alone, even if it meant pretending to be on good terms with Fox.

The trip passed smoothly, with Andrew and the duke doing most of the talking. Fox sat too calmly and later insisted on helping his dear Aunt Ida from the carriage.

Andrew and the duke spared a glance, and Andrew wondered what Beatrice had painted. She'd wanted him to view it so he was hopeful it would be something which would help her image. Only Fox's insistence on the trip convinced him to be wary.

Once inside, the floor-to-ceiling artwork of Somerset House's exhibition almost flowed out the door. The windows directly overhead gave pleasant views of the paintings.

His mother looked up, then around. 'I had no idea they could get so much artwork in one room. It must be five hundred pieces.'

'Close to a thousand,' Andrew replied, standing with his hands clasped behind his back, examining a rendition of the Thames.

He stood on one side of his mother, the duke on the other, Fox behind them, his innocent liar's countenance again telling far too much. Every time Andrew could catch Fox's eye, he gave a glare of warning.

'You might find someone to patronise.' His mother spoke to her eldest son as she stared at the art above them.

'Yes.' Fox sniffled the word out, squeezing his lips closed, eyes watering with the wrong kind of tears. 'I think I could suggest someone.' He opened his eyes long enough to look at Andrew. 'I am trying to think of the name as we speak.'

The duke examined Fox, his own lips becoming a straight line.

They continued to make their way around the room.

An elderly matron moved beside them and Andrew held his mother's elbow and moved her further along, past a couple talking animatedly about some portrait they were staring at.

'We could use something fresh for the sitting room...' the duchess said.

His mother's words stopped, and her jaw went slack, as she looked beyond him to the painting the couple had been examining. Her eyes were wide.

He turned his head and saw a larger-than-life painting of a female holding a sword across her chest—which was a good thing, as the garment she had draped over her had merely exaggerated that part of the woman's anatomy. In fact, all the coverings over the woman's body helped the viewer's mind embellish what lay beneath.

Andrew drew in a breath.

Fox's choking laughter and the duke's gurgle caused Andrew's eyes to move to the warrior's face and lock there.

'A depraved artist painted that heathen warrior woman with hardly more than a silk handkerchief covering her.' His mother let out a deep breath. 'Boys.' She grabbed her son's arms. 'Turn away. This is not for a male's eyes.'

'Aunt Ida, it's...' Fox choked on his snuffling.

Andrew grabbed Fox's arm, ready to put a fist in his cousin's face. Fox shook with the effort to control his voice. He glanced at Andrew. 'Boadicea...'

Andrew squeezed Fox's arm with enough pressure to silence him.

'It is not humorous to see so much of a woman, Fenton Foxworthy.' His mother marched for the door and the muffled voices around covered the sound of her leaving.

Andrew thrust Foxworthy's arm aside, giving him a look of promised retribution.

'...the Beast.' Foxworthy squeaked out the word, then turned to follow his aunt. Andrew looked to the duke and saw his brother staring at the painting, memorising it.

'Lionel,' Andrew snapped out his brother's hated given name. 'We are leaving. Do not leave your eyes behind.'

Andrew sat in his study, the image of the portrait locked in his mind for ever. He'd returned to the display after his family left, half-expecting to see the duke again as well. At least there was no true signature on the painting. Just an illegible line.

He returned home to find an unopened lavender-scented post waiting for him. If he shut his eyes, he could bring the scent of baked goods to his memory. Instead, he pulled the note to his nose, inhaling—inhaling deeply just for a moment before he looked at the folded paper again. The floral pulled him in and the feminine loops of his handwritten name set the snare.

He slipped a finger under the seal, unfolding the paper.

My muse,
I really did not think I would be portrayed quite so hideously in the last engraving. I do not know how it was construed so inaccurately. The caricature of you was unfair.

I've left my brother's house so that I might return to my former home and begin anew. Especially as I have convinced Mother she must see her sister so I will be alone.

Please consider visiting my home so we may begin work on the portrait. I cannot sleep for my dreams of having you as a subject. I feel your face would inspire me to greatness.

Of course, I would like to see more of you.
Beatrice the Demure

His fingers caressed the flourishes of her words and the sketch at the top of the page. She'd drawn a small profile of him.

But even as he traced the likeness of himself, his mind filled with *Boadicea*. The artwork had not been lit by lamps, but from overhead windows. He'd not thought a flat plane could be filled with curves, but the portrait had proven it could be done.

He wanted to see Beatrice again. Needed to see her. He had to explain the finer points of discretion. *Beatrice the Brazen* would sell more copies than *Beatrice the Beast*. She must understand the need to change her outward behaviour.

In her own home, she could slide down the banisters. But in public, she had to find a way to get pleasant views. Respect. He stood, pleased with his plan. She would want respect for her works. In order to do that, she must gather respect among the *ton* for herself.

He sighed. He must ask Beatrice if she truly wanted to change how she was seen. He wanted to see her again. This woman who had captured his thoughts in the same way Boadicea had led her impassioned soldiers. He just did not wish to have the same fate as the men led by the warrior queen.

Andrew decided he'd travel to Beatrice's home after he took one more trip to Somerset House.

As soon as possible, he would see Beatrice. And he would not think of her barely concealed breasts. No. He would not think of her curves.

He would see Beatrice and be extremely careful.

He never wanted to hurt her, in any way. She'd already been through so much with Riverton.

He did not know if she had read of his father's mistress and doubted she would have paid much attention even if she had. It had hardly made more than one or two lines of print. But they would be engraved in his mind for ever.

Chapter Nine

After he put away the shaving supplies and extinguished the lamp, Fawsett pulled the cravat out of the wardrobe. Then he closed the smaller drawer, and stepped back, pushing the door shut.

Andrew pulled the shirt over his head and Fawsett stepped in front of him. The valet worked efficiently to get the cravat tied, then held the waistcoat for Andrew to slip his arms into. While Fawsett retrieved the coat, Andrew did the buttons.

Then Fawsett held the coat for Andrew to slip his arms into. 'I do appreciate your giving me a break from the carpentry while you visit your beloved's house, but I am not sure you are making a wise choice.'

'What do you know of my private business?'

Fawsett's chin dropped an infinitesimal amount. 'You are visiting Lady Riverton. At her house.'

'And how do you know this?'

'Mary Ann and Hester are sisters. Julia is the coachman's niece.'

Andrew looked closely at Fawsett. He had no idea who the women were. 'Indeed.'

'Cook agrees.' Fawsett said.

Andrew stepped directly in front of Fawsett. 'I insist on discretion in a valet.'

'Sir…' Fawsett's shoulders rose with the puff of his chest '…I merely listen.'

Andrew didn't move from his proximity to the servant. 'You are not to discuss my life with anyone.'

'I was the same with any enquiries as I would have been with a magistrate. I speak many words with only enough truth to add credence to the lies. Not that I am adept at—dodging magistrate's questions.' Fawsett's eyes flickered away momentarily. 'And trust me, they are more determined than the maids.'

'Fawsett,' Andrew continued, watching the valet's expression. 'Have you been ill?'

'No.'

He raised one brow and locked eyes with Fawsett. 'Why did my man of affairs receive the bill from the physician?'

Fawsett's pointed nose again moved upwards, offended. 'I take my duties seriously. Seriously. And I have decided I am quite fond of the new maid and now I do not intend to lose this post.'

'Charging your bills to me is not the way to keep it.' Andrew frowned.

'The bill is completely for you,' Fawsett said, 'and I did not think I would need to explain.'

'You do.'

'I have had a brief instruction on quick wound care. Although…' he looked aside, shuddering 'I will *not* be able to apply leeches or do any sort of blood-letting, but I'm assured that can wait until the time of a physician's arrival.'

Andrew examined Fawsett's face. The man was serious. 'Why…?'

'Your activities. I warrant, the carpentry work is bad as one might expect. But the other danger—'

'There is no danger. Lady Riverton is a fine artist. She has asked to paint my portrait and we are to discuss many things.'

'You say she's painting you?' Fawsett had puzzlement in his words.

'We are to discuss it,' Andrew answered, looking to see Fawsett examining him.

'On what part is the paint applied?'

'The canvas.'

'And why would she wish to paint...when there are so many more enjoyable ways to spend a moment?'

'My face. She likes it.'

Fawsett snorted.

Andrew inwardly started. Was it that odd that a woman might like his face?

'So you expect me to believe,' Fawsett continued, 'this is a journey simply to have your portrait done? Sir, I am not a magistrate. You do not have to recite Byron to me. You remember I did accidentally see her request and I can read—and not just the words written on the paper.'

'Yes. That is all.'

'Do you mind if I watch?' Fawsett asked innocently. 'I don't think I've ever seen it done that way before.'

'Fawsett. You are sacked.' Andrew said. 'You have your wish.'

The valet smiled. 'If I am sacked, then I will no longer be under the valet's code of silence. But still, I will silently take your secrets with me...

Throwing myself into the streets, a fallen, broken man, begging for Cook to toss a few morsels to me and hoping with my last breaths for the safety of my much-missed former employer, whilst I burn the saw and hammer.'

'You are merely sacked as my valet. Not my carpenter.'

'I do not know if I can remove myself until I am certain of your sanity. A sensible man does not go alone into a room with a woman to sample her paintbrushes. Cook would laugh at me for believing such nonsense, and if it is the truth, I will be extremely embarrassed.' Fawsett glanced across at Andrew. His voice lowered and he frowned. 'It is the truth.'

Andrew glared at him.

'Blast.' Fawsett hit his own forehead with the palm of his hand. 'I should have known. You do not spend your nights gambling, but bang nails into wood. You get caught with a woman called the Beast and you spend your time with her discussing her palette, and not the right kind of palette.' He sighed and put the back of his hand to his forehead. 'Have you not heard tales—tales of the debauchery of the upper classes? Of idleness? Of drunken revelry?'

'Have you not heard of servants who work?'

'At your house they do.' He wrinkled his nose and then his face completely changed and he smiled. 'Except on the rare occasions when my beloved and I spend a few stolen moments together.' He spoke with precise assuredness. 'We do not paint.'

'Perhaps you should.' Andrew smiled, giving his manservant a knowing smile. 'There is something quite…intriguing about private art.'

Fawsett raised his chin heavenwards. 'I suppose, if you can be *painted* by Beatrice the Beast and still retain the necessary equipment for a repeat performance, I must bow to you.'

Then Fawsett turned to him and his voice softened. 'I would not like to see parts of you strung out like clothing to dry. I caution you to be extremely courteous when you bid her farewell.' He smiled. 'I assure you this is good advice—and no matter how well she agrees to the parting—escape like the demons of hell are after you. And you should do this soon.'

'Lady Riverton and I have a complete understanding.'

'Yes, but you and the duke do not. He is planning to introduce you to the lovely sister of Lord

Dumonte. It is a surprise.' Fawsett bowed his head and let his voice become melancholy. 'And I have ruined it.'

Andrew drew in a breath. His brother took his duties entirely too seriously.

'And should you decide to pursue Lord Dumonte's sister, who is quite enthralling from all accounts, the understanding you have with Lady Riverton might become crowded,' Fawsett asserted before Andrew could speak. 'We do not know what Lady Riverton is capable of.' His head tilted and his eyes narrowed as they raked the area of Andrew's chest. 'Or perhaps we do.'

Andrew growled, 'When Cook throws her scraps to your body in the mews, it will be quite cold.'

Fawsett looked at Andrew as if his employer had no sense. 'I suppose you will be safe as long as you tread carefully and do not tarry afterwards. I have seen the scar—I know you like rough love play and I am a firm believer in romantic exploration, but my tastes do not go to the length yours do. I am but a simple man.'

'Fawsett.' Andrew used all his strength to keep his voice moderate and his jaw fought the effort. 'I do not like being bitten, I assure you.'

'It is not my concern how you conduct yourself in the bedchamber. When the speculation reached my ears on what you and this woman do in private, I did acknowledge you've come home rumpled on more than one occasion. It's to be expected. I now have a few tinctures and instructions from the physician should things become—overenthusiastic and...' he opened his coat, revealing a pair of scissors poking from a roughly sewn interior pocket '...should you need to be quickly untied.'

'Fawsett. You are daft.'

After letting the garment fall back in place, the valet did not blink. He patted his coat. 'I, too, have been in love.'

Andrew turned and shut his eyes. He had never been in love. Wasn't sure he believed in it.

'I expected you to be more like the old duke.' Fawsett's musing voice reached Andrew.

Andrew stilled. His fists clenched and he turned, ready to thrash Fawsett. But the valet rummaged inside the wardrobe. The comment had merely slipped from Fawsett's lips and meant nothing.

Idle chatter.

Andrew ignored the sweat on his brow and left the room. In the hallway he stopped, remembering the moment he'd discovered the name of his father's mistress. He'd been home on his last school holiday and finishing a book by Defoe. His mother had been reading, shuffling pages of newsprint. Her gasp had caught his attention and he'd looked up. He'd thought her choking and rushed to her side. She'd been trembling and crashed her hands together, still crushing the paper in her grasp.

Not a word was spoken, but her face turned ashen. He'd never forget that. He'd reached for the paper, but she'd not released it, pulling it close to her body, refusing to loosen her grip.

But he'd not backed away. He'd snatched the sheets, ripping them from her fingers.

'What?' he'd demanded.

She'd still not spoken and reached towards him, trying to keep him from seeing. He'd turned, keeping control of the scandal sheet, his back broad enough to prevent her from taking the rag.

She'd cried out and run from the room.

Then he'd seen the print and even though the names were not completely spelled out, he knew. His father. The mistress. The birth of a child.

Chapter Ten

Andrew stepped into Astlin Manor, the house the architect had skilfully bargained to have built for his sister during the marriage settlement with the earl. Andrew had seen sketches of the Palladian staircase, heard stories of the gold trim on the ballroom ceiling and seen a drawn version of the alcove.

He ran his hand along the banister as he ascended the stairway. The home was fairly small in the number of rooms, but big in scope.

Each craftsman had been presented with a drawing of a lace design and instructed to do a one-of-a-kind creation they would give to a lover for her home. Chairs' legs had the tiniest trails of lacework carved into the legs. Sconces had the pattern as well.

These kinds of details were what Andrew insisted on for his own home as well. Unobtrusive but visible treasures around him. Items with stories behind them. Fixtures that went deeper than their obvious need, but nourished the spirit as well.

Directly in front of him, the first steps rose up in the same way of a usual staircase, but then two separate curving paths split from it, circling behind and up, meeting slowly on the first floor, like the curve of a giant tiara. A walkway at the top circled the cut-out of the staircase, making him able to walk completely around the banister overlooking the ground floor. Palladian columns rimmed the overlook and the structures reached to the second level.

The butler stopped, giving Andrew a chance to take in the surroundings before leading him on to the parlour.

Slippers clattered across the marble tiles. He looked up in time to see Beatrice, her brown hair piled into an unruly mass of curls, moving towards them. But he couldn't take his eyes from her. The image of her Warrior and the true woman melded in his mind.

He could not speak. Perhaps he did believe in love.

'Lord Andrew.' She swirled forward, her moss-coloured dress fluttering about. The last few inches of the hem had been decorated in yellow fabric cut in circular shapes, adding weight which caused the flare around her feet, concealing her slippers. 'We meet again.' She walked to him.

Then she looked at him and an eyebrow rose in anticipation of his answer. 'What did you think of the…?'

He missed what she said next, expecting she would ask him what he thought of the portrait and knowing he could not find the words to tell her how the portrait had affected him. Then he realised he'd misheard. 'Pardon?' he asked.

She leaned forward. 'What did you think of the stairs?'

'Magnificent. Beyond belief. Two points of splendour. A pathway to incredible wonder.'

'I think they're a bit overdone myself and a long way to get a short distance, but they work for me.' She moved back to the circular area of the stairway. 'Come along, I'll show you the owl cove.'

Then she led him to the white alcove. He could almost reach from wall to wall should he stretch his arms. Bas-relief trees surrounded him. Several marble owls perched around the area, just above the viewer's head. The creatures' eyes were tinted glass and hollow behind. 'I can have the candles lit if you'd wish,' she said.

He'd been told of the hidden-access passageway behind the alcove.

He shook his head. 'No. I can imagine their eyes flickering.'

She nodded. 'I once had the candles lit at night. Once only. I did not expect to feel frightened at all, but somehow, the sight of all the eyes glowing did not impress me.' She turned. 'Now the ballroom. My personal favourite. This way.'

She turned away, moving with the freedom of a youth, taking him down a wide hallway into a grand chamber.

He turned his head to the left, noting the fireplace large enough for four chairs inside.

Then she moved into the centre of the room and looked up, spreading her arms. 'But there's where the purse emptied, or so my husband said. Eight thousand and ninety-three pounds on the ceiling alone and the artists worked for almost nothing. Lived here and I fed them, clothed them and gave them the good wine and brandy when they'd been working the hardest. But Riverton made them cover up all the indiscreet parts.'

He looked up and took a few steps backwards

while his eyes searched. He realised he could have spent hours, days, examining the ceiling.

'No two cherubs are alike,' she said. 'I had them named once upon a time, but I've forgotten now. Even that many little angels watching over me didn't bring happiness. I could not imagine…' she extended her arms and twirled around. 'I was a countess. I had a home like this. I had the finest clothing. A staff to meet my needs. And I was not one bit happy. My husband had been gone for months. He lived with his mistress, or so I thought. I decided to have a house party with only a few people to attend, Tilly being one—so now I know how the tale was spread. I stepped out of the gardens to see his carriage roll up at my home with a woman bringing her trunks. No one even knew where Riverton was at that time.'

'You attacked the vehicle with the woman inside.'

'I only broke a window when she was trying to pull her belongings out. She would not leave. She kept insisting I had Riverton hidden in my home and claiming he'd given it to her.' She shrugged. 'My grandmother was in the house. My husband most definitely was not. I could not possibly let the woman move in.'

She paused. 'Once he returned, months later, dressed in rags, I did try to keep him home, but let him do as he wished. His mind was so…sad, that I had to stay near him to prevent him from getting worse. In his corner of the house, he could do as he wished. With my acceptance of his actions, he was less likely to get his throat cut in Seven Dials and servants could pick him up from the floor. I didn't want people to see him so, yet it appeared I was supporting his problems. Again, I was portrayed badly, but I could not let him die in the cold.'

'You cannot think about the past, you must concentrate on the future if you want to change it,' Andrew said. He could not imagine living so.

'I am. But that part of my life is in my memory every day.'

'Push it aside because it is not who you are to be now.' He moved to stand in front of her. 'Beatrice. I saw the painting at Somerset House. You were barely dressed. You are not helping change the perception.'

'You recognised me?' The words squeaked out. Eyes widened.

'It is a wonder I looked at your face at all, though I suppose most men wouldn't. But I knew instantly.' He frowned. 'It is a self-portrait. How could I not recognise you?'

'No. It's not me. The woman in the painting has red flowing hair, a delicate nose and much bigger—everything than I do.'

His thoughts jumped to her words. Beatrice had ample everything, she did not need to change them.

He stared at her face. She had not expected to be recognised? 'I knew you instantly. And Fox led me right to it.'

'Tilly,' she grumbled. 'Tilly knows him, and Tilly, well, she may have been in my studio when I worked on it.'

'You cannot paint portraits like that and have them displayed—' his voice toughened '—if you wish to change your image.'

She blinked up at him. 'What did you think of it?'

He didn't answer. Just stared at her.

She prodded, brows tight. 'Andrew. What did you think of it? I worked very hard on the hands.'

'I...any man looking at it would want to kiss those fingertips, Beatrice.' He kept his gaze on hers.

Her voice changed, became soft, sad. 'It is not

about kissing. It is about strength. A woman's strength. If you did not see that, I failed.' She stood, took a step and wobbled. Andrew caught her arms, steadying her. His palms burned in the most pleasant way.

'It is not in your best interest to have that artwork on display,' he said.

She swayed sideways and he kept her upright. 'Pardon me,' she said, reversing her hand so she gripped him. She leaned down, removing one slipper while teetering.

He put a hand at her side, helping her remain standing. She removed the last one, stumbling herself right into his arms.

'That was no accident,' he said, extracting himself, but only partway. Their clothes still touched.

'I'm getting my coin's worth for those torture-chamber shoes I paid well for.'

'I cannot believe you are so comfortable with notice and notoriety, yet you wear slippers that hurt.'

'They make me more visible. Taller.' She raised her chin. 'Powerful—when I do not stumble. I feel like they are my soldier's boots and I am an eminent leader in them, announcing my arrival.'

'All leaders are not great. In fact, it may be quite

rare to be a great leader. Even a mediocre leader with the perception turned his way can sound like the best superior.' He wanted her to understand how important it could be for her to turn the talk in her direction. Her art would receive more notice. She could do more, in whatever she chose.

'You do not want to be Boadicea, leading yourself into a fight you cannot win,' he said. 'You must plan ahead so you can be a better Beatrice.'

'I rather like the warrior.'

'Now is the time to finesse. Not storm ahead.'

'The picture is art. Some day I wish to be known all throughout England for my portraits,' she said, holding her chin high.

He could not keep himself from smiling. 'Your brush is wicked.'

She narrowed her gaze. 'It is a very sincere painting.'

His eyes stayed on her when his chin briefly darted sideways. 'I will not argue that with you. I have no complaints at all about the painting, except that she decidedly resembles you and it could gather attention we don't wish for. I thought you might paint, perhaps, some flowers. A landscape or two with baby rabbits or baby chickens. Clothed people even?'

'I am not inspired to paint fluffy things or landscapes in the same way I wish to capture the likenesses of people. Faces and bodies are intriguing. Each person is a masterpiece in his or her own way. But you are more than that. Your face inspires me in a way no other ever has. Go with me to my studio and you will see what I can do.'

He met her eyes.

She blushed. 'With a paintbrush, unless you wish otherwise.' Taking his arm, she moved towards the studio.

Beatrice took Andrew down the path set among carefully tended grounds and walked to a cottage surrounded by overgrown ivy, edged by a field. Five cattle grazed in the distance. Two were obvious milk producers. None were impressed by visitors or even seemed aware of the soft breeze which flowed in the air or the chip-chip call of a chaffinch.

Sorrel, with its deep veins, and pineapple sage grew at the edge of the rock pathway. Many times she'd painted the pineapple-sage plants when they reached their height and had burst into their crimson flowers.

The cottage was another work designed by her

brother. Shaded by sycamore trees and oaks, it would fit nicely into the landscape of many paintings as a crofter's home. The arched windows added a whimsical look.

Having Andrew walk to the path of her studio made her feel the lightness of the world she'd lived in before she'd been introduced to stays and corsets. In those moments, she no longer cared that Tilly had not been a true friend and that Riverton had betrayed her.

'When I married and needed to escape Riverton,' she said, 'sometimes I lived in the cottage and shut out everything but art. The servants would know of his ways, but we were in the country and that was safer for him.'

She stopped on the rock path, staring at the structure. 'It is quite plain.' She'd hardly let a servant in to even clean it, preferring the solitude and dust over interruption. Splotches were here and there inside, and nothing was suitable for entertaining or guests. Yet it was her refuge. Her sanctuary. She missed it when she was at her brother's house, but sometimes the solitude became too great and sometimes her mother became too motherly.

'Mostly it is quiet, but sometimes too loud when

Mother begins regretting her decision not to have grandchildren. She believes it was a grievous error to let me remain unmarried after Riverton died and to let Wilson remain unattached.' She wrinkled her nose. 'The servants respect my privacy and Mother mostly tolerates it.'

She paused before opening the door, wanting him to see the studio in the same light she did. But then she rushed forward, hoping he would understand.

'I live here for weeks on occasion when I want to immerse myself in art. It is a perfect place to escape into painting. Servants bring meals and water at regular intervals, otherwise I am completely left alone, except for an occasional request—with teeth—that I join Mother for tea.'

The scent of linseed oil welcomed her the minute she stepped over the threshold. She moved to unlatch the windows and push them open.

One easel stood with a small painting, half-completed, of a dragon. On a table beside the easel, Boadicea's sword.

He picked up the weapon, enjoying the heft of it in his hand.

'The sword is from a museum in Piccadilly,' she said.

He placed it back and continued examining the room. A roll of canvas stood propped against a wall and an artist's stool sat near the easel. A sofa finished the askew tableau, the resting place of an unframed painting of a garish woman. Resting on the cloth upholstery of the sofa sat two skulls— one rather large and, he supposed, bovine. The other smaller, an animal he could not guess.

'Inspiration?' he asked.

'I'm sure scandalmongers could have quite the print space for that information, but you cannot paint something without knowing exactly how it looks. How it fits,' she said, picking up the whitened bone and letting her fingers trace the seams. 'Imagine trying to paint a cow's eye and not knowing the size in relation to the rest of the animal.'

She held out the skull to him. Andrew took it from her hands, not looking at the object, but at her. 'Today I am completely comfortable with not knowing the exact proportions of a bovine.' He placed it back on the sofa and put a hand at the small of her back. 'Should we begin?'

She nodded, turning. Having him in her studio was more intimate to her than a bedchamber. Taking the paint-stained and dried cloth beside her easel, she brushed the dust from the two skulls and then wiped her hands.

'Because of what you said at the theatre,' he said, 'I wondered if you might wish to maintain the notoriety you have.' He clasped his hands behind his back. 'Is that true?'

Beatrice shook her head. 'I cannot like being the Beast.'

When Riverton was alive, she'd been bombarded by so many feelings, heard and lived so many lies she'd really not concerned herself with the print much. How could she when she was living an even worse nightmare under her roof? 'I am just now becoming myself again and am able to look at the past more objectively. Perhaps those tales in the sheets are helping me open my eyes. To see that it truly doesn't matter so much what others think of my past. It will never go away. It will not be forgotten.'

'You can make new memories in their minds. You can temper the responses. Images can be softened. Blended.'

'Oh, yes, I know. I am looking at the past very differently than I did before. I shrank from it. Wanted to hide in my art. My studio. I could not face the theatre again. Perhaps I was wrong. Perhaps I should embrace the little tufts in the drawings. Those memories are far kinder than the ones I have from behind the closed doors of my marriage.'

'It is the past.'

'The past. But it is my past. My husband confessed to me that he'd only married me because his parents hated me so much—and that they'd been right. He said he preferred the taste of poppies far above the taste of my lips and he preferred to be insensible than to remember himself married.'

She hadn't minded so much hearing the words. They'd been a relief almost. She'd already known it by then and had been pleased he saw the truth of it.

Silence filtered into the room much like the sunlight from the windows.

His face had the look of stone again.

This time she didn't mind. 'I have to admit, I probably would have preferred poppies to marriage at that point, too. Or arsenic or laudanum or gunpowder. But instead, I chose to immerse myself in the scent of linseed oil and pigments.'

A blank canvas stood on her easel. The one she planned to use for Andrew.

Her voice tightened. 'It's best to know how things look to paint them. If you guess the proportions…' She shrugged. 'And the shadows. Light is so important.'

She ran a finger over the canvas. 'Andrew.'

One brow flicked up. The smallest shake of his head. His body stilled.

'You will be a grand subject.' She breathed in deeply, her imagination taking her senses closer to him, pulling the barest whiffs of pine, leather and maleness and immersing it into her brain with the tones and hues of his skin.

'Andrew.' She stepped closer, her body responding to all the parts of him, both real and imagined. 'I would so love to paint you as you were created.' She focused on the threads of his coat sleeve, touching only one finger pad to the cloth and absorbing as much of the fabric as possible with the briefest touch. 'Imagine, the Andrew Nude.'

His face tilted down and he quite looked over his nose at her. One emphatic shake of his head.

Her skirts swirled around the legs of his trousers and an awareness flowed through the material. 'I simply could not ask a footman to remove his shirt and, if I remember correctly, you were willing to remove clothing, or at least push it aside, when we first met. I would like to paint all of you.'

'I will not ever pose without clothing. Even for Rembrandt.'

'I am extremely fascinated by the male form.' Her hand touched the buttons of his waistcoat. 'And this would be of no prurient nature. We are not talking of base natures and leering eyes. We are talking of art. Grand and majestic.'

She reached out, touching his chin. 'Your nose—straight, flared but not overly so. A mouth, wide enough. Teeth—amazing. And your hair— the way it falls across your face. That dark hair overwhelms me. Women would never see Fox standing beside you if you would just flash them a smile. Only because you hide within yourself do you keep women away from you. I've never seen a man so well formed as you—' She locked eyes with him. 'And I certainly have looked. You've shoulders to spare and hips not too lean, but a perfect base. And muscled in the right amounts. Greek statues pale in comparison.'

'You flatter me.' He smiled. 'You can continue. I'm just not taking off any clothing.'

She shook her head. 'No. I look at you with a

critical eye. I would wager no one has ever peered at you so closely as I have and seen so much.'

Her hand slipped under his waistcoat, palm flattened, captured by the close fit of the material. Only her fingers could move. 'You are exactly what I want in a model.'

She rested her head against him, taking her palm from beneath his clothing and letting it float along the cloth, shutting her eyes, trying to memorise each turn of his body. Feeling the proportions of his height and his shoulders. All of him she could press against her and wishing she could hold him close for hours, hugging it all into her memory.

Chapter Eleven

There were worse things in life than to be the object of an artist's attention, Andrew thought as Beatrice hugged herself against him.

He took her shoulders in his hands to scoot her back from him, but once his fingers gripped they floated down her back. His cheek rested against her hair and he realised art had much to offer. Shadows and proportions were part of it. The curves and textures and warmth another.

If she painted him without clothing, he would face the temptation of her eyes, her lips and he was sure there was more. Much more. Days would pass when he thought of nothing else but her. Already he wondered if she had not shown him a part of himself that he had not known existed.

He wished he had been there on the night she'd taken the scissors to her husband.

To bed her on the first night they met would have been safe—when he did not know her. But now he saw the person she was—someone who'd suffered because of Riverton's actions.

'Andrew, you've a bone structure better than I've ever seen. Your body is magnificent, joined together in all the right ways—at least what I can see of it. Those eyes of yours—unfathomable—except when your mask falls away and I see the gaze of a hungry male.' She pulled away, but as she moved, his hands slid down her arms, stopping to clasp her fingertips.

Beatrice looked him over top to bottom. 'Arousing. If I could capture that look from your eyes. If I could put your form on canvas in your most natural state.'

With all the other thoughts and sensations at war within himself, the only one with an easy answer was the question of a nude painting. 'I will never agree.'

'True. You wouldn't. I realise that.'

Standing in the room with her was all the adventure he wished for. The thought crashed into him. He had felt the wind from an erupting storm blast against his face and body with such force it almost took his feet from under him and that was nothing compared to the vibrancy unleashed from her.

'No one would ever have to see it but the two of us,' she said.

He spoke loudly, to make sure his words reached all his extremities. 'No.'

She slipped her fingers from his and moulded against him, shuddering. 'I understand.' Her voice soft. Her hand soft. Every part of her body against his—soft. His body—hard.

But he did not want to hurt her. He did not.

Boadicea. The female leader who could stir a thousand—no, a hundred thousand men to do her bidding. But it didn't change the battle.

A battle. Uphill. Defeat.

More than ever, for his own children, he wanted what he had once had. The quiet order of the world from his early memories. The soft voices. The muted light bringing everyone close so they could see their books in the early winter darkness.

Boadicea might well have loved her daughters more deeply than any mother ever could, but it did not mean their lives were kind and gentle.

'Beatrice. I will pose for a clothed portrait only.' If he disrobed for her to paint him, it would be difficult to— Impossible to— Impossibly hard—

He shut his eyes. He hated his self-control, but it was necessary. Not just for himself, but for her as well. She must understand the need to keep her name from gossips. Some day she might have children. Or Wilson would have children. They would not want their children to have to listen to sordid tales from the sheets. The stories already published needed a chance to fade deeper into the background. That was best for all concerned.

He felt his shirt rising from his trousers, pulled upwards, long fingers slipping on to his skin. Burning a trail across his stomach. Fingers which practically took him to his knees.

He grasped her wrist, stopping her movement.

'I am only learning your body,' she said. 'I am seeing you with my touch.'

'Perhaps that is what your eyes are for.'

'I suppose.' She stepped back, using her hand to fan her face. 'Inspiration is so overwhelming.'

She shivered, then walked to a container of brushes, tips pointing upwards, and pulled out one. 'If you will not have the grace to pose for an unforgettable piece of artwork, then I will paint a formal portrait of you. A gift. For both of us. The pose, a present from you to me. The canvas from me to you. I will put all my feelings into the creation.'

Gentle raps sounded while she tapped the wood handle of the paintbrush against the table. 'I shall need a large amount of black pigment for your coat and some white for your cravat.' Her voice softened. 'No one has ever been proven to have an apoplexy from wearing other colours, Andrew.'

She talked of hues when he could only think of the subtle movements beneath her clothing. He would need more caution than he had ever used in his life. He would be building castles to remove Beatrice from his thoughts.

But he did want to see what she would put on canvas. To have a memento of their time together for the rest of his life. One portrait. Skin she had created on the canvas. A face she fashioned. A way of binding them for ever.

And he would pose because no man could say no to this woman, not the one in the painting in Somerset House, nor the one standing in front of him now.

Beatrice could stand across the room from Andrew and feel him as if she touched him. He would make the most perfect portrait. She had created her version of a woman with strength in her Boadicea painting—her rendition of all that a woman was meant to be. Now, she wished for the male complement to the painting. No one else in the world could be that person, but him.

She imagined the finished product. Could see the form of it clearly. Needed to see the exactness of it. Needed to capture what her mind saw and put it on canvas.

She whirled around so she couldn't see him, and yet, he remained in her vision. She pulled strength from inside herself so she wouldn't be too awed when she turned again.

Distancing herself from the emotions buffeting her, she walked forward and reached up. 'Pardon me.' Her hand touched his chin, moving to go over each plane of his skin, feeling the barest hint of whiskers. 'Your valet does a close shave.' She gave a sniff. 'And what is that scent he uses after he shaves you? It's quite masculine. Reminds me of forests.'

His eyes narrowed. 'I don't believe touching is necessary to painting.'

She smiled. 'No. But I rather like it.'

He bent forward, speaking softly. 'So do I. That is why you must not do it.'

'Well, then.' She ducked her chin. 'I suppose I must not touch you—as you know, I always follow your direction.'

In that section, their gazes held for a moment and acknowledged what she had truly said. She turned away first and pointed to a small pedestal by the window. 'Stand there and prop your elbow on it. Look thoughtful—not as if you are going to your own hanging.'

She recognised that stone-cold uncaring look—the one she now suspected appeared when he felt things most intensely.

Frowning, she studied him, looking for imperfections. A flaw, a scar—the man could not be this perfect of form.

'Let me see you...' she said, stepping forward.

Nothing on his face changed. She shook her head. 'Snarl or something. Pretend you're the beast this time. I want to see the muscles move on your face.'

'First you ask me to disrobe...' he muttered. He showed her his incisors.

She examined him. Proportionally, he was exquisite. She stared at his ears, but they were half-hidden under hair. He closed his mouth into a sharp line—which immediately wrested her attention from his ears. Little lines did appear at the side of his eyes—but not severe ones. They only made him seem wise, somehow.

'I must touch your hair,' she said.

'No.'

Her hand stopped in mid-air. 'Your ears. I have to see them completely. You must have a flaw of some sort.' She dropped her hand to one side.

He reached up with one hand, threading his fingers in his hair and revealing his ear, but just as soon he released the locks and they fell into the same ruffled disorder that gave him the roguish look she preferred.

She examined. 'Remarkable, in their own way. Just the right size. Not too big. Perfect lobes…'

She walked to stare at his profile. He gazed heavenwards for a second and then frowned at her.

'That night, the night—I saw you truly for the first time, in the light of the candle—I could not believe the perfection in your face.' She stood on tiptoe and peered into his eyes. 'Lovely flecks of light and darker colours mixed.'

'I am not a horse at Tattersall's. And you were wearing someone else's spectacles that first night.'

'Which I peered over.'

He gave a sharp nod. 'Beatrice…' He lowered

his chin and moved, propping his elbow on to the pedestal. 'If the paint does not start to flow in a heartbeat, I am leaving.'

'Very well.' She stepped to the canvas, tipped her head at an angle to look at him and reached for her sketching pencil. 'Be still.'

He would be aghast if she painted his waistcoat vermilion.

She perched on the three-legged stool and the only sounds in the room were the whispers as the graphite of the pencil brushed against canvas.

Beatrice made the flowing strokes which would give her the outline of his form, imagining the lines of his body—wishing she'd not let her desires overwhelm her when she'd had the chance to view him unclothed. And wishing she'd had a whole night to explore all of him.

Keeping her eyes in motion, she switched her gaze from Andrew to the canvas and back again.

He raised his hand, moved it into a fist and propped his chin on it, shutting his eyes. He looked so dear, even with the grimace on his face. How fortunate she was to have been born in the same world as him and to find him, basically, on her doorstep. It was destined for her to capture the man. This would be her masterpiece.

She kept sketching, but took a moment to savour the look of his lashes reposing on his cheeks.

Her hand worked furiously, trying to pull each nuance of him on to the canvas, making sure to get the proportions just right, the lines close enough, and when they weren't, she moved, changing, making another darker line nearby.

Time flowed as quickly as her pencil. Then she reached for the paints.

She looked at him, then touched her brush to canvas, gliding the colour on to the surface with precision, biting her lip. 'Uh-hum,' she muttered, feeling a calming oblivion with the stroke of the brush.

Andrew sat still and she realised he now watched her as closely as she studied him, but it didn't matter. Nothing mattered but the art. The paintbrush controlled her thoughts and her mind focused simply on transferring her vision from sight to canvas.

When she painted, and her mind and hands joined into the skill she had practised, the process she felt was not the slow application of colour to a surface. The world around her ceased to be.

She couldn't see a seed take life—the process happened at such a different rate that the mind could not capture it. The plant would sprout, the stem, leaves and then a flower would burst forth. Painting took her inside the process so that she could feel and see the growth of the art. To experience the same thing in the garden would have meant she would have been inside the seed and felt the changes of it from the beginning until the final roots were formed.

Each brush stroke absorbed her and she worked, not from conscious thought, but letting her eyes guide the brush. She didn't think of what she did—she let the brush free.

'Beatrice,' she heard a voice and realised Andrew spoke.

Shrugging away the minor irritation of being interrupted, she looked at him.

'We've been here hours,' he said, 'and if I don't move soon, I won't be able to.'

'That can't be true,' she spoke, turning her head to see the clock. He told the truth. Hours had passed. She gave herself a shake.

'One bit more,' she muttered, clenching her teeth softly on her tongue while painting the top of the eyelid. She wanted eyelashes, but not visible—as the human eye might distort them when viewing. 'I just need to redo this lid. Your eyes must be correct, Andrew. The eyes are everything to a portrait, although the hands are important as well.'

He stood and stretched, arms unfurling, reaching out, an explosion of man in front of her, bringing her from the trance of concentration into the world of different sensations.

His arms stretched. His back lengthened and swirled, and his eyes shut briefly when he blinked. Her paintbrush stopped, forgotten.

She'd never known a black coat could have so much vibrancy. Each twist and turn affected the earth in some way because she felt herself move with the coat.

'Beatrice...'

She raised her eyes to his face.

'You have been staring at me with your brush poised in the air.'

'Oh.' She shook her head, not in disagreement, but as a way to return her mind to the real world. Cleaning the brush, she put it in a glass, bristles up. She picked up the flannel and wiped the pigments from her hands.

'Beatrice, I must go.' He yawned, then moved more, muscles stretching again.

She drank in the movements.

He adjusted his waistcoat twice. His sleeves. Again.

She paused in her view, remembering the post she'd received that morning. She spoke in a pained voice. 'Unfortunately, my mother has seen the papers and has decided to return here. She is concerned that she might miss out on something. She likes to be in the thick of things. She is planning to stay with me and I'm sure she'll meet you.'

'I have no issue with that,' he said.

'I do,' she muttered. 'Mother always has her own idea of how her children's lives should be lived. You never know what she might say. I was so happy when she decided to live with her sister for a time.'

'I am not the least concerned.'

'Perhaps you might invite her to live with you, then,' she suggested. 'She hardly takes up any space and eats very little. I will even send staff along to see to her needs.'

Her mother would take one look at Andrew, realise he was the duke's brother and so forth, and be planning a marriage. If she found out Andrew wanted her daughter to improve her reputation,

Mother would be willing to finance the special licence herself. Hopefully she would not propose on Beatrice's behalf.

After Andrew bid her goodbye, her world darkened when the door closed with a gentle snap, but when she looked at the canvas, it was as if he remained in the room. She smiled.

She examined the face taking shape before her, unaware of any world beyond.

Inspiration plunged into her. She brushed a hair back from her face and moved to the door, locking it.

She went to her easel, took the canvas of Andrew and propped it on the sofa, concealing the dried one behind it.

Then she scurried to her supply room and clattered around among the various plaster casts of body parts she had purchased to give her proportions. She moved aside an abandoned half-finished painting and reached behind it to the canvas lying horizontally. She'd had it stretched at the same time she purchased the one for Boadicea. She turned the canvas so the length of it was vertical. A perfect fit. A perfect fit for a life-sized portrait.

Her easel was too small, but she didn't care. She'd prop the canvas against the frame of it and make it work just as she had with the other one.

Time passed while she stared at the whiteness before her. Her eyes imagined the ratios, the pose, the variations of light she'd need to capture.

She would create a masterpiece. Her shining moment. This would be the best work she'd ever done.

Reverently, she picked up her brush. Astounded by the prospect before her. The gift she had been given and the prospect of a lifetime.

A painting for her eyes only. A painting only she could paint. She would capture a man's desire and strength in his expression, and create a vision a woman could not forget.

Something only to be viewed long after the present time had passed. Not something for this generation, but art to let the future discover the man of today.

It only saddened her that she would not be able to share the painting with Andrew and the world.

Chapter Twelve

When Andrew next arrived at Beatrice's home, the butler was leading him to the sitting room when a voice interrupted. He carried the latest scandal sheet. The one with a story relating to Beatrice's recent visit to Somerset House.

'I suppose you are here to see me.' The shrill pierced his ears and the cackle which followed made the hair on the back of his neck stand at attention.

He turned to see an older version of Beatrice standing in a doorway and the years had been kind to her. The weight of her necklaces alone could have stooped a lesser woman. Although her eyelids drooped, the sparkle of azure beneath them jabbed. He supposed she still would be considered attractive—if it weren't for the sense of unease one felt when looking at her.

'Beatrice told me to expect you.' She frowned, touching the pearls around the silver knot of hair she had piled on her head.

At first, he thought she might be walking so delicately because of her age, but when her hem moved, he realised she also perched on tall slippers.

He moved towards her, taking her hand to bow over it, and noticed a whiff of tobacco.

'I suppose we can talk in the sitting room. Beatrice's busy.' She moved to a doorway, and whirled around, putting both palms on the facing. 'You know I want to welcome you into the family. I want you to marry my daughter even though she claims it will never happen.'

'One never knows what the future holds,' he said.

'Oh, that answer is so full of nothing.' She smiled. 'I like that. It would work well for a son-by-law. I can overlook that you are related to Foxworthy, who does manage to get himself in trouble. You know he is quite bold. It is said he has consorted with the likes of Sophia Swift.'

Andrew let his head fall sideways, expelled a breath and raised a brow. 'Sophia Swift? Should I know of her?'

The woman pursed her lips. 'I would not lay it on so thick. You might be able to pull that off with others, but not with me.'

'Well, I have it on good authority Foxworthy is not fond of Miss Swift.'

'It is a good thing for him. I have heard her personal diary is quite revealing.'

Crashing cymbals could not have overridden the thoughts in his head. A diary?

She frowned, bringing the wrinkles around her eyes into prominence. 'It is hard to believe Foxworthy is your relation.'

'I have trouble with it myself.' Of course, if Sophia kept a diary, that could all change.

'But you are acceptable,' she said. 'I believe in arranged marriages and have no problem with doing the work myself. Unfortunately laws and such get in the way. A mother simply cannot force her daughter into marriage as one could in the old days.' She paused. 'You can nod at any time.'

'I doubt that would be safe around you.'

'Doesn't matter, I will take your silence as agreement.'

'Then you will be mistaken.'

'What's that in your hand?' she asked.

He did not hold the paper out. 'Just the last print-ing of a scandal rag.'

'I'm sure if it's important I'll hear of it,' she mut-tered. She lowered her arms and waved him to follow her into the room. Once inside, she made a non-threatening fist that she put to her chest.

'My Bea is simply not understood. She is not. She tells me you only wish to help her be recog-nised for her art. That cannot be true.'

He didn't answer. He would not discuss with her what he didn't fully understand himself.

'Riverton said he loved her dearly. He did not. I thought her marriage would be the best thing for her and it nearly crushed her. I so wished for him to be converted to an angel—either by prayer or ambush. Took a while, but wishes do come true.' Teeth flashed. 'I actually cried when I received the news of his death. I was so happy. A first for me.'

Beatrice's mother made a rough, clearing-her-throat sound. 'May his corpse rot with such a stench he can smell himself in death. Not that I bear him any ill will, of course,' she said, her eyes widening. 'I asked that he be laid to rest with a boulder on his chest, should there have been a mistake and he be alive when he was put away.'

She looked at Andrew. 'So how soon before you propose?'

'Neither of us is inclined to marry. And I know you want your daughter happy with her choice.'

'Happy?' She shrugged. 'I just want her married to a man we are disinclined to dismember.'

'That would be for the best.'

'I thought because Riverton was older, yet so much like her in many ways, he would be perfect for her. Perhaps if he had not had that one little problem. Of being born.' She rubbed her chin as if checking for stubble. 'I see now I was mistaken.'

'Perhaps she would be happiest of all painting.'

'Perhaps. She assures me you will help change the cruel way the scandal sheets refer to her with your quiet ways.' She shook her head. 'I did all I could to bring her up strong. I saw that she was taught fencing, painting and how to load and fire a flintlock. All the things I missed out on because I was female. I encouraged my daughter to do as she wished. It is hard for the world to accept.' The older woman shook her head. Straightening the strands of a necklace, she said, 'I do not meddle in my children's business—any more than is necessary. I mention small motherly concerns and try to give them a kick in the right direction. But do they listen?'

'My mother would say the same about us, I suppose.'

'Possibly. Sometimes it is a waste of effort to speak to children.' She touched her fingertips to her forehead. 'And men.'

He became aware of movement in the doorway and looked around to see Beatrice. She again wore a dress dotted with paint. In her hands, she held a cloth, muddyed by colours, and rubbed it over her skin, trying to remove stains.

Her mother brushed by them, marching to the doorway. 'Dears, do be discreet,' she called over her shoulder. 'Spend all the time alone together you wish. Pretend I am not here. I will not speak of it.' She walked away, humming.

'Mother can keep a secret,' Beatrice said, leaning towards him. 'However, she rarely chooses to do so. I have told her this time she must because of how you are assisting me and she's agreed because she hopes it might lead to my marrying again, either to you or someone else. Strategy is very important in my family.'

She arched a brow. 'Do not play cards with her. Do not be misled into believing she hardly knows any game she might ask to play. She is quite skilled and even cheats when she is winning.'

'Is anyone meek in your family?' He stepped closer to Beatrice so his voice would not carry into the hallway.

'My aunt. But we cannot figure out what caused it.' She turned towards her studio. 'Follow me.' Her shoes clattered away.

Andrew only half-heard them. The little smear of blue on the *derrière* of Beatrice's gown when she walked away had caused everything else in the room to dim. He took a moment to appreciate the moment. The graceful twitch of the blue paint lingering in his mind.

'Have you worked on the portrait?' he asked, following her and imagining his Boadicea.

'Care to see?' she asked, taking him down the path to the studio. At the cottage, she opened the door and moved to the easel.

The new scent he associated with her swirled around him—not baked goods this time, but the brush wash and lavender. Nothing had been straightened while he'd been away. If anything, more disarray had appeared. One window was open, but even that didn't take the scent of oils from the room.

'I think you'll be pleased.' She frowned. 'Mostly.' She twirled around, putting enough distance so she could look at him from top to bottom. And she did, slowly, all the way to his boots. He felt he should cover himself, her eyes were so direct.

'I hope you do not look at all men this way.'

Lips parting, she hesitated before speaking. 'And what is wrong with it?'

'Too direct, Beatrice.'

'Not—' she raised her chin high '—for an artist.'

He gave a deep bow. 'My pardon. But I do not think Lawrence looks at the men he paints with quite the same intensity.'

She shook her head and laughed. 'I cannot speak for other artists, but I do take my research seriously.'

'You have work to do. And not on the painting.' He handed her the newsprint in his hand. She would never be a meek woman. A woman who was right for him so he could continue the work he loved. And if he did not give his heart to her in all ways, then how could he be certain he would not become like his father? The image he saw when he looked in the mirror.

She looked at the story. 'I read it. Isn't it what we wished for? I was merely enhancing my image as an artist and wished to find a particular painting.'

'Beast hunts Boadicea?'

'I only went because I do not believe the artwork looked as much like me as you claim and I wanted to examine it again. It wasn't there and I made a bit of a stir.' She preened. 'See, Andrew. It is a beautiful painting. A patron of the arts has taken it.' Her eyes looked downward. 'But I so wished to see her again. The sad part of painting is that you must sometimes see your best work go away. It is like losing a friend, but you cannot keep them all. '

'No one would argue your skill. Your subject is the only thing in question. And the attention you received was not printed as we would have wished.'

'Everything has been exaggerated...mostly.' She shrugged. 'I merely jumped to a few conclusions.'

He tossed the paper on to the sofa, watching it land near the skulls. 'So does everyone else. You must remember that.'

* * *

Andrew walked to the undraped window and stood, his back to her. She stopped. Memorising. Shoulders—in proportion, but leaning to width. Shape of his head—hair falling into a picturesque disarray.

Beatrice's stomach tumbled pleasantly. She'd not lied to him. His form arrested her in a way none other ever had. She must do him justice.

'What is the Newgate incident, Beatrice?' He turned slowly. 'I saw the reference and had not heard of it in the past.'

She plopped the cloth she carried over her shoulder, motioning him to the pedestal. 'I met a man—a sort of criminal, I suppose. I conversed with him, quite politely, as he agreed to pose for me.' Her voice tightened. 'It is hard to find a suitable male to paint. And his eyes were quite attractive. The scar on his face, so fascinating. But before we settled on the details, he ended up in Newgate. As I was getting him released, someone hoping to curry favour with Wilson sent my brother a note. My brother forbade releasing the man and managed to raise such a fuss, I could not continue in my efforts.' Looking at the pots, she continued. 'Wilson claims to want a proper family, one accepted by society, but if he had kept to himself concerning Newgate, it would certainly have drawn less attention. And finishing the portrait was not easy as a result. I managed, of course.'

She picked up the paints, adding bits to her palette. While she mixed the flesh tones, she grumbled. 'The man from the gaol—I would have paid him well enough to satisfy his greed. Harming me would have ended the funds he stood to make. I wasn't worried and told him he must leave his cudgel at home. I had a stable man nearby to keep an eye on him. My brother overreacted.'

'Strong reactions are common in this family, I'd say. But you must be sure to remember how they will be exaggerated in print.'

She did not mind the unappealing words about her as much as the gnawing knowledge of his desire to change her.

Andrew could never understand. He was the opposite of Riverton, yet Riverton did not love her for the person she was. Andrew could not love her for the person she was. They were both equally disastrous.

But it did not matter. She shoved away those

thoughts. This was about something bigger than either of them. A masterpiece.

He stood behind Beatrice's shoulder and stared at the canvas. She'd completed the head and shoulders outline of a man, filled in with base colours only and pencil streaks showing dimensions. His eyes were there, but he could not see that she had painted at all in his absence. 'I assumed you would work on it while I am not here.'

She picked up a brush and clamped it in her teeth, crossways. She scooped up the palette and knife, tapping at the colour, stirring it. She pointed. He saw his perch—a stool which looked to have been cobbled together in a hurry, but would put him almost at the same height as if he stood.

She put the knife aside and took the brush from her mouth, staring at the tools. 'I do work on it while you are not here.'

Andrew took his place. His back hurt from lifting boards. He tried to get comfortable on the stool. Beatrice peered around the canvas, the look of a disgruntled tutor on her face.

'I did not mean to criticise, I just thought it would go faster.' He moved his boot heel on to one of the rungs.

'Art takes effort and time.' She peered around the canvas again for only long enough to speak. 'And passion.'

'You are a very passionate woman.'

'Of course. I must be to create. One has to be driven to sit for hours on end, trying to translate the subject from their mind into a view others can see.'

'Why do you feel that way about art?'

She held the brush between their line of vision for a moment and he watched the wistful expression on her face. 'I don't know. Perhaps when I was a child and practising with my watercolours someone told me how fine it was and I thought that nice and did more. Or perhaps I loved art from birth. Perhaps I was complimented on several things, but only the memory of the praise of drawing remained in my mind. Do you not think it is the same with your architecture?'

'The houses I improve make better homes for people to live in. They are more comfortable. Warmer in winter.' He blinked the words away. 'And it's profitable. I did not wish to change my brandy, leave Hoby boots behind or find a new tailor when I left the duke's household.'

He had also liked the privileges of his youth and

wanted to give his children the same advantages he'd had. His house was not as grand as the ducal residence, but the nursery was better. He'd even made sure its windows looked out over the best view so he could have something to point out to his children while they grew.

She turned to her tools. 'You could have just married for money.'

'I've heard ninety-five-year-old heiresses with waning senses are in short supply and I think Foxworthy would not let an opportunity like that escape him.'

She laughed. 'I wondered if funds made inevitable my tumble into an unhappy marriage.' She wiped the tip of her brush into a fine point. 'I loved my husband—but if he had not had so much status and wealth, might I have seen his weaknesses sooner?' She placed the brush in the holder, the wood clinking against the glass, and picked up the larger one. 'But I learned from that dreadful experience. A woman should not let herself be blinded, either by a man's wealth or—anything else.'

'I agree. Completely.'

'When I look at you, my artist's vision takes over. And when you look at me, you see someone

to change. The first night you thought I was someone else. A mild companion and that entranced
you. Only moments later, when you found out who
I truly was, you began trying to alter me.'

Her head tilted around the canvas. 'Palmer sent
me a note.'

Andrew did not move. He exhaled a rumble
from his throat in acknowledgement. That was
almost as good as a proposal from Palmer if Beatrice wanted to turn it into one. The other man
would not be able to be near Beatrice without falling under her spell.

He stared at the back of the canvas, noting the
wood and the easel.

'After I finish your portrait,' she said, 'I might
ask him to sit for me. It will not be the same, but
he is… He mentioned he has been quite forlorn
since his wife died.'

'Perhaps he might pose for your warrior painting.'

Her sigh filled the room. 'Perhaps. I do not think
he would mind to be seen in such a light. I think
he would be proud.'

Chapter Thirteen

He heard another little moan. Not really much of a sound. But she painted, then gave a short murmured commentary on her work. Not words, just mumbles. The whispers captured his imagination.

He leaned more into the pedestal so he could see around the canvas and have a better view of her face. Her eyebrow would quirk. Her lips would part and then compress, and she would look at him with absolutely no expression, then look at the canvas and her face would reflect her thoughts—but he didn't think they could truly be her thoughts every time. She frowned, pursed her lips and then peered over at him. Dissecting parts of him.

He crossed his eyes and she didn't seem to notice. He touched his nose.

She gasped and moved backwards. 'You need to sit straight and still.'

'Certainly.' He moved back into position.

He crossed his eyes. She peered around the canvas and never noticed. He bit his bottom lip. Nothing. He scratched his nose.

'Pul—*eese.*'

'Pardon.' He regained his stoic look. 'Are you working on my nose?' he asked.

Her head darted around again. 'Yes. How did you know?'

'Fortunate guess.'

Her eyes tensed, her mouth firmed and even the paintbrush in her hand tensed. 'We will get nothing done today if you don't co-operate.'

Then next time she stuck her head around, he crossed his eyes. She didn't notice. Still working on the nose.

She moved back into her thoughts, and his thoughts moved the length of her body and he felt himself smile. He kept his nose perfectly still.

He shut his eyes, very carefully moved his fist under his chin to prop himself up and relaxed, listening to the occasional sound of her wordless commentaries. The act of posing for her captured him in a way he'd never expected. To be the centre of her concentration for hours on end brought to life a connection that flowed into him.

Without the scar on his chest, he would have been tempted to remove his clothing and see the outcome of her brush. He could simply have made certain she changed his features and waited some time before she displayed the piece.

No, he thought, inwardly shaking his head. He might be comfortable with her capturing him bare, but he could not ever be comfortable with anyone else but his or Beatrice's eyes on the artwork. Not even if the face were someone else's completely. He would know, and when the eyes gazed at the flesh it would be his image they saw. He could not live with such a thing.

'We're done for today.' Her words shocked his eyes open and he raised his head from his fist, flexing his fingers. He felt he'd been compressed. Perhaps he'd dozed off. He wasn't sure.

He stood, loosening his muscles, and looked across to see her stretching. He wrinkled his face, letting his nose know it could now relax.

Walking to the painting, he saw the sketched outline of his face and now he had a nose—although he wouldn't have been able to tell if it was anyone else's nose.

She looked at him, eyes waiting.

He gave a nod. 'Very good.'

Then she reached up, put her brush back in her teeth and grasped his chin, turning his head first one way and then the other. 'Uh-huh,' she mumbled around the brush. She removed the obstacle to her words and spoke softly. 'You do have a remarkable nose,' she told him, imparting some artistic knowledge.

He looked again at the painting. Nothing. A nose. Simple. Two nostrils. No bulb at the end. No bump at the ridge. No twist at the side. But perhaps that was what one wanted in a nose.

He took her chin, lifted it and she stilled. He examined her nose. 'Then you have a remarkable nose as well.'

She blushed and he would have supposed she blushed to her toes, but his thoughts were sidetracked by the tops of her breasts.

And then the memory of how they'd looked when she'd lowered her gown popped into his mind and he didn't need her to sit hours for him to be able to recall them.

Posing wasn't the chore he expected. For hours as he posed, he watched her. Every instant that she was lost in concentration, her face was unguarded. Without words or touch, he could feel himself being pulled deeper and deeper into a connection to her.

He should not have agreed to it. Watching her paint was drawing him to her in a way he could not have expected. Gone was the little bird who'd fallen from the nest and the Beast. She watched her canvas in the same way a mother would look at a babe. He could not take his eyes from that sight.

'You've paint on your cheek,' he said.

'It would be odd if I did not.' Her words were hardly loud enough to hear and her concentration never left her task.

He stood, took a step to her, then used his thumb to brush away a colour which really hadn't been but just a speck in the first place, and watched a hint of red grow, blending well with the almost invisible dusting of freckles at her nose.

'Oh, Andrew...' She gazed at him and almost gasped out the words when she turned her head back to the portrait. 'You're looking luscious.'

He didn't think the words were truly directed at him, but at the painting. He stood in front of it and examined the work.

She had done a good job, he had to admit. All

the parts were there and looked amazingly like him. Nothing particularly fascinating. He'd seen the same face in the mirror countless times.

'Let's go a little longer. Please.' Eyes the shade of azure pleaded and no one could think her anything but demure if they'd gazed at her now.

He gave a quick nod and an inspection of her dress. The one with the mark at the breast. All the paint on Beatrice's clothing drew his eyes.

'There is just one problem,' she said. Her voice faded, much like an absentminded tutor's might. 'I must now see your chest in good light—without your clothing.'

'Beatrice.' He examined the canvas. She'd already outlined his neckcloth in pencil and filled in some of the darker strokes of his coat.

She pointed a brush to the cow skull. 'An artist needs to understand more than the outside.'

'If that were the case, then you could not paint me fully well until the skin was taken from my bones. I wouldn't agree to that, either.'

She smiled, perfect lips, perfect teeth and an imperfect grin, then turned her paintbrush towards the man, not the canvas. She trailed the rounded end of her paintbrush against him, starting at his ear and tracing his jawline, sending pulses into his body. 'So, if I said I'd just like to see you without your shirt?'

She wove the brush around him like a sorceress's wand.

'I had a long night, Beatrice.' Because he could not sleep for thoughts of her.

'I lit the lamps and painted. I risked ruining my eyes but I could not stop. I've been awake since one.' She indicated the inner doorway with a quick nod of her head. 'Soft bed. We could both rest.'

He shook his head, but the image of her clothes sliding from her body flashed in his mind. Her skin would be silken under his touch and he could bury his face in the tendrils of her hair.

He looked into her face, examining her with the same intensity she used on him. Comparing her to the *Boadicea,* aware that she had chosen the perfect theme for a reproduction of her likeness.

She was the vermilion of an explosion and he was the tones of the forest at sunset. He might watch an eruption, be fascinated by it and drawn to it, but he could not live inside it. He pushed away the regrets of life. He had only to think of the day his world had changed for ever with the daubs of a few bits of ink on paper. The words had the strength of being etched in steel.

Instead of pulling from his gaze, or showing discomfort at his scrutiny, she paused, looking as if she absorbed his view in the same way one might feel sunlight.

He could not help himself. He bent down, not kissing her cheek, but letting his cheek brush against it, feeling the roughening on his cheek against the smoothness of hers.

Andrew pressed his lips together. His control could not desert him, but he was not fond of it any more. It seemed to be getting in the way of so much.

Slipping the brush from her fingertips, he opened her palm. With the rounded end, he traced the ridges of her palm, then flipped the brush around to put it back in her grasp.

His eyes told her what he didn't put into words and he saw the flush creep into her cheeks, and the flash of agreement and anticipation.

She stared at the form taking shape. 'But I am close to finishing.' She frowned. 'I'm torn. I want to linger over this and yet...'

'Just finish as you normally would.'

His defences had dashed away, but not completely and he would not let them. While being close to holding her unrestrained in his arms, at the same time he mentally prepared to leave so he did not become entangled.

She stared at the work.

'It's just a painting,' he said.

'No. It's not. Not to me. It's so much more.' Pulling her hand away at half the pace of her normal movement, she looked to the portrait. 'You do like it?'

'Yes. You're an accomplished artist.'

'I so wish to finish this so I can continue—another.'

The thought of Beatrice looking forward to painting something else didn't relieve him as it should have.

'You must take care with your next portrait. It must be something to enhance your image. Something you can show the world.'

She lowered her eyes and, in that moment, he saw a different person. The other Beatrice, and he could not guess her thoughts in any way. He moved to see her face better and her expression changed. Her smile fluttered in place—a guise to distract from her true thoughts. She had ceased to think of anything but charming him.

She touched his cheek and then her forefinger traced the seam of his lips. 'In truth, I only think of painting you.'

'Beatrice—can you live a sedate life?'

The words stopped her hands in mid-air. He saw nothing in her which could be satisfied with serene. Behind her eyes glistened so many different bursts of energy. She couldn't even keep silent or still when she painted and her curls kept rearranging themselves when she moved just the slightest. Beatrice had been created for life, liveliness and adventure. She was a spirit of her own. Something designed to bring the world around her alive.

Her paintbrush returned to the portrait, dusting at the paint, blending. 'Perhaps I was put on earth to create vicarious adventures for others.' Her laugh sounded fluid, touching him in a palpable sense.

But her words echoed the truth throughout his body. Beatrice flourished with adventure.

'One way to change perception is to use your art to paint some pictures of children, or baby chicks or lambs. Gentle subjects,' he said.

'Who will care about boring subjects?'

'You are painting a very boring subject now.'

She lowered her chin and raised a brow, but then her face relaxed. 'I'll make you interesting.'

'Now I'm concerned.'

'Perhaps you should be. Perhaps I should be. Artists let bits of their own feelings towards a subject show in the work. It cannot be prevented. Colours are mixed a bit darker before you realise it. A placid face becomes a scowl.'

'Then I will look forward to seeing if I have a halo or horns when you finish.'

She looked at him, thinking of his words. 'I think you have a bit of both in your eyes.' She moved to let her fingers trail down his face, starting just below his eyes and ending at his chin. 'You are rare to me. The men in a few sculptures I have seen almost have no expression and that is a beauty in its own way. To make the model into a form that is encompassing art and not an individual. But I want you to look like the person I see. I want a picture that one hundred years from now someone can look at and recognise you as if they know you.'

'You are expecting a lot of canvas and paints.'

'I am challenged by your form to do my best. I have practised all my life so I might paint you. You are my muse.'

Chapter Fourteen

Beatrice continued painting in the hours after Andrew left, letting the vision surface and watching his face before her. Pleased with what she saw, but unable to stop, even for water. Wanting to see him closer, to have him before her in the exact way she saw him.

When she heard the maid knock and enter, she smelled meat pies. She looked up long enough to acknowledge the woman holding the tray. 'I'll eat when the light fades. Let Mother know I'll be painting longer.'

The maid nodded, completely unsurprised with the statement, and placed the tray on the table by the door.

Beatrice frowned, irritated. The light would not last long enough for her to continue as she wished.

She needed to lock the door and switch to the other canvas soon.

Andrew was the muse for the rest of her life. In wanting to change her into a better version of herself, he had shown her that she was the person she wanted to be.

She bit her lip. But she would miss looking at him. She had to have the painting, the large one, to keep for ever.

She must make it so real she could look at the likeness and the luscious eyes, and smell the woodsy smell. Standing inches from it, she wanted to be able to know the touch of his skin again. His eyes needed to be so real she could feel the gaze.

Brown could be so many shades and picking the right ones for his eyes had been difficult. It seemed they changed with his expression. Vibrated intensity. Her brush fought with her, but she would not give in.

Then she stood and reached for a lamp, stumbling over the slippers she'd left in the pathway, and righting herself to stand in front of the art.

Only the canvas likeness could accept her as she was. Andrew could not. He desired a princess sort who could curtsy well and glide on her golden slippers.

She would always have the painting, and when she felt alone the eyes looking back understood her completely.

She had put the large portrait away and worked on the smaller one when Andrew walked into the room for their next session. After her mother had met him that one time, Beatrice had asked him to find his way to the studio for the future sessions and let himself in.

She could feel him studying the work. She was so close to being finished.

'Can you make me look a pirate?' he asked.

'I could,' she muttered. 'But you are not a pirate. You are the knight. The strong knight.'

She picked up a dry paintbrush and stopped in front of him. She ran the brush along the bristles of his chin. 'You did not shave this morning.'

'I did not have time. I could not wait to see you. Lady Riverton, you are capturing more of me than just my image.'

As her brush left his face, she turned the rounded top to let it flicker along the folds of his cravat, click down one side of the buttons of his waistcoat and then move back to the centre of his chest.

Her brush stilled. 'You must know something I have decided as I painted. I have thought about it well into the night. My art will be viewed more as the Beast's. Perhaps that is truly who I must be. I don't want to change it. I think, if I let the notoriety continue, my art will be noticed more. I will not have to hide behind a signature that is nothing more than a straight line.'

'Are you certain?'

Sadness caused her stomach to churn. She could not destroy the spirit inside herself that made her see life differently from others. The spirit that drew eyes, but yet, was what made her like her life.

Riverton had tried to quash her, but Andrew could actually do it. He was her knight and he wore the armour. She could almost hear the metal ring when he walked. She could not get past the breastplate over his chest. With one swipe of his eyes as he cringed because of her actions, her blood would slowly seep from her body. He abhorred the experiences that nourished her spirit.

She could bear the condemnation of strangers. But she could not pretend to be someone else. Little fissures that seemed insignificant before marriage grew each day after the vows were said.

The years of censure by Riverton and his family, whom she did not care one sniffle for, had taught her that she could not bear to live in a home where disapproval followed her.

Well, except her mother's. That she was used to.

She would stay Beatrice the Beast, as much as she hated it—the person the scandal sheets had created. She wanted the applause, the notoriety. She might sometimes regret her actions because of her impulsiveness, but she loved her art. She loved the freedom to create as she wished, what she wished, and to stand up with arms outstretched to the heavens uncaring who saw. She wanted the storm and the splatters of rain to coat her face, the lightning to scare her and the thunder to vibrate her senses.

She twirled the brush, watching the rotation. 'Yes, I will remain the Beast. I know it is not the answer you wish for. Not the path you think I should travel. But it is my road.'

Andrew knew Beatrice was finished with the portrait, or close enough that he need not pose any more. She had asked him to arrive for one last sitting.

His mind was taken by brunette curls, a rosebud mouth and a voice which would mellow into a most arousing murmur as she stared at the canvas.

He could think of nothing else but seeing her again. Surely, once they parted, he would be able to put her out of his mind. He now had every copy of every scandal sheet that had mentioned her. He had read them all over and over. Each story, reminders—and an affirmation that she was not right for him. The words he had memorised could be reviewed in his mind at any time. Perhaps now he would not hate the print so much. They reminded him of the truth of the world.

His white cravat was tied perfectly and his black coat pristine when his carriage arrived at the front of his home for the trip to take him to Beatrice's estate.

When he arrived at the grounds, he bypassed the estate to walk directly to the cottage. Beatrice reached for him, grasping his fingers, and sending warm jolts through his body.

The knowledge that the newsprint was directing his life flared within him again, but suddenly he did not know if it was for good or ill.

'I do want you to see what I've completed on

the portrait, Andrew. I'm very proud. I think it's the second-best painting I've ever done.'

He examined her, hoping he never forgot the sight of her excitement and freedom. 'I suppose I should be offended not to be the very best painting you've ever done.'

Her eyes darted away. 'I would not complain too much.' She glittered up at him. 'I misspoke. A jest to see your reaction.'

She looked at him with the same intensity as she'd gazed at her canvas—aware, by the flush to her face and the way her breathing increased, she didn't mind.

She stepped closer and touched his cheek, letting her hand fall flat against his skin.

He took both her hands and she moved forward. He bent down, his lips grazing hers for a taste, and savoured the luscious warmth of her mouth, tasting the sweetness of a confection and having a feeling of moving into a realm of femininity which sated him completely—if he moved forward.

He pulled back, surprised. She'd not moved, except for kissing him in return. He'd somehow expected hands tugging him closer, or feeling her press her body against him. Instead, she stood, looking at him, with her lips parted and her eyes—slightly lost.

Just looking at her eyes—seeing the dazed reflection…and he reached out.

Dipping to her mouth again, he took advantage of her stillness, pulling her against him, feeling the press of breasts against his too-thick coat. He put his hands lower, running the length of her, holding her bottom closer, her body heating his arousal.

He shut his eyes and put his forehead to the side of her head, letting skin touch skin, letting their hair mingle—feeling her in a way he'd never felt anyone before.

Her hands pushed against his chest, not shoving him away, but moving herself back. She stumbled, hair bouncing, eyes wide and lips parted.

He saw her give herself a shake, a shudder of control. 'I have learned I am not quite so unaffected by soft words and gentle touches as I thought. You've been my muse. And you fascinate me immensely. How you can be so happy with the flavour removed from life, I'll never know. But please do not say nice things to me now. I might remember them later, and it would be bad…'

'I understand, but I might not be able to help myself.'

She reached up, patting his face with a bit of strength. 'No kind words like that either.'

'I will try.' She was right. He touched over his chest again. The reminder.

She waved a hand, dismissing the subject. 'But, the picture,' she said. 'I want you to see the finished painting. I will only need to spend a few more days and then let it dry.' She moved to the door. 'I only know a painting is completed when I look at it and think the brush strokes I'm adding are making it worse. Then I know it's time to stop.' She shrugged. 'The fingers are not—' She stopped, gave her head a quick shudder. 'See how out of sorts I am. I didn't put your hands in the portrait.' Her voice became light. 'How ridiculous. I meant your earlobes. I simply didn't do them justice.'

Andrew reached out, grabbed her wrist, sliding his hand to hold hers, and pulled them facing each other. Beatrice. He could not bear the thought of not seeing her again. He could not.

She shook her head. 'The portrait first. I put it aside so I could be certain of watching your face when you see the completed work.'

Whirling around, she walked from the room and returned, putting his likeness on the empty easel.

She stood back, waiting. Andrew moved to look.

'Looks like me.' Andrew said. He stared at the painting. Suddenly, he hated it.

'That's all you have to say.' She gave a sniff.

'Well, it does look like me.'

'Do you *like* it?' She stepped back to see him better, studying his face.

He reached over, lifted the art and examined it. 'You are accomplished. Talented.'

'Thank you. I would have appreciated the comments more if you'd been a little quicker with them.'

He heard the ire and, putting the painting back on the easel, turned to her. 'How can I appreciate it justly, when I see that face every day of my life?'

It was the image of his father.

One side of her lips turned up. 'So it is the face you see in the mirror.' She gave a soft slap to his arm. 'You do like it?'

He nodded, taking her shoulders, moving his hands to push the light fabric of her sleeves up, so he could hold her.

'I don't see any roguish stare or anything out of

the ordinary. I admit, I was concerned when you said you wanted me to have a halo and horns.'

She shrugged. 'This one only shows the outside. The exterior everyone sees.'

'None could have done better.' He looked into Beatrice's gaze. Eyes so soft he could have fallen into them. Even the upsweep of her lashes brushed him with warmth.

He touched Beatrice's cheek. He needed to have something to take away the sting of the view he'd had when he saw the portrait. The feel of Beatrice's skin was the only thing in the world that would do what he needed at that moment.

He burned his face against her, holding her against his heart. Her hands touched his hair, his back, his shoulders, and clung to him.

But she didn't still and pushed away to loosen his cravat, pulling it from his neck. He felt the sliding cloth even through the collar beneath. He never saw what happened to the stock, but he grasped the curve of her waist as she reached for his buttons at his waistcoat. He knew when her hand passed above the scar.

'Andrew?' The words came from somewhere. Maybe the next room. Maybe inner London. He did not care.

His mouth fell to her lips and she tried to ascend his body. He had no time to help her climb him. The fastenings at the back of her dress, each one felt like a little lock which had to be picked, but he was almost at the very end of south. Now he had corset ties and he'd have to change plans if they were tangled. There'd simply not be enough time to unknot.

She pushed back with both hands and he stared at her. His jaw dropped. Surely she was not going to change her mind.

'I don't want to wait any longer,' she whispered. 'I have waited a lifetime for this moment. It is as if the portrait I painted has appeared alive before me.'

His lips touched hers and he felt no different than she. His Boadicea had appeared in his arms—in all his senses, only she would rise victorious.

He watched her, this inspiration, reach to slide her bodice downwards, her chemise coming loose as well, breasts revealed freely—nipples erect. He would never look at her painting again without seeing this version of her.

He couldn't form words. His mouth kept moving towards her nipple and when his lips closed around one, he heard a groan, and it wasn't from him, he felt certain, but he wouldn't swear on it. His tongue swirled, his lips closed and he felt her hand moving to his buttons. Both hands.

Then he stopped.

'Where is the bed?' The most important question he'd ever asked.

Her fingers twisted around his waistband and she began to tug him forward in tiny steps.

He pulled back, seeing her dark hair unleashed to her shoulders, better than any image in reality or imagination. Lips full with desire, blue eyes darkened. No artist on earth could recreate what he saw in front of him.

'Bed,' she whispered.

'Direction?' he asked.

She pulled her skirts up, which had sagged with the loosening of her hooks, and moved to an open doorway.

He followed.

Inside, he saw the tester bed and imagined it a cloud.

He couldn't help himself. He shut her door, dropping down the tiny latch, even while keeping his head half-turned to her.

Beatrice wriggled her dress the rest of the way to the floor and her corset and chemise followed, movements more alluring to him than any siren's. Her body seemed a sliding, heaving, pulsing delight to his eyes.

Boots. Boots. Boots. He didn't take his eyes from her as he did something he never remembered ever doing before. He effortlessly slid his boots from his feet.

Trousers followed, hitting a bed post.

She grasped one fist on his shirt front and pulled him forward as she fell back on to the bed.

He stopped his momentum to land just above her, pausing only a second, but the moment would be in his mind for ever. Beatrice. Hair splayed. Eyes locked, a thousand, thousand unspoken words flowed. He'd never looked so deeply into another person.

'I know,' she said and reached up, touching his face.

A kiss deeper than any other. So much more than the first night he had seen her.

And time. Time outside the door stopped and inside himself. He could linger and savour and his dreams of her became more than reality.

Beatrice brushed against him, moving inside the world she tried to capture on canvas. Skin wasn't just a hue of colour any more. Just as every leaf on a tree was truly different, every brief skim of her fingers against his skin revealed a sensation she'd never known. She could feel each trace of him in a way that blossomed into her mind, all the hues of life revealed to her with only a sweep of her fingertips across his body. Individual nuances of him exploded into texture under her hand. His scent wasn't only pine, leather and male, but masculinity. His throat pulsed. The razor had left a trail, from sharp edges which awed her, and led her to the softer skin just below, a downy infinitesimal trace of hair lying on the surface to give more texture to her touch.

A roughened ridge of flesh at the contours over his ribs alerted her to a memento of his past, some scrape that he possibly didn't remember, but an added imperfection that heightened her awareness of him. Now she'd touched a part of him, this scar from his past, a moment of accidental injury which proved he was mortal.

He pulled away as she touched it and took her fingers to his lips, then slid her hand to his side, moving to lie in her arms.

Every bit of him was individual from every other part of him and she did not want to miss any sensation. Her body woke more to him, aching to be closer.

She'd only captured a wisp of him on the canvas and his body alongside hers showed her how little her art could compare with nature's brush. The warm room and the moisture of their breaths created a connection between their embrace that melded them into one entity long before they slid into passion's complete embrace.

She gasped and cried out in his arms. His life flowed into her and he shuddered, shuddered into a climax she'd never felt before.

Her hands clawed his back, pulling at him with all her might, pressing her face into the moisture-coated skin of his shoulder. She gasped, lost in the magic around her. She screamed her release.

And then she bit him.

Chapter Fifteen

Beatrice opened her eyes and forced herself to raise her head. Andrew stood at the side of the bed, getting dressed. He'd already donned his trousers. He tugged the shirt over his head and tied it.

'Normally,' she stated softly, not wanting to hurt his feelings, 'afterwards—a man might at least roll over and fall asleep.'

'Thank you…very much…Lady Riverton…for that information.'

Beatrice, she thought. She was not Beatrice any more?

He turned, snapping his waistcoat from the floor and pulling it on.

Whatever he lacked in sweet endearments, he made up for in well-proportioned form, she decided, letting her breath out with a whoosh. And the thin lawn of his shirt showed those shoulders quite well. She compared the reality with her art, examining the true masterpiece and so hopeful she could capture at least something of him on to the canvas. But flaws. They always had to be present.

He didn't sit on the bed to don his boots, but in a chair. He looked at her. His jaw clenched. His eyes had changed into those pit-dark orbs she couldn't see past.

She could not figure out what she'd missed.

She pushed herself up on one arm. 'Is…something wrong?'

He slipped one boot on to his foot, tugging, then the other, before answering 'Women tend to use teeth in the act of lovemaking. Can you explain that?' Dark eyes rimmed by darker lashes met hers.

'Teeth? I don't know what you mean.'

He pointed to the area of his shoulder and then his midsection, then splayed his fingers and raised his hand questioningly. 'Teeth.' He clasped the ties of his collar.

She twisted around, rolled on to her stomach, propped up on her elbows and faced him. No tender endearments. No sweetness. Now she knew why he was a virgin. The man was daft. He lost his mind when he completed the act.

Apparently, unsettled men were attracted to her. Riverton with his wish to numb his mind. Andrew with his intense beauty, his intense thoughts and his intense ability to escape the act of lovemaking. The ones…not quite perfect.

But this was not so bad. Not so wonderful, but not completely unworkable as long as one understood it. This did not have to end their friendship. His instability when he finished lovemaking could somehow be directed to a gentler conclusion.

She pulled the covers from the top of the bed, wrapping them around herself. She spoke ever so delicately. 'I see you are flawed—'

'Lady Riverton.' The words snapped out and he jumped to his feet, his right hand pressed over his ribs. 'Just because it happened once does not mean I have a proclivity for it. I am a normal man, I assure you.'

She would not wager the silver on that. The room became chilled, then fiery hot. He was not taking the loss of his virginity well. 'A proclivity for such *is* normal.'

His face paused as he took control of himself. His face calmed. He relaxed back into the chair.

'Thank you for explaining that.' He shook his head. His lips moved up in one of those smiles that was more apology. 'It, however, does not suit my nature.'

She'd been foolish. She'd misread his reluctance. It went far deeper than anything she could have imagined. And how much more insensible she felt to be foolish as a widow than as a green girl. At least she had an excuse before, and now, she had none. The papers were right. She was merely some creature that acted on impulse.

Abandoned. Again.

'Go.' She spoke clearly. 'Leave. Now. I cannot bear you to be in my studio.'

'Beatrice.'

'I simply—it's the way of an artist. I thought to touch the painting and then I discover it's no different than canvas. Reality can never touch the splashes of paint the artist has daubed around. Sad. But that is the way it is.'

He nodded, eyes on her. 'I understand completely.'

Then he turned to the door and raised the latch.

His eyes ran the length of her one last time, a caressing farewell.

Anger, hurt, disappointment—everything surfaced in her body. Just as it had before. Rejection. Again.

She pulled herself up and swung her legs around, sitting on the side of the bed, never taking her eyes from him. 'I am pleased we waited until the portrait was finished.'

She took a slow, deep, lingering breath and put her palm on to the bed, then leaned sideways, letting her arm brace herself, letting the covers fall from her body. Watching his eyes. Feeling a quiet satisfaction at the way they lingered.

'Goodbye.' Quiet words, shouted from the heart.

He nodded. The door shut ever so softly, a slam in its own way.

Andrew left Beatrice's house, trapped in the carriage with his thoughts. Her nails had scraped his back as her teeth had pressed into his shoulder. He could still feel the impression of the marks on his skin. She'd reminded him. With her teeth, she'd reminded him. She was the tempest and he was the calm.

He'd not expected Beatrice to be calm, but neither had he planned on gathering any more scars.

He was certain Foxworthy had none from the

women he'd bedded or Fox would have told him when Andrew had shown him the blemish.

He crossed his arms, leaning back against the squabs, memories of the earlier moments with Beatrice resurfacing.

After Beatrice finished the painting, her visit to Wilson's house had not gone well. Her mother had flitted back from a visit to her sister, become upset when she discovered Andrew was nowhere about and sulked away to Beatrice's house.

Beatrice, her brother and her aunt all appreciated the others' residences from time to time and they'd all offered to assist her mother with finances for a home of her own, but she'd not thought it a grand plan. Not wanting them to waste their funds, she'd claimed.

Beatrice had not been able to hold her mind to anything but Andrew. His parts, all of them, remained vivid in her memory. She could recall the stubble, the chin and the individual aspects of him one after the other.

She should be thankful they had actually made it into the bedchamber before he rejected her. All along she'd known he would not be satisfied with her creative side—the side of her that gave her

life. She'd just not expected him to be so uncom-
fortable with lovemaking.

Riverton had been flawed. Andrew, with his
silent nature, which she had thought hid more
sensual parts of him, was just as unsound. He
probably drew stick figures on his walls and slept
on a rug in his bedchamber. Just like Riverton.

But Andrew stirred her to create in a different way than Riverton had. With Riverton she
painted to escape. With Andrew, to experience.
She wanted to rush back and look at the portrait
and prove that her imagination hadn't transformed
him into a creation not humanly possible. Surely
her mind had taken some fanciful leap and put
him on an artistic pedestal that no man could
belong on. She had to see his face again. She'd
forced herself to stay away for the time it took the
oils to dry—painting a miniature of Mrs Standen
instead. Oddly enough, the housekeeper's face
looked more like Andrew's.

In a few days, she would be seeing Andrew
again to give him the finished portrait. She'd written him a note telling him the paint should be dry
and the portrait ready to hang. No matter what
else happened, she wanted to present the work to
him. He was rational with his clothing on.

Rushing into the studio, she stopped at the small formal portrait, going into the magical place inside herself where she could mentally see each brush stroke, each nuance.

He truly looked better to her each time she saw his image. It was not fair to women that a man should be created so. It simply was not. Men should be most unattractive so a woman could look at them with her mind and not get muddled by—everything else. Andrew was the perfect combination of what an artist would want to paint.

And she couldn't fall in love, particularly with another irrational man. She imagined her heart again as the charred mess. That was best. She could not care. She could not spend the next years of her life in her studio, holding a paintbrush and managing no more inspiration than a yellow, five-petal flower on a green stalk. That had taken her a year to paint and she'd slashed that canvas herself. She could not go back to that.

Love caused things to get all tangled and mangled and messy. She'd been eviscerated before. Granted, Riverton was different than Andrew, but it wasn't only the man who caused the problem. Something happened to her when she fell in love. Something wobbly.

The emotions took her over and made her dream and eat and think differently. The world turned fuzzy everywhere but in her affection's embrace. It consumed her. She hardly slept. She floated. She hardly ate. She stumbled right into a quagmire of despair.

When Riverton had courted her, her curves had fallen away. And her brain had dropped to the size of a pea.

She should have seen Riverton for what he was. Should have been able to grasp that the rosewater he used was to cover up the scent of more unpleasant activities. He'd even had a small pink feather sticking to his waistcoat when he proposed. How likely was that to happen during the normal course of events?

And when she finally couldn't believe anything but her eyes, and had to accept him for what he was, the marriage ate her away from the inside out. She'd not been able to sleep. She'd feared for her own sanity.

Months had passed. She thought she'd be stuck in Riverton's mire for ever. And when she finally could sleep again and her mind worked properly, she'd sworn never, ever again. No more love. No more being dragged to the pits. No more suffering for someone else's sins. No more living with daggers in the heart.

After Andrew left, she'd painted again as quickly as she could. She couldn't let the thoughts lock into her brain and destroy it along with her heart. But she couldn't rinse Andrew out of her thoughts in the same way she could dip her brush in linseed oil and leave the pigments behind. Instead, she'd immerse herself in a new project and pour her emotions on to the canvas.

She shut her eyes and touched the stiff canvas, running a finger along the dried paint creating Andrew's lean jaw. Andrew truly was the most glorious man she'd ever seen and she had captured him on canvas. Twice.

But she didn't know for sure if her eyes saw reality. She couldn't trust herself. Maybe his hair was normal and maybe he—no, she shook her head. He was a treat for a woman's senses. She'd watched the heads turn and the eyes devour him. Bosoms bobbed higher when Andrew walked by.

A tiny shiver of pleasure went through her when she thought of the other portrait. It wasn't exact, she supposed. Not entirely, but a woman's imagination could be impressive. And she knew she'd reached close enough.

She went to the door opposite her bedchamber. The door stood open. Chills covered her, even in the heat of the day. She gripped the door handle, shock plummeting her breath away. She walked inside and stopped, feeling the air in the empty room. Gone. It could not walk away on its own. The painting was gone.

She stepped back until the wall crashed into her back. This couldn't be. The painting was life-sized.

She could barely lift the canvas and it was gone.

She clasped her throat and then, knowing it made no sense, she pulled the other paintings aside, hoping that by some unknown act of nature the painting had fallen to the floor and her eyes were deceiving her.

Then she ran back to the main room of the studio and her eyes traced every outline in the room. Paintings just did not walk away.

Nothing else had been disturbed.

Her heart thumped in her ears.

The room had been locked. The servants had no fascination with the place.

She clutched her stomach when she rushed into Astlin Manor.

The housekeeper started, jaw slack, as Beatrice ran towards her, almost careening into the woman.

'Lord Andrew?' The words felt the size of a boot and couldn't be pushed from her lips fast enough. 'Has he been here while I've been away?'

'I can't think so, but a man arrived for the painting. The big one.'

'But...' Beatrice stopped, controlling herself so she wouldn't grab the woman by the shoulders. 'Who has been in my studio?'

The woman took a step back, realisation causing her eyes to widen. 'Just the man.'

'Man?' Beatrice gasped. *'Man?'*

'The one for Lord Andrew's painting.'

'I did not...'

'Oh, yes.' The housekeeper's cheeks reddened. 'I made sure. I asked him to describe it before I dared let him into your studio.' The housekeeper could not meet Beatrice's eyes. 'I had not thought that man you painted so bold, but I knew he had posed and his manservant arrived and told me the painting was to be taken...' She squeezed a glance at Beatrice. 'And I suppose a man knows what his own...' she extended her arm away from her body, but waved a hand in the general direction of her torso '...area looks like so for him to have a painting of the area...' Her chin raised. 'I do not pass judgement on art, Lady Riverton. And I do not understand what kind of a man would wish for such a painting, but I suppose he might want to remember when he is older...'

'The smaller one? The smaller one? You did not give him the smaller one?' She put her fisted hands to her own cheeks.

The housekeeper shook her head. She widened her arms, stretching her hand over her head to indicate size. 'I went in the room where you store the paintings. I could not miss it.'

Chapter Sixteen

'Sir.' The butler stood at Andrew's door. Obviously something had stirred him from his bedchamber.

Andrew raised his head from the paperwork at his desk, blinking away the fatigue of the day. The servant had forgotten his cravat and his face was puffed from sleepiness.

Andrew stared. His household never disturbed him after the hour was late.

'Lady Riverton to see you.'

Andrew raised his brows.

'I will inform her,' the man said, 'that you are not receiving callers if you wish.' He paused, thinking. 'She has a portrait with her, and she appears…distraught.'

Andrew brushed a hand across the day's stubble. His own cravat was draped across the back of a chair, under his waistcoat. He stood. 'Show her to the sitting room.'

He'd not expected this. He'd thought of her so many times and he could not force her from his mind.

He'd had Fawsett bring every copy of the scandal sheets printed since he'd left Beatrice's studio and not one new mention of her. Well, there had been the one, but he'd had Fawsett check on it and the story was entirely made up. Beatrice had not been in the Thames.

Andrew found his neckcloth, put his waistcoat on, but did not bother with a coat. Propriety had well escaped between them and now Beatrice was arriving at his house alone at this hour. He sighed. She would never be demure. It would take a better man than he knew to make her so.

He walked into the sitting room, lights already relit by the butler. She sat, perched on the sofa. Beside her, his portrait was propped, facing him.

Inwardly he smiled. That was a damn good painting.

His world brightened to have Beatrice in his house. 'You did not have to bring it at this hour,' he said, after greeting her.

'Well?' she asked. She blinked three times and

stood, leaning a bit forward as if she needed spectacles to view him.

'I do like it, Beatrice.'

Her smile burst on to her whole body. Her mouth moved, forming words, but she didn't speak at first.

'Oh, Andrew.' She lunged forward, grabbing him around the waist in the tightest hug he'd ever had. The gust of woman moving forward caused a quick intake of his breath.

'You do, truly?'

'Of course.'

'Andrew.' The word had thousands of others behind it, but she collapsed into his chest and he had no choice but to catch her.

Warmth changed into the power of the sun. His body changed faster than hers had. The waistcoat had been a bad idea.

His fingers traced up the hooks of her gown.

Perhaps being bitten wasn't so bad, he decided, slowly moving his hand down the clasps. One fell undone under his fingertips.

He found the top clasp and held her against his body, but he didn't have to. If he'd taken his hands away, she would have remained, hugging and squeezing.

He held her, shutting his eyes, letting the wisps of her hair tickle his cheeks. Scents of lavender and pigment brushed against his nose and he wondered if he could ever again smell linseed without becoming aroused.

His hands trailed up the back of her gown, past all the closures that had opened, and tangled in the ties of her corset.

'Andrew. I am so relieved.' She sniffled. 'I did not...'

Tears.

Tears?

He moved to find his coat pocket and pull free a handkerchief, handing it to her. She brushed it across her eyes.

His eyes moved over the picture again. 'I told you that I liked it before.'

She stilled.

'Before?' she asked, her voice the merest whisper.

He didn't answer, gathering her back into his arms, kissing in the salty taste of her lips, looping one of the tie strings tighter and tighter around his finger while he nipped down,.

Moving back, fingers still twined in her ties,

he moved enough to speak. 'I plan to put it above the mantel.'

She jerked back so quickly, she took his hand with her. The momentum, with the tie still in his hand, caused the unknotting, and the dress sagged at her shoulder. He couldn't take his eyes from the creamy skin.

'Tell me exactly what you think of it,' she said. 'Exactly.'

He looked over her shoulder, enfolding her into his arms and holding her tight. His eyes examined the painting and his hands slowly worked the corset loose. 'Very kind to me.' He shut his eyes, moving to bare her shoulders so he could savour them with his own skin. 'Not as lovely as *Boadicea*. But they could hardly compare.'

'Tell me...'

'I don't wish to talk now, Beatrice, except to tell you how to feel, taste—the scent of your hair—'

She pushed back, creating a cool chasm between them, but he didn't care. So much of her warmth remained against him.

'What did you think of the—chest?'

He shrugged. 'I suppose the folds of the coat are just as they should be.'

'Oh, no, no, no,' she said, her hands against

his torso, pushing herself from him. 'No!' she screeched.

He'd never heard quite that sound from a human.

She raised her hand, using her fingertip to point over her shoulder and behind her. 'You do not have another portrait I have painted?'

He smiled at her. 'I did not know you realised I have it.'

'Oh, you do? Truly?' The light returned to her face.

'Yes.' He pulled her back against him. *'Boadicea.'*

'Dash it.' She hurled herself from his reach.

She stood back, sorting, holding her dress against her chest. 'You did not send someone for the painting?'

The shudder of a head shake. The question in his eyes as he looked over her shoulder at the artwork behind him. 'No. I knew it needed to dry and you sent the note saying you would bring it to me.'

'Oh.'

He took a step towards her and she moved back.

'There is something, perhaps, you need to know.' Beatrice looked at Andrew. This was the moment of confession. The moment of truth.

She blurted out, 'Mother is afraid I am with child.'

She saw the look on his face—not really an expression, more of an absorbing stare. The masked, unmoving look.

'But it's not true.' She rushed to grab his hand. Then she reached to his shoulders, grasping both. 'Breathe, Andrew.'

'Beatrice.' He pried her fingers from his shoulders. 'I would do what is necessary should you be—in that state. You should never doubt that. Your words surprised me and, of course, I should have thought of the possibility of a child.'

'It's not true—just a concern of Mother's, you understand.'

'Time will calm your mother's worries.' His hands slipped to hold hers.

The touch soothed her. But how could she let her actions harm someone like Andrew?

Beatrice double-blinked.

His hands tightened at her back, rotating circles which sparked like embers with hot breaths blown over them.

'Beatrice.'

She looked into his face—eyes with lashes long enough to keep a woman warm on any cool evening—and he mesmerised the truth from her. Not from her lips, but from her head.

She could not bear to see his face look at her with the anger he might feel simply because her muse had taken control of her paintbrush.

'Andrew. I have been trying to keep quiet and garner no attention. I truly have. I thought…' she paused, stumbling over her words '…painting keeps me busy and away from scandal.' Her head tilted. 'This all began when we met and somehow I can't stop it from getting worse. I wouldn't say it's your fault, but it is not completely mine, you understand.'

His fingertips clasped her shoulders and she could feel his touch through her light sleeves, and the warmth tingled down, hitting all the important places in her body.

'Oh, Andrew.' She looked at him. 'This is not something I can speak of.'

'You can tell me anything.' He studied her face. 'You can. We've shared… We've shared so much.'

'Of course I can tell you anything.' But if he didn't react well to a little love nip, he might not react well to a detailed study of the human form, surprisingly like his own.

She spoke before he could ask questions. 'Andrew, I committed an indiscretion. There is evidence of it.'

Something behind his eyes changed. Flickered with thoughts. The stare again. He put a hand to her chin. 'Whom did you attack?'

Her brows knit. 'No one. It is nothing like that. But these things just happen to me.'

'Yes. They do.'

'Do not worry. I will figure it out. I will fix it.'

'Tell me what has happened.' Andrew's face had no more emotion than a wall. 'I will take care of everything for you, Beatrice. Tell me about it.'

She shut her eyes briefly and waved a hand. 'I am overwrought. The travelling. You understand. The concern about…whether you'd changed your mind.'

'Beatrice. I can help.'

She would tell him. 'Something I have…um, painted, has potential for embarrassment, and I would truly not like it to become public knowledge. Such as another Boadicea, but perhaps more…beautiful.'

'Another Boadicea?'

She clamped her teeth together. 'Yes.'

'With less clothing, I would wager.' His shoulders seemed to become broader, his head taller and his eyes darker.

'Yes.'

His voice softened, but still had censure. 'Clothes are not a bad thing in art. They show the style of the age. Show more of the person. They are an ornament and give the viewer more knowledge. I do not understand why artists decide something private must now be shared with the world just because they can do so.'

She took a breath. 'You must know. This one was not to be displayed. No one was to see it but me. For now. Maybe in a hundred years... It was my private painting. My masterpiece.'

'Where do you think it is?'

'I do not know.'

'And this will embarrass you?'

'I'm not sure,' she grumbled.

He gave her a direct appraisal. 'Whatever has happened, no one will believe you above suspicion.'

'I would say not since I signed my real name to it.'

Andrew kept his voice gentle as he pulled at the corset ties, correcting them. 'At any moment did you take seriously my intentions to improve the reputation you'd gathered?' Every day of his years plunged into his body and the long nights spent working, and the moments of pleasure he had not chased because he planned for his future.

Beatrice turned and spoke to the head-and-shoulders portrait. 'Yes. I thought it a grand plan. I did not quite see how it could be accomplished, but I was willing to try.'

He finished the hooks.

'No,' he whispered. 'You were not. You were willing to let me try. To get myself embroiled in your activities, but not to alter one moment of your plans.'

He strode beside her, gently taking her shoulders and turning her in his direction. 'Did you hope that I would garner you more attention and not care at all about what kind it would be? Did you think a romance between us would simply add more notoriety to you and ignore how it would impact on me? I did not mind a few blemishes against me if it helped you, Bea, but you did nothing—not one thing to soften the words against you. You did not pull yourself up, Beatrice, you merely wished to drag me into scandal with you.'

'I was trying.'

'Trying. I have heard that word from many people. *I am trying to learn a new language. I am trying to drink less. I am trying to make peace with my family.* It is an admission of failure. A person intent on success will tell themselves *I am drinking less* and hopefully they will not even need to speak the words to others because it will be so obvious. Those silent words are the most meaningful, Beatrice. Did you speak them to yourself?'

After a moment of silence, she said, 'I am trying to like you, Andrew.'

Chapter Seventeen

Beatrice rushed into her brother's house, glancing about. The butler appeared before her, not looking a day older than a century.

'Everything in order, madam?' Arthur studied her face. 'It's half past bedtime.'

She brushed a hand through her curls, knowing she could not make herself look composed. 'Tell me quick,' she whispered, eyes on the stairs. 'Is everything the same as before?'

Lips tight, he nodded. 'My back hurts. My elbow hurts. Your brother does not pay me enough. I am the most handsome man in all England.'

'Anything—out of the ordinary? Among the *ton*. Any talk of me?'

Arthur shook his head and, even though his lids more than half-drooped over his eyes at the edge, she saw interest spark. 'Should there be?'

'Where's my brother?' she asked.

'Safely asleep.' He gave a slight shrug. 'Everything's the same—up to this moment.' His chin went up and his lids lowered so much she could hardly see his eyes at all. 'But I see you are about to change that.'

'I am hoping my brother has one of my paintings, or he knows of it. And I must also check Somerset House in the morning. I had a picture of an old harridan I had hoped to display and perhaps they thought I meant now and sent someone for it. I might be in a mess again, Arthur.'

'You'll have to call me Arturo if you wish for my help.'

She growled before speaking. 'After your father died, I asked how you would like to be addressed as you are dear to us. You said there was only one Standen, and you would be pleased to remain Arthur. Then you started correcting me every time I use it, telling me Artemus, several times, Aristotle once. I asked Mrs Standen. Your real name is Arthur.'

One brow raised enough that she could see an entire eye. 'My dear wife also believes I am the most handsome man in all England and that I am the by-blow of a duke.'

'If you do see a rather large painting about—and this must be handled with the utmost of stealth—I will pay handsomely for its discreet return.'

His lips bunched and his eyes squinted. His chin gave an upturn of agreement. 'And what is this painting of?'

'A male's most private parts.'

'A male's most—?' He studied her face. 'Attached?'

'Yes. To a complete person.'

His eyes widened and so did his grin. He looked twenty years younger. 'You didn't.' He chuckled. 'And it is lost?'

'One should never confess until one is completely presented with the facts and perhaps not even then if a good story of innocence hasn't been fashioned.'

'Lady Riverton. It is an honour and privilege to work for you.'

'But you must not let anyone know.'

'I will not speak of it. Surely no one would be interested in such a painting. No one would be so depraved as to view such a thing.'

'Mr Standen, you are not to make me feel worse. If you see the painting arrive here, you must alert me immediately.'

'I will.' He smiled. 'But I might also show it to Mrs Standen. I would not want her to miss something like that. She will, of course, be aghast at such impropriety.'

'Arthur.'

He bowed quickly. 'Lady Riverton, I cannot promise to keep such a thing from my wife and you know we are both deeply devoted to you. You can be sure if even a whisper of such a painting is made and I hear of it, I will immediately alert you and do all I can to assist.'

'And if Lord Andrew sends a sincere apology, I might like to hear of it.'

'Of course.'

'Or if he arrives looking a bit overwrought, perhaps innocently send him in a direction away from my true location and alert me.'

'I suppose I do not have to ask whose most private parts have been painted?'

'Please do not.'

Arthur's head creaked up and down. 'I will do all I can to help. I will have a trunk ready in the event you need to leave the country.' He smiled. 'Mrs Standen and I will both travel with you and we will make sure you are quite comfortable. And if Lord Andrew arrives, I will be sure to handle the questions as you wish.'

Near Foxworthy's house, Andrew stopped the carriage with a thump to the roof when he saw Foxworthy walking.

Andrew pushed open the door, Foxworthy jumped inside and the carriage wheels rolled again.

'You were right about Tilly,' Foxworthy informed him, grasping his own coat at the lapels, pulling it straight so he could sit comfortably beside Andrew. 'And that there is a parcel which seems to be of import.'

'You discovered this so soon?'

Fox stared at Andrew. 'I work best when naked women are involved. You should know that.'

'And did Miss Tilly have anything to say of import?'

Foxworthy smiled. 'Correct of you to think of her. My good Miss Tilly seems to know quite a lot about what goes on in Lady Riverton's world.

It seems her mother and Lady Riverton's mother are quite close sisters.'

'Does anyone know where Lady Riverton is now?'

'Her brother's house. She is trying to make certain the portrait does not arrive in London without her knowledge. Tilly is watching every move anyone makes.'

'So you keep me waiting.'

Foxworthy gave a la-di-da wave of his head.

'Do the men with the carriage know what the package contains?' Andrew asked.

'I'm not sure. Tilly is trying hard to get the information from her mother, but they are not exactly on good terms because Tilly upset Lady Riverton. Tilly's mother refuses to tell her what is going on.'

'How unlikely is it that Tilly will not find out all she wishes to know?'

'She will find out. She is begging her mother's forgiveness every day. But the important thing to note is that Tilly suspects Beatrice's mother of taking the art.'

Andrew waited outside the door of Wilson's house, hearing a scrambling noise just before the door opened with a quick snap. The servant stumbled backwards, in the way of one whose momentum had suddenly changed from full speed to rapid stop. He gulped for air.

'May I speak with Lady Riverton?' Andrew asked.

'She is not at home. She did not inform the staff of her destination.' The man's chest heaved.

Andrew nodded, not believing him for a second. 'Is Wilson here?'

'No. He is away as well.'

'Might I wait for him?'

'Oh, I could not let you do that. The cat has died.'

'My sympathies. I will wait though.'

'The stench might be a bit overwhelming and I could not let you suffer so.'

'The stench?'

'Dear Fluffy somehow got into the walls to chase a mouse and was not able to escape. The yowling was atrocious and then it stopped, only to be replaced by a distinctly foul odour, which permeates all the upper rooms of the house.'

'That is so strange. But do not worry, I can handle a bit of a stench.' Andrew bounded up the stairs.

'I hope so,' he heard muttered, mixed with the man's steps, behind him.

In the room, Andrew sat on the sofa, extended his arm across the back and challenged the butler with a glare.

'I will see if Lady Riverton is returning,' the servant said. He moved out of the line of Andrew's vision at a sedate pace, but as soon as he rounded the door, the sound of footsteps on the floorboards quickened.

If Andrew admitted the truth to himself, he wanted to see her. The painting did not interest him overly. Then he stopped his thoughts. That was not entirely true. If Bea had painted another portrait of herself, perhaps wearing even less clothing than before, he would certainly like to see it.

But if such a thing came into public view, Beatrice's reputation would never recover. She must learn to control the storm and to create rainbows. Perhaps she could do a series of rainbow paintings in different settings. A boy looking from the window at one. A mother holding a child and pointing to the colours overhead. A crofter walking from his doorway to look at the sky after crops had been watered by the heavens.

He realised he lied to himself. Beatrice could no more paint a rainbow than she could paint a daffodil. She liked portraits. She liked flair. One did not collect skulls in order to better paint flowers.

He sighed. Beatrice enjoyed notoriety.

She was the storm and rainbow all in one. But he could not have his life a tempest. Even now he should be checking out some properties he'd heard about in Bristol. He did not trust the drawings he'd received of them, and his man of affairs was not experienced enough to make a decision on such a large purchase.

Andrew sniffed. The air in the room didn't move, but it did have the scent of cleaning. No perfume to cover anything dead. Even the servants around Beatrice did not seem able to concoct a suitable fable. He should have said she'd been called away to visit an ailing relative or had a megrim. Something suitably dull.

Movement from the doorway caught his attention and he looked up to see Beatrice plunge into the room, her dress a blur of blue. His heart stirred.

She had the side of her skirt loosely grasped and released it.

He stood, pleased he had the likeness of her to keep. 'Your mother may have the missing painting.'

Instead of the relief he expected, she reacted much the same as a chicken might who'd just had a major feather plucked, including the squawk.

'Mother? Oh, this could not be worse.' She lowered her voice. 'This could not be worse.'

'I said your mother may have it. Your mother.'

She tumbled forward, reaching out, both hands landing on his chest without force. But the blow tingled in him.

He clasped her elbows, holding her steady.

'Andrew. My mother has it?' She stared at him.

'I'm uncertain. But it's possible. We must ask her.'

'I suppose.' She knocked her head against his shoulder. 'A man in a carriage came for it and I had assumed it was you. But Mother could have sent someone.'

'Simply ask her. We can leave now. My vehicle is waiting.' He slid his hands up to her shoulders, aware of the thin fabric and the energy of her beneath it. 'I'll escort you and return tonight. We'll get this settled.'

'I don't think Mother lets things settle well.'

'Can you leave now?' he asked.

'I can go alone,' she said, stepping back, reaching out to pat him. As if he were some puppy she wanted to appease. Except she patted too quickly. Too something. Her head turned away.

'I'm going with you,' he said. 'Or alone. Now. The carriage is ready and, by coincidence, I have nothing better to do.'

'I'll gather my things,' she said. 'There is something…' She paused. 'Perhaps I will show you the painting when we recover it.'

He took her arm. 'You can be sure when we recover the art, I'll want to see what has caused this uproar.'

She stopped all movement. Wide eyes caught his. Her mouth opened but no squawk, or whisper or purr.

'Bea,' he reassured her, 'don't concern yourself that I will be shocked by what you've painted. Remember, Foxworthy is my cousin and, disreputable though he may be, we are friends. I have travelled the same trails as he, I have just not detoured into all the bedchambers.'

Fox had once been the patron for an artist. Fox ended up with quite a collection of sketches which would never be on a wall, but had been passed around in a few taverns.

'You say that...' Beatrice let the words trail away.

'We will concern ourselves with it later,' he reassured her. 'The first step is to have the image back in your hands. Now, we must proceed in that direction.' He put a hand at her back and moved her along.

When they left the room, he didn't lessen his touch. The gesture gave him a connection with Beatrice that settled into him and he didn't want to lose it.

She sighed, slowing to relax against his side. 'To be travelling alone with you at night. What of my reputation?'

'I assume it will help it.' He chuckled. But she didn't. 'I'm jesting, Bea.'

'But it's true,' she said. 'I cannot quite stop being who I am. I am not sure I wish to try any more. I gather even more notice as I try to have less.'

In the carriage, Andrew turned to her. 'No one wants you to stop being who you are. I wish everyone could see the truth of who you are.'

'Truth?' Her fingers lingered against the wood of the window frame, bouncing with the movement of the wheels. 'The truth is in the scandal sheets. That is why it is so damaging. I did hurt my husband with the scissors. I did break the glass on the coach. I did marry Riverton and he was above my station. I closed my mind to everything but love.'

'That cannot be so wrong.'

'You've never been in love.'

The carriage turned and then he answered, 'I'm not certain.'

'Oh, no.' She shuddered. 'Love is why the little cupids on my ceiling all have arrows. Sharp.' She raised her brows. 'Pointed. Something that hurts. I wanted to be able to see the beauty of the ceiling. The pretence at love. Little floating cherubs. And then the arrows to pierce the life right out of me.' She shrugged. 'You're the first person I've told. I don't think I needed the reminder above me, but it was nice to have my own private thoughts on the ceiling.'

'The mythical Cupid did not want his wife to see him,' Andrew said. 'He preferred her to think him a beast than to see the truth, and he was not hideous at all. He merely presented himself that way to her. Perhaps he wanted to see if her heart was true.'

'If you think you are convincing me that I am a good sort on the inside, then you are wasting words.' She relaxed into the seat. 'I am quite sure of that already. But it is not me you think to convince, Andrew. It is the world.' And himself, but she could not say that. 'When Psyche saw Cupid's true face, because she had disobeyed him by viewing him against his wishes, he felt betrayed and deserted her.' She shrugged.

Perhaps Andrew was her Cupid. But Andrew was not comfortable with his passions. Riverton had doused his in smoke and women. Andrew hid his under a black waistcoat.

The comparison of Andrew and Riverton resurfaced her memories of the past.

Her husband's passing had filled her with relief, guilt and very little grief. The day after his funeral, she'd overheard a servant humming and noticed a fresh brightness to the house. Laughter from below stairs had even wafted up through the walls. That had never happened before.

'Riverton deserted me on the day of our marriage, or at least immediately after. He wasn't sober as he said our vows. I was stunned. When we courted, he had stumbled a few times from drink, but nothing, nothing like what I discovered after we wed.'

She stared at a bit of road dust on the panes. 'Riverton did not care at all for himself and if he could not think anything of his life, how could he love anyone else? He would have liked to, I'm sure. He would have preferred not destroying so much. But he could not help it.'

'Are you making excuses for him?'

'No.' She touched the back of Andrew's hand. 'He could not help it. He died. Simple as that. If you are willing to sacrifice your life for moments when you have lost sight of the true world, then certainly, you cannot help it. You die for an imagination while you ignore the truths around you. The sun may be shining, birds singing and spring bursting from all corners or a snow may be covering the world with a different kind of magic, but he ignored that because it meant nothing. The truth inside his head was more real than life. Even his own.' She clasped Andrew's hand. Fingers lean. Strong. 'It does not change anything. It does not change how I wanted to dip his head in a chamber pot, along with the rest of him. Can you guess how that would have sounded, my drowning my husband in a chamber pot? Don't think I didn't consider it.'

Love was no different than the imagination Riverton sought. A swirl of magic the same as a night-time dream. She tried to create it much in the same way he tried to live in a sotted world and claim it correct. But her imaginations did not work as strongly as his and she stepped away from them.

If she were to love someone like Andrew, he would be constantly trying to change her into a simple, unassuming wife. He was chasing the same smoke vapour she'd been lost in. Only his surrounded her.

How could she enjoy the sparkle in her world if someone tried to quash her?

'Do you ever wear any colours but black and white, Andrew?'

'They do me well.'

'Vermilion suits me.' The words were true. But it was soft colours concerning her now. The flesh tones.

Chapter Eighteen

Andrew clasped her fingers, stilling them. The whole of the time in the carriage she had tapped her foot or moved her hands or changed expressions.

'If your mother has the portrait, no harm will be done.'

'You can believe that. I don't. But if she took it, then I will have a better chance of finding it and taking it back. I hope.'

Even as he held the fingers immobile, he noted her slipper tapping again. 'She can't want to cause ill to you. You're her only daughter.'

'Ha. She claims to have had others, before me, but drowned them at birth. She said she only kept me because it was a slow year.'

Her hand slid from his and now her fingers clasped over his. He didn't think she was aware of the movement. But she didn't want to feel captured.

'Beatrice. Her sense of humour is cracked.'

'So is her sense of motherhood.' She swayed his hand slightly as she talked.

He leaned back, leaving their hands together, listening as she told tales of her mother's infractions during Beatrice's childhood. Beatrice had no anger or resentment. In fact, she chuckled a few times at her mother's exploits.

This was not the world he had known. The duke's household could not waver in its perfection, at least on the surface. Even though Andrew's father had died, the household continued just as his father would have expected. Andrew's choices with his inheritance had been questioned, but he'd risked his brother's censure, and the family had accepted his need to have the living he wanted. Andrew needed secure funds to continue in the world of the *ton* and he had not wanted to step out of it.

His father had given all his sons the same education, training and discipline. He'd said all his sons were extensions of the ducal heritage. A father did not only give his sons names, he also gave them preparations to be men.

Secretly, Andrew hadn't wanted to be so far surpassed by his older brother. He'd been determined to create his own elegance around him. He wanted the finest carriages and a home just as well equipped as any ducal residence.

He looked across at Beatrice.

She'd taken off both her gloves and fanned herself with one, wafting the scent of lavender towards him.

'Do you think we could go faster?' she asked. 'I just do not like to think of Mother...'

'We'll get there in due time.'

'I suppose. It's just... Mother.'

'You shouldn't paint anything you wouldn't want the whole world to see.'

The fanning stopped. 'I...agree.' She looked out the window. 'It's the reactions that concern me. I personally think it is quite beautiful and something the whole world *should* see. I just do not think others will share that opinion.'

'Rainbows,' he instructed. 'Paint rainbows, flowers, bunnies or cherubs with their arrows only you know about. There is a whole world of things which do not cause grief which you can paint.'

She put the gloves together in her lap, straightening them. 'Artists have suffered for their creations for quite some time. Just to show teeth in a painting can cause such an uproar. It is seen much the same as showing a corset.'

'So you did as Vigée Le Brun and showed the smile.'

'No, I did not. But she is my inspiration. We even have the same curly hair and the same love of fashion and art. I hope to meet her some day. She is much underrated.'

'She's painted nobility.'

'Still underrated, but if she saw this portrait I completed, I think she would understand.'

'The important thing to do is find the portrait and destroy it if it can cause you that much grief.'

'That is not an option.' She put her gloves back on. 'I cannot destroy what I have created. This one must be protected.' She stared at him. 'Riverton sliced some of my best paintings. I could never forgive him, nor could I forgive anyone who did that to this one.'

An impassive face stared back at her, but she did not care.

The carriage turned to the drive of her home. 'I suspect,' she said, 'even without checking for her carriage, that Mother is here.'

His coach stopped at the front of the house and Andrew helped Beatrice alight from the steps.

Beatrice whisked into her house, hoping the portrait would miraculously have been returned, but she doubted it. Not if a carriage had arrived to remove it in the first place.

How foolish she'd been to think her mother would respect a locked door. But her mother avoided the studio house. Complained of the lingering smell of paint thinner in the air.

They moved up the stairs. After Beatrice instructed a servant to ask her mother to join them, the maid returned to tell Beatrice her mother was unwell and not receiving visitors.

'I will speak with her,' Beatrice said, standing to go to her mother's chamber.

Walking into her mother's room, she saw her mother on the sofa, reading the *Times,* scowling. A lingering hint of tobacco rested in the air.

Her mother sat straight and threw the paper to the side. Her nightdress flattered the silver streaks of her hair and she twirled a pair of spectacles in her hand, though Beatrice knew her mother would rarely put on the eyewear, only hold them in front of her face when she wished to read.

'Where is the painting?' Beatrice asked.

'Painting?' She squinted. 'Which painting?'

'I know you took it, but I don't know how you discovered it.'

'I can tell when you're up to something. I've known you since before you were born and I do like to keep aware of my children. I was walking along, peacefully on the path to the cottage, minding my affairs, and I knew how you must paint in the light, and so the window was there and I was there and you'll never guess the shock I received.'

'I know exactly what you found and removed.'

'I have the portrait, Beatrice.'

'I know.'

'You do?' Her mother smiled, one a dedicated executioner might use. 'Oh, and I so wanted to keep it private. I've known about it for some time. I just had to let you finish it and let it dry, and wait for you to leave. Details.'

She tensed. 'Where is it?'

'I could not have something like that lying about. Your brother would try to kill that man if he saw the picture.' Her mother stood, and walked behind the sofa.

'Think of Andrew.'

'I did, Beatrice. Very much so when I saw the painting.' She gave a discreet cough, covering her mouth with her fist, and eyeing her daughter. 'Which is the reason the portrait isn't in front of your brother right now.' She tossed the spectacles to the table beside her and clucked her tongue. 'He'd burst into a rage. Might have an apoplexy.' She looked at Beatrice. 'He will explode and shatter bits of himself across the *ton*.

'He need never know.'

'I only plan telling him about it if I have to. And if he doesn't grasp the import, then I'll show it to him.' She shrugged. 'I don't think this is something a man should view, however.' She gave her daughter a wink. 'It almost caused me to stop breathing.' Her voice softened so much to make the words almost invisible. 'Is the painting to scale, dear?'

'Mother—I don't trust Wilson not to hurt Andrew. He had Riverton beaten.'

'No, he didn't.' The older woman frowned. She wrinkled her nose. 'I sent the toughs after Riverton.'

Beatrice's jaw dropped.

'For Riverton's own good,' her mother insisted. 'Wilson was going to kill him, but he couldn't very well kill a man who was recovering from a beating. It gave Wilson time to cool off. I didn't

want my son having a murder on his conscience.'
She shook her head slowly from side to side. 'A
murder isn't an easy thing to live with.'

'Mother, perhaps you should let us have our
own lives.' Even as she said the words, Beatrice
knew they dissolved in the air before her mother
heard them.

Her mother's face pinched. 'And neglect you?'

'I don't want Wilson going after Andrew because of this,' Beatrice said. 'My brother knows
Andrew and I have been close. This painting
should not be made public. It's my private work.
Which I secured in a locked room, with half-a-
score of other paintings.'

The older woman reached for the spectacles
again and stood. She straightened her back, using
the eyepiece as a pointer. 'It's not yours now,
Beatrice. It's mine. I do like Andrew. And he obviously has some feelings for you and you him.
You need to marry him. He got the best of his
bloodlines. His father's looks and his mother's
respectability. And he's not an arrogant peacock
like his brother.'

'I don't want to marry him. He would make me
miserable.'

'He is perfect for you. Your residences are a

good distance apart. You could hardly know the other existed. It is not like the past when Riverton kept causing notice. This one practically buries himself. Would save us the trouble.'

'He would make me miserable. He thinks women should be demure. He does not wish to marry Beatrice the Beast. I am shunned by men.'

'You're also Beatrice with her head in the clouds. If it weren't for Wilson having such a temper and everyone knowing it, and Riverton ending up beaten—Beatrice, child, the men of this town drool when they think of bedding the Beast. Your brother and I frighten them, though. Except Lord Andrew.' She waved her hand. 'It was much the same in my day. A good set of curves, glorious hair and a hint of brazenness and they line up. Your father never let me out of his sight.'

'Mother,' Beatrice snapped.

'Beatrice. You need to be married.'

'No. I don't. A widow can have liaisons.'

'You aren't listening.' She lowered her chin. 'It's not good for the family name, or for Wilson's future, for you to remain unwed. I'll be your mother until the day I die, Beatrice, and I don't see myself stepping aside. You've had a difficult first marriage, to be sure. And you're reluctant to marry again. You should have a second husband. Perhaps a third one later. You can't just stop at one. Your grandmother had four and she lived to be ninety-two years old. The trick is to bury them quickly.'

'Mother! How would you feel if Wilson and I took it into our heads to see you married?'

'That's ridiculous.' She stood. Then she paused, her brows softened and her voice lowered. 'Who do you have in mind?'

'Mother,' Beatrice growled.

'Beatrice. I have seen the painting.' She shut her eyes. 'And frankly, dear, you could do worse.' She opened them. 'You two just need a careful nudge in the right direction. You've obviously bedded him, now get the paperwork taken care of. Need I remind you, Beatrice, I have the painting? If you do not marry Andrew, I will turn the painting over to your brother. And you know he will not be happy. Nor will Andrew's family. He has a mother. A brother. A very ducal brother. But it won't matter, will it?' She put a pitiful pout on her lips. 'Because you don't care for the man. To see his life in upheaval because of your painting would not mean anything to you at all. And frankly, he shouldn't have allowed you to do such a thing. I can't feel badly for him—a man who poses nude knows what to expect.'

'Mother, he doesn't know.'

'About the—?'

'Portrait.'

Her mother's eyes widened. She put a hand at her chest. 'Oh. Would you like me to tell him?'

Outside the sitting room door, Beatrice slowed her steps. She'd been rushing, hurrying to get back to Andrew, but she wasn't sure what to tell him.

She could waltz through this incident if it weren't Andrew involved. All of him was involved, except the toes of one foot. She'd let them be draped by silk to give her more time for the other details. If he discovered the truth, he would find anger he didn't know existed within him and the sight wouldn't be pleasant.

When she walked through the door, he stood. Face expectant.

She decided to take her chances. Anything but the truth.

'Mother will be with us in a moment. She had already prepared for bed, but insists she must speak with you.'

'Does she have it?'

'Mother is not above blackmailing me, Andrew.' She whispered out the words.

'How could she wish for something that might cause problems for her child?'

'What I see as a problem, she sees as an opportunity.'

The image of the painting flashed through Beatrice's mind. Pulses of satisfaction curled in her. Yes, she'd captured exactly what she wished. She shouldn't have. But she did.

'What is the price she's asking?'

'She wishes for me to marry.'

'Anyone in particular?'

'Yes. A very particular someone.' She told him with her gaze that he was the object of her mother's selection. Her mother did not see how mistaken she was.

'We will just reason with her.'

Tilting her chin down, she looked up at him. 'Reason? This is not a simple woman. It wasn't Wilson that had Riverton beaten. It was Mother. She said she did it for his own good. She sees things—differently. To reason with someone they have to understand what the word means. Mother is not of that temper. She doesn't take no easily. She doesn't even understand compromise. She believes her motherhood entitles her to whatever means necessary to sway her children. '

He took her fingers. 'Beatrice. We do not live in a time where mothers can force their widowed daughters to marry.'

'I know. But blackmail never goes out of style.'

Still holding her hand, he moved his upwards, using her own fingers to shush her. 'Beatrice. If you have decided not to concern yourself with the scandal sheets, call your mother's bluff. Surely she would not embarrass you.' He frowned.

'No, but she would see me wed.'

'Is it very much more revealing than the other one?' Then he paused. 'It would have to be, wouldn't it? To concern you.'

She pulled her hand from his, the darkness magnifying the sadness in her eyes. 'It is rather.' She put on her calming face. 'I told her I will convince you to marry me. I need time to find the portrait.'

'I'll talk to your mother,' he reassured her. 'I'll explain I've no wish to marry you. That you have no choice in the matter.'

'For me, and only for a moment, please let her believe what she wishes so I will have time to find the painting,' Beatrice suggested.

'I'll see if I can persuade her.'

'Andrew. It's just that—' She looked at the ceiling. 'As I said, I may have made some mistakes in my past.'

He gave a huff. 'Other than my brother, who hasn't? Although I would say this is an error on your mother's part.'

'She sees it simply as a manoeuvre.'

He kept hold of her fingers, waiting.

'Some of my mistakes may have been recent.'

She moved, placing a small chair very close to an easy chair. She sat in the stiff-backed chair and tugged him to sit across from her, the skirts of her dress only a hint from his knees. 'Andrew.' The word had a persuasive lilt. She would have added violins and harp music if she could have. 'Please go along. Only long enough to give me a chance to retrieve the painting. It cannot be hid that well. It's rather large. Mother would need to secure it with someone.'

He didn't answer.

'You did rather reject me,' she said. The barest of smiles, the most hopeful of eyes and a squeeze on his fingers.

'I did not.' His voice struck the air.

A lift of her eyebrows in disagreement. 'Felt like it to me.'

'It should not have.' He lifted her fingers for a kiss.

She couldn't speak for a moment. The rendition of him had been frozen before her eyes for days. Now, to be so close again to the real image was taunting her. 'If that painting is damaged in any way...' she muttered. To destroy her work was to destroy her. And he would. She knew it.

He caught the look in her eyes and his smile told her he would go along with the ruse. 'You'll have to find the painting fast,' he said, 'and convince her not to have the banns read yet.'

She nodded.

'And one other thing,' he said. 'I'd like to see it.'

Her lips thinned and then she answered, 'Remind me after it's safely returned.'

Beatrice bent forward and tapped his knees, and the natural readjustment behind her bodice as she moved all but erased the next words from his hearing. 'Think of a reason to convince her the date must be put off a while.'

He examined her eyes. All of her face. Feminine. Delicate. Her body seemed almost in argument with her personality. This Beatrice could never wield a club or protect a maid, but yet, she had.

She kept talking, but he couldn't follow the words. This woman was nothing like the caricatures. Nothing. She wore silk and lace, smelled of flowers, wisps of hair floated around her eyes, brushing against the skin. This woman surely could not…bite anyone.

'Marriage.'

The word jerked his attention back to the conversation, dousing his thoughts with a thunk against his ears.

'—marriage and keep from attracting much notice. As soon as I find—' She moved back in the chair, her bodice following her, and becoming discreet again. 'When I get it returned and lock it securely away, then I will tell Mother we are not to be wed.'

She reached and gently tugged at his arms. 'You must believe me that I am sorry you are embroiled in this. You must remember that—should things not work out well.'

'This will solve itself. Your mother will come to her senses or you will simply weather the storm. You've been written about before and I believe it is likely to happen again.'

'I suppose I could—' she stared into his eyes

'—except this time there might be more censure than I want. Perhaps a lot of censure—from…'

'You can survive it.'

'I know.' Her eyes wavered. 'I think I could use some respite from it.'

'Perhaps once you get through this you will decide to truly embrace improving your reputation.'

Her eyes only minimally changed.

He knew she'd not had an easy time of things and he really couldn't blame her for what had happened. 'I have to admit I admire your courage in the way you've handled the reports in the newsprint. I have not been so comfortable with thrusting their words aside.'

He reached out, running a finger along the soft skin of her upper arm, and let his voice soothe. 'Never think I am not carrying around admiration for you even though we are so different. You amaze me with your spirit.'

'Oh, Andrew.' Distress showed in her eyes. She stood, her skirts swirling so fast he moved back to keep the flounces away. 'You have no idea how determined my mother is to see us wed now that she believes she has the means to procure a wedding.'

She moved behind the chair, her fingers clenching on the upholstered back. 'I wish I'd told you to take a few swallows of brandy before you met Mother, breathe garlic on her, have dirty hair and cast up your accounts on her shoes.' She raised a hand above the chair back. 'She hardly likes anyone. Half the time, I think she doesn't care for Wilson or me.' Her voice fell so low he could hardly hear it. 'And yet—she is taken with you.'

He didn't appreciate the amazement he heard.

'Your mother is straightforward. Bold.' He paused. 'So unlike the others in her family.'

She reached up, pressing at the back of her neck. Then she fixed him with a dead-on gaze. 'Or perhaps she shares my fascination for eyes that once you look into them, it is as if you can see every shade of the earth ever imagined.'

'Beatrice—' He tried to put as much persuasion as he could into the word and saw it totally miss the mark.

'Mother has chosen you now.' Beatrice raised a hand to silence him. 'She said nothing on my marriage to Riverton when he courted me. But now, she has her heart set on you as my husband. I don't know how to discourage her.'

He leaned so he could lock eyes with her and

stare intently. 'I could still cast up my accounts on her shoes.'

'This is not for jesting, and besides, I don't think it would work. We must outwit her.'

'Do not let her control your life.'

'I suppose it's not my life I'm worried about. There may be more to it than that.'

She had his full attention. 'And why is that, Beatrice?'

Chapter Nineteen

Her mother's shoes tapped in the hallway like little woodpecker raps on the floor. Beatrice whirled around, facing the older woman.

Her mother wore longish sleeves woven so fine the slightest movement fluttered them. Her hair was pulled to the top of her head, similar to Beatrice's own crown of curls. Yet, the look in her eyes had the definite flair of a witch mixing potions.

Andrew moved around Beatrice and walked to her mother, taking the older woman's hand in greeting and giving a brief nod of his head, surprised again by the lingering wisp of tobacco scent in the air.

She examined him, the silence a way of trying to take command of a conversation, a challenge for the other person to speak. He waited.

'I supposed you've heard that my daughter has misplaced a canvas,' she said finally, all innocence.

'Where is it?' he asked, his tone matching hers.

'In a safe place.'

'The best place for it is in Beatrice's care.'

'I would have to disagree,' she said. Her brows notched up almost to her hairline and her voice floated like petals on the wind. 'Have you seen it?'

'Mother.' Beatrice rushed forward. 'You simply cannot.'

Her mother's eyes, moving slower than a general waiting on an enemy to raise its head, turned to her daughter. The voice again an ode to sweetness. 'I do intend to give the painting to him, Beatrice.'

Andrew didn't relax at the words. Her eyes were too focused—and her words too buttery. He waited.

The older woman purred to him. 'As a wedding present. It's time the family tree stopped having cracked branches.' She lowered her chin and levelled a gaze at him. 'Of course, if you don't wish to marry my daughter, I'll happily give you the painting if you wish to marry me.'

'Mother,' Beatrice snapped.

The duchess shrugged. 'Giving up grandchildren would be a sacrifice, but the boasting rights alone to having a husband such as him would make my friends forget how to count. They'd be too envious.'

'I will find it on my own,' he said.

'You don't wish to marry Beatrice? She really is lovely, even if I do say so myself. You could hardly do better. And I don't see you stirring her to violence.'

'Is the art in this house?'

The lined eyes roved over his face 'All I ask is that you marry her. You should thank me. Art does make a lovely gift. To a woman and her husband. I might even throw in some silver candlesticks for good measure.'

'I don't think a mother should endeavour to force her widowed daughter into a marriage as you are doing,' Andrew said.

'Of course not. It just isn't done, is it? But...' she waved a hand about '...I am one of those meddling mothers. The kind whose name is mentioned with a shudder. The kind who...' she smiled '...gets her way.'

'Not in this. A lady shouldn't resort to blackmail.'

Beatrice's mother took a deep breath, digesting the words, and her face registered carefully constructed surprise. 'Nonsense. One uses the methods at hand. I've decided you'd make the perfect foil for Beatrice's lively spirit.' The dowager's eyes sparkled at Andrew.

'I am quite taken with Lady Riverton, but don't you think we should decide on the minor details of our life?' Andrew's voice flowed through the room, rich, comfortable. Not threatened.

Her mother raised a brow, giving her face a look of whimsy. 'You may as well call her Beatrice. You're among family and I can't believe you call her Lady Riverton when you're alone.'

'One likes to keep tender endearments private.' He turned enough so Beatrice's mother could not see his expression and smiled at Bea. Beatrice's cheeks blossomed. What he'd not expected was an accompanying blossom within himself.

He turned back to see a pleased sputter from her mother's upturned lips. He imagined her already selecting names for the grandchildren.

'The two of you will marry,' her mother decreed. 'I won't hear otherwise. And apparently Beatrice has told you I have the means to bring about such an event.'

* * *

Beatrice caught her breath, bracing for her mother to speak of the painting. Her mother's mouth opened. The words were forming.

Andrew's voice softened to a rumble more appealing than distant thunder with a light spring rain. 'I can understand your wish to find her settled and I must say I'm honoured to be the recipient of such trust. But we are both of an age where we decide such things ourselves.' He moved forward, easily, leisurely, a gentle step, and closer. 'Although I think you would make quite the charming mother of the bride.'

Her eyes widened, she coughed and then she fluffed at her locks.

'Normally, I could agree with that,' her mother said. 'But only if I said it. I know nonsense no matter who spouts it. I don't care how old you are, if the means to secure such an event falls into my hands, I'll use it, be you five or fifty-five years of age. I think you will make a fine husband to my daughter.'

He put a hand to his heart and Beatrice thought of the stage. 'Think how I would feel, knowing my beloved only wed me by force. I would be wounded deeply. Could you do that to me?'

Andrew might have some of the actor in him, but from the gristle in her mother's eyes, not enough.

'When the children arrive,' she said, 'you'll forget about the methods used to secure the wedding. You'll be too busy making sure you have their lives planned out for them. I'll help, of course.'

Andrew reached to the side, taking Beatrice's hand. 'If your daughter and I marry, it will be because we decide on our own. Nothing you can say or do will force the issue for me.'

Her mother's eyes reflected the look of a gardener completely at ease with snipping off the heads of roses in perfect bloom.

'You think so now. And I will give Beatrice twenty-four hours to change your mind. After that, things will become more apparent. You might find this worth the negotiations. Of course the best part will be that you will get to marry into my family.'

She nodded to Beatrice. 'Twenty-four hours to convince him. Another day to get the special licence. You should certainly thank me for this. And I will expect a gift while you are on your wedding trip. And a grandchild. One of each. You don't have to name the boy after me, but I would so love to see a little Euphemia.'

She left the room.

Andrew looked at Beatrice. 'We'll find it. First, we must search this house. We only have to open the door and sniff. Any closed-up chamber will smell of the fresh oils. She may have taken it in a carriage, but perhaps she keeps it close. We have to make certain.'

Beatrice took a breath. There could not be another Euphemia. Ever.

The upper floors had a few rooms used for storage of furniture and trunks. Beatrice led Andrew to the chambers. She followed him, each of them carrying a lamp and facing mounds of covered and dusty household articles.

She sneezed as she raised her lamp. The air smelled of musty coverings and old clothing. 'It's not here.' She walked through the stacked and crated items. 'And I doubt it can be in the house.'

Andrew didn't pause in his perusal. 'No matter. We need to search.'

She went through the house, even knocking at the rooms in the servants' quarters, making sure no scent of paint lingered when the door opened.

Sniffing. Satisfying herself with the innocence on the faces and the lack of evidence in the air.

Each time, Andrew watched as if he must also ascertain the accuracy of her search.

At the end of the hunt, she could see the fatigue growing under his eyes, hardening the determination behind them.

'She could have also hidden it in plain sight,' he remarked. 'Your painting room.'

Giving a quick upturn of her head, she acknowledged his words, moving to go to her studio, carrying a lamp.

She didn't know what time it was, but looked to the sky to see if it lightened in the east, but she couldn't discern the morning glow.

Walking to the cottage in the darkness, she could feel him behind her. She stopped, turning. She could see the same memories behind his eyes that she felt. The last time they'd been in the cottage had been heights followed by a crevasse.

'I don't know what to do or say or think,' she said. 'Normally, that doesn't happen to me. But I do care where you're concerned.'

'It's the past. Means nothing.' He shook his head. 'Nothing that hasn't—'

'I'm really not a bad sort of person.' Even as she spoke, she puzzled. Nothing that hadn't happened, he'd said.

'Of course I know that.' He walked around her, opening the door for her, and she realised he'd shut another door at the same time. Her apologies would fall on deaf ears.

'Has something happened, in the past? Someone bit you?' she asked.

He paused and one blink shuttered away his answer.

'Beatrice. Some things are best left unsaid.'

'I suppose.' She wiggled her head. 'But I usually say them.'

'I don't. I'm a private person.'

She could not think he would view her painting quite in the same way she did. 'Do you have a temper?' she asked.

'Everyone has a temper.' He chuckled.

She had to get that painting back.

Moving past him, she went inside to make certain her mother hadn't had a once-in-a-lifetime conscience flare-up and returned it.

A casual glance in each room told her the creation wasn't there. Andrew kept moving things, looking, putting them back. Not really searching for the painting, she suspected, but perusing the situation, or her, through the art and the heart of her world.

Sitting on her painting stool, she watched the black coat moving over the broad shoulders, flexing as he searched. The thought returned to her mind that he always wore the same style of clothing. Always. Except in her painting.

She tried to imagine him in any other colour but black and couldn't. But she could still see the man as if he wore nothing underneath. The years of studying forms and shapes did her well.

Her brushes had been magic. They'd moved exactly as they should.

The formal portrait was good. Her best, in fact, except for the other one. The nude was her masterpiece. And she doubted she'd ever be able to recapture the spirit of the painting again. Not that she thought her work would be inferior, or that she wouldn't paint quite well. But her paintbrush had pulled Andrew's spirit on to the canvas. A person could look at the nude and see the true form and beauty of the man. Could almost feel his breath in the air. And if a hand reached to touch the oils, the fingertips would be surprised to feel paint instead of warmth.

She'd painted the man beneath the mask. If he saw that…if he realised how she had truly bared him to the world…

The weight of what she had done crashed into her body.

She had to get the painting in her possession and quickly. She didn't want anyone else seeing it either. Not now. Not for centuries. But her, only her.

And perhaps the painting wasn't just of him, but had the mists of her feelings for him woven into it.

That portrait was more than art to her. She was certain it would be at Tilly's mother's house. Oh, that could be sticky. Tilly would not wish at all to relinquish it, if she'd seen it. But her aunt. Her aunt would. She always could be counted on to do the right thing.

Now that she thought of it, she could not imagine her mother taking it anywhere else. The coach could easily have been her aunt's.

But if Tilly knew Beatrice was coming for the painting…

'You understand, the only way to keep the portrait from being seen once it's discovered is to destroy it. Burn it,' he said.

Destroy. The word hit her thoughts, but bounced back out again. *No.*

She had to find it first and not tell him where it was. She could not. She would find it and this time she would lock it away and keep all the keys, or hide it at the back of another painting and secure it. She would let everyone think it had been tossed into a fire.

She would need it for the nights Andrew was not in her life. To burn it would be like removing Andrew and her feelings for him from the world. She had poured her spirit and passion into the art, and she could not lose it. She must keep this tie to him.

'I'm searching your brother's house,' he said. 'It could be there.'

She took a deep breath. 'If you return to London tonight, then I will let Mother think you are getting the special licence and, perhaps, I can convince her to drop the blackmail idea.'

She knew Arthur would have alerted her if he'd found it. The painting could not be in that house without the butler knowing. But if Andrew travelled with her to her aunt's house, he'd find the painting and get rid of it.

'I'll start at first light. Do you wish to go with me?' he asked.

Conscience tore at her, but she swatted it to the

ground. She had to let him go in the wrong direction and she couldn't follow.

'I will question Mother again in the morning.' Her hand waved a bit as she talked, misleading in its own way, helping her pretend an unconcern she didn't have. 'I will ask the servants about every place she could have gone. Not just what she says, but where she could have secretly gone. We have two days.'

But she would find it at her aunt's house. She knew that was where her mother had to have taken it.

The portrait was the one link to Andrew she could keep for ever, unless he found it first.

She'd only meant to doze for a few moments, not even untying her corset. But when Beatrice awoke her eyes opened to harsh light beaming into the room—showing everything with all the softness taken away. Within moments, she'd summoned the carriage, only to learn her mother had left in her coach. Beatrice couldn't follow quickly because a wheel to her vehicle had apparently decided to leave when her mother did.

By the time Beatrice walked into her aunt's

house, she already suspected the painting would be gone.

Her aunt, ever the opposite of Beatrice's mother, greeted her niece, arms outstretched, handkerchiefs in both hands, chattering welcome.

As soon as Beatrice could become untangled from the lilac perfume, the questions about the trip and the comments about how lovely she looked, she asked, 'Did Mother borrow your carriage recently?'

'Why, yes. She needed a parcel from your home and at the same time wanted us to take a ride though the countryside.' Then her cheeks flushed. 'Amazing portrait she retrieved. She insisted I see it. I cannot believe you did that.' She leaned forward. 'How delightful it must be to paint. All the lovely hours in a day to work on such a thing.'

'So where is the painting now?'

'Your mother returned for it this morning. She took it.'

Beatrice had never known the very air one breathed peacefully one second could choke the next.

She regained her composure. 'Did Tilly see it?'

The time between the question and the answer couldn't have been long, but gave her aunt time to glance at the ceiling and at the side, but not at Beatrice. 'It's unlikely.'

Pop. Pop. Pop. The little bubbles of hope in Beatrice's heart vanished. She took a chair. Andrew would never forgive her if the painting became public.

'You do not have to worry about your mother relinquishing that painting.' Her aunt patted Beatrice's hand. 'She promised she will take excellent care of it. I quite believe her.'

'And where was Mother going next?'

'She planned to go to Bath, but at the last moment said she'd changed her mind. I asked her if she was returning home and she said she'd never seen Scotland and might be eloping to Gretna Green with the portrait.'

'So she would not tell you?'

'No.' Her aunt's eyes twinkled. 'But wherever she is with that splendour, I'm sure she'll be happy.'

Andrew sat at his desk, his pen in his hand. The ink untouched on his desk. Silence. His world had quieted since he'd left Beatrice. But that didn't stop him from thinking of her bouncing footsteps, brown curling hair and the shriek of her voice when she exclaimed. He absently twirled the pen.

He would find the painting and present it to Beatrice as a gift. It would be the right thing to do. Fawsett would enjoy the task of discovering it and surely it would not take much time.

He used his left hand to pull open the drawer and slide out the paper inside. He looked at the page, feeling a range of emotions. He'd completed a quick sketch of Beatrice, arms open to the sky, standing in a thunderstorm, absorbing the energy.

He'd drawn it because he wanted to be reminded of her and because he needed to be reminded his decision was the proper one. For them to marry would be like trying to put her in the cage of his life. She should fly free and keep her spirit about her. Her mother didn't understand that. But he did. He'd seen the collapse of a marriage of two people perfectly suited for each other when one gave in to impulse. To have two people of different temperaments joined together, one who could not say no to her whims and the other following his urges by the very act of the wedding, would lead to certain disaster.

The tales that had been reported would be nothing compared to the new ones and Andrew could not see his children grow knowing they would be exposed to the sight of their parents' lives put about for all to see, yet have that be only a hint of the heartbreak going on in their home.

He'd sent his valet on a mission to the architect's house and Fawsett had returned, assuring him that no maids had noticed any arrival of a new painting. Because Beatrice's paintings in her brother's home were older, they would have noticed the odour of a new addition.

Bursts of sound caught Andrew's attention and he stilled. A raised voice. Thumps. Thundering steps up the stairs.

He dropped his pen and stood. The butler shouted *no*.

Wilson lunged into the doorway, one hand grasping the frame. He stood, bear-like, spotting Andrew, the butler stopping at Wilson's back.

'You vile heathen.' The architect moved into the open doorway, his eyes bulging in rage and hair flying wild. He clasped wadded newsprint.

'Leave,' Andrew spoke to the butler. After squinting to make sure Andrew looked at him, and receiving a brief nod, the servant departed, leaving Andrew and Wilson alone.

The architect's voice blasted and he held a scandal sheet crumpled in his hands. Walking forward, he sputtered before he could speak. 'Your last breaths will be taken as you choke on this. You let my sister...'

Fawsett bounded into the doorway from the opposite side.

'I cannot imagine what you are talking about.' Andrew shook his head, raising a hand in supplication, trying to calm Wilson enough so he could figure out the problem. Then he realised. The portrait of Beatrice. He could understand her brother's wrath.

'It was not something I asked her to do.' Andrew stepped towards Wilson. He'd never seen a man so lost to his rage before. He saw Fawsett reaching for a lamp behind the architect. He caught Fawsett's eye and gave a snapped shake of his head.

'You cannot expect me to believe that. First you have her dress in *clothing* unbefitting her and now this. You will die.'

'I did not know anything of it,' Andrew said. 'I did not.'

'It is all across London. Everywhere,' the architect said. 'And you say you did not know? My sister painted this and you did not know?'

The architect thrust the wadded paper forward. 'Did you have your eyes closed?'

Andrew reached to the paper. He pressed his hand over the newsprint, smoothing enough to see the engraving. To read the heading.

He stepped back, the invisible blow of the sight rocking him. A likeness of him—supposedly an engraving of a portrait—stark naked except for a strategically drawn bit of foliage. Above it the words: *Beast Bares Beloved.*

He faced the raging eyes of the architect and his mouth opened but he could not speak. He shook his head, and forced his mouth to form words. 'I am—'

'You're wearing a damn flower over your private parts.'

Explosions louder than any Vauxhall fireworks, even ones setting the stages alight, rocked inside the confined space of Andrew's mind.

The architect's head twisted sideways, but his eyes never left Andrew's. His hands shook. 'You— Beatrice— This is— They even spelled the names.' The wildness of his hair was calm compared to the rest of him.

'I assure you. This was not my idea—'

'You let her paint you—naked.'

'No.' Andrew forced himself, while trying to gasp in deep breaths of air, to look again at the article. But he'd already grasped the whole of the story. In three words. *Beast Bares Beloved.*

'I didn't pose—for that,' Andrew said. 'I would never. Never.' He looked at the architect. 'Never.'

Calm entered his body. A semblance of it anyway. He could breathe. He could speak. He could form sentences. He could see red-tinged shapes. 'This is the first—'

'I cannot believe you would let her—'

'Oh,' Andrew bit out the words. 'I posed. But I did not even remove my cravat. A formal portrait.'

He pointed to the picture on the wall.

'Then this is a lie.' The architect jerked a hand to the paper.

His vision finally lost the red tint. He could see lighter colours now. 'I somehow doubt it.'

The architect took the biggest breath Andrew had ever seen a man inhale. 'Why?'

'I do not know why. Beatrice listens to her own voice and her own ideas. She does not follow rules. She does not know the rules even exist.' He sat at his desk, elbows on the wood, and used his fingertips to massage his temple. 'I would like to talk to your sister.'

'You—' the architect pointed a finger '—were supposed to be a calming influence. To keep her from the scandal sheets.'

Andrew raised his eyes. 'Boadicea herself could not do that.'

Merde. He looked at the print again. His face was there. His body was there. But his clothing?

'I cannot believe she painted such a portrait and you did not know.' The architect didn't stop moving. He paced the room, fists at his sides.

Andrew stood, leaning forward, using splayed fingertips against the desk to help hold him upright. He kept his voice low.

'I can.'

Beatrice had whims and acted on them. She'd had an impulse for the artwork and before she'd known what had happened the thought had taken over her mind and controlled her. A flutter of an idea had captured her like the flutter of a woman's skirt might capture a man's eyes and cause him to forget all the years of his life before. Rash behaviour and thoughts. An innocent mote of an idea and it grew and grew, taking everything along with it. A grain that could turn into a massive storm. A whirlwind destroying the very beginning of its existence. Not stopping until it devoured everything good around it.

Andrew looked to Fawsett. The valet's eyes looked as if he felt superior to everyone in the room and his hand hadn't strayed from the lamp. Andrew frowned.

'You will never speak to my sister again,' the architect ground out to Andrew.

Andrew snorted and moved within an arm's length of Wilson. 'I will speak to her as soon as I can find her.' He flung the paper from his hand.

The architect took a step closer. Their noses almost touched, both men leaning across the desk. 'I…' Andrew thumped his chest '…am in the scandal sheets. *I* have been wronged by your sister. *I* will be getting my hands on a certain portrait and I will personally destroy it.' His voice trembled with rage. 'And if you try to hinder me, I am quite certain the scandal sheets will quite enjoy the tale of how your face became black and blue and you ended up tossed from a window.'

'You would not dare tangle with me.' A fist swung Andrew's direction. Andrew dodged.

Words fled Andrew's mind after he heard *dare*. *Dare* registered. His fist answered, moving forward before his mind alerted him of the action and warned him from it. He connected with the architect's jaw even before he realised he'd moved. The architect's head snapped backwards and Fawsett stepped aside as Wilson dropped to the carpet.

Wilson lay there, breathing hard. Fawsett looked at Andrew and he raised the lamp in his hand. 'Sir,' he said softly to Andrew. 'Lamps break. However, they do not feel bruised the next day as your hand will. And I would have taken care of that for you.'

Andrew looked to the architect, but spoke to the valet. 'With my luck a blow to the back of the head would have killed him. I did not want to see a caricature of that in the shop windows.'

Wilson pushed himself to his feet, checking for blood and missing teeth. A drip of red formed at the slice on his cheek from Andrew's ring. His mouth was slack and his eyes wide. Andrew doubted anyone had punched him before.

'I don't know how to destroy a man twice, but I will find out.' The architect's eyes flashed. He rubbed his jaw.

'You're too late,' Andrew said, giving a hollow laugh. 'Your sister has beaten you to it.' Andrew nodded to Fawsett. 'See that my carriage is readied—now.'

Fawsett scurried away.

'But,' Andrew continued, almost quivering in his own anger, 'I will be speaking with your sister. Is she at your home?'

'I will not tell you.'

Andrew reached for the architect's coat, fisting his hands in the fabric and pulling them face to face. Even though the architect blustered, Andrew kept his grasp on the coat. 'I swear to you I will not hurt her, and I swear to you I will hurt you if you do not tell me.'

'You are destroying your life and your reputation.' Blood trickled down his cheek.

'No.' Andrew tightened his fists on the fabric, pulling them closer. 'Your sister did that to me.'

'Not alone.'

Andrew thrust his hands from the architect's coat and both men stepped back.

'You will pay for this,' the architect snapped.

'I already have,' Andrew said.

'She truly did this on her own?'

He nodded.

Realisation dawned on Wilson's face. He touched his cheek lightly, checking the damage. 'I can believe it. She is off the rails. A fool without a care in her thoughts.'

'Do not speak of her so.' Andrew turned to the architect. 'It is my bare arse on display. Not yours.'

'She—' the architect speared the other man with a look '—is my sister. I can speak of her any way I wish.'

Andrew's fist clenched. 'Not if you don't wish to find yourself on your back again.'

'How did she? How did the scandal sheet find out?'

'You mother stole the painting.'

'Mother?' The architect uttered the word softly. Then his eyes shut, his jaw clenched, his head twisted up and he spoke the word again towards the sky—hardly moving his lips. His face relaxed and his words were whisper-soft. 'You were in my house and I thought it a wonderful opportunity for Bea. I thought—she needs to marry again. She's not living in her own home and she flits from one place to another. And she was being indelicate with someone so particular he used his handkerchief to dust off a drawing I placed on his desk. He would *never, ever* cause scandal as Riverton did. No. No.' His voice rose. 'He's a duke's son.'

'Who put you flat on the carpet,' Andrew said. 'And it was Aubusson. And now it'll need cleaning.'

'If you take a brandy…' Wilson pointed a wavering finger at Andrew '…you never even empty the glass. You can't have posed like that. Not you. Not the man who counselled the workmen to keep their waistcoats buttoned because a maid might pass by.' The architect nodded, dropped his hand and his head tilted to the side as he turned to Andrew. 'You really didn't pose. You couldn't have.'

Andrew shook his head.

Nodding as he spoke, Wilson said, 'I think she might owe you an apology.'

'You could say that.'

The architect stepped backwards. 'I'm seeing things more clearly now. Brilliant plan, Lord Andrew. You certainly diverted some of the talk of her.' He snorted in laughter. 'I can hardly wait to read the next mention.' He grinned. 'I'll do all I can to help you in your quest to take the notice from her. I'll purchase another copy of the paper to show *The Naked Knight* at the taverns. Wouldn't want anyone to miss hearing about it.'

Andrew watched the architect's retreating back and, when he disappeared out the doorway, Andrew heard another snort of laughter from Wilson and the words he called up the stairway as he exited echoed in Andrew's ears. 'She's at her house, Sir Knight.'

Seconds later, he heard the thump of the door closing.

She didn't. She couldn't have. But she did. She must have painted him in the same style of her *Boadicea* painting, only—

Surely the scandal sheets had subtracted the clothing. He wanted to believe it, but couldn't. The stories printed of Beatrice had been based on truth. Perhaps they had wavered a little, but were still accurate underneath.

He shut his eyes, capturing control.

Forcing himself, he swiped a hand to the floor, picking up the scattered paper. Nothing about the engraving looked like him. Nothing, except the face.

Yet the words.

Reading quickly, he read hints of many painting sessions followed by *unknown activities of the smouldering sort*. A brief recounting of Beatrice's past followed, then a lengthy mention of him. It read almost as if he had died and they were recounting his life.

Almost. No. He had died. His life as he had

lived it was a thing of the past. Now all, even in death, would be overshadowed by this.

Clenching the paper in his fists, he ripped it apart and slammed it to the floor.

Beatrice. She had destroyed the order of his world. She had taken scissors to him as well, cutting the clothing from his body and brought the eyes of the *ton* to him, exposed.

Temples pounding he stared at the shreds in front of his feet, seeing only the caricature of himself.

She had taken his life and done the same to it as he had to the paper.

He left the room, forcing each footstep to be unhurried and each breath to go in and then to leave his body.

He would see her and hear from her why she had done such a thing.

As the carriage pulled to the front and he stepped towards it, he saw Fox, coat-tails flying, riding his horse in Andrew's direction. He had newsprint in his hand. 'Andrew,' he gasped, holding the paper up, eyes alight. He slid from the horse, still holding the paper out. 'You devil, you.'

Andrew brushed by him. His hand was already throbbing. His head pounded. His teeth ached.

And he could even feel the puckered skin of the bite mark.

He heard Fox chuckling. 'I'll leave the paper with Fawsett. You'll want extra copies.'

Beatrice looked at the curtains and wondered if the house had been worth it. She had made a monumental mistake in that marriage.

Then she heard the sound of a carriage in the drive and she immediately went to the front door.

She didn't know why her mind didn't accept the threat of impending doom, but perhaps her arrival home had filled her with such trepidation, she couldn't feel anything else.

Or so she thought, until she opened the front door—and saw the murderous face of Andrew.

At that moment she looked into his anger-glazed eyes and she realised she truly loved him. That was indeed unfortunate.

Andrew stopped. He breathed as if he'd rushed a long race. He stood less than an arm's length from her.

His face emitted anger, except for what could have passed as the hurt of betrayal.

He knew. She bit the inside of her lip. He knew. He stopped, his hair completely disarrayed, and his clothes continuing the windstorm look. He'd never looked so creased before—he even had bruised and bloody knuckles.

Her courage, her voice, deserted her.

This didn't seem to be the time to admit anything, or deny anything. She opened her mouth, thinking to choose her words more carefully than she'd ever done in her life.

'Might we speak a moment?' Andrew's fury blasted through his face, causing his eyes to darken, his lips to thin, and everything about him flashed blackness. He emphasised each word.

Andrew continued, his voice thunderous. 'You painted me—without my permission—didn't you, Beatrice? You bared my person to the world.'

'I did paint you. Your form is better than Adonis.'

Andrew didn't move forward.

She looked at his face and realised he had no intention of stepping foot in her house. No intention of staying. Her heart beat, even though the little pierced, charred bits of it were hardly big enough to matter.

'Would you come in?' She moved her hand only a fraction towards the house.

'Why?'

She looked back, making sure no one was listening, and moved a step closer. Andrew inhaled sharply, eyes dark and lips thin. Riverton had not looked so coldly at her after she'd stabbed him.

'I could not help myself, Andrew. The brush worked of its own accord. You were my masterpiece. Like Michelangelo's *David*, but in oils.'

'Why didn't you put another man's face on it, Beatrice? You certainly couldn't have been using my body?'

'Your face. It had to be your face and it is your body. Maybe imagined in places, but I've touched you. I know your shape. I watched when you posed and not only your face. I saw the muscles and form through your clothes.'

He shook his head, side to side. 'No. You do not know my body. We have been intimate, but you do not know my body.'

'I look at you with an artist's eyes.'

'Nonsense.' He looked at his carriage, still waiting, and then turned back. Examining the house, he said, 'I would like nothing better than to leave. To step into your house, under these circumstances—it feels like the bowels of hell and I am immersing myself.' His eyes. Cold. Hard. 'But I must have that painting and it must be destroyed.'

'No.' She put her hand to her heart. 'It's my masterpiece.'

His chin went down and his eyes snapped into hers. 'Then you had better plan on painting another one, Beatrice, of someone else. Of this one thing, I am sure—I will find the painting and destroy it.'

'You don't have it now?' She could not believe so much grief—if he had not seen the painting.

'Of course I do not.' If anything, his fury increased.

'Then how do—?' She feared the answer.

'The scandal sheets.' His lips closed on the words and his eyes condemned. He continued. 'I guess you've not been reading them here. But there's a small story concerning a certain painting of the Beast's. You will be pleased to know not much was written—' His voice might have been considered a purr, but one to cause the hair on the back of the neck to rise. 'Because they needed the space to display the caricature of the painting.'

He turned back, and with a wide sweep of his arm, he indicated to his carriage driver to take the horses to the stables. 'I am going to search this house again.'

Beatrice would not have thought there was room

for him to move by her without touching her because of the posts on each side of the steps, but he had no trouble.

When he passed by, she turned, seeing the broad shoulders, the dark head, the man of any sane woman's dreams, and one particular daft woman. And she had stabbed him in the back. She could imagine the splashes of vermilion on his coat.

Chapter Twenty

Walking into the parlour, Andrew lifted the decanter, staring at it, and crashed it down with a thud after filling a glass.

'Mother has the painting and she will correspond with someone eventually and I have let everyone know they are to send me her location. It's Mother. She will not be able to remain from my life long,' Beatrice said. 'Then we will retrieve it.'

'I do not think it matters so much now. The damage is done.' Andrew held the glass and looked at Beatrice. 'But I want that painting.'

The painting was not all he wanted. He wanted the comfort of Beatrice's arms, but he could not allow himself to touch her.

'Say, Beatrice…' Andrew's eyes turned mild. 'Is there foliage in the original?'

'Foliage?' Her brows creased. 'It is not of a tree.'

His head tilted and he smiled. 'No flower.' He clicked his tongue. 'I thought not.' He tapped a finger to his lips. He shrugged. 'Vauxhall Gardens. Could your mother have displayed it there?'

Beatrice ignored the sarcasm. 'She would not let it away.'

Andrew swallowed his drink and smiled at Beatrice. 'I'm afraid the painting must be destroyed.' Andrew's voice turned musing. 'Before the prints start selling in the shop windows.' He paused. 'How many copies would you like? Even if I buy the whole print run, they'll just make more.'

Andrew stood, staring at the tumbler. His lips turned up, but it wasn't even meant to be a smile. He looked at his empty glass and spoke towards it. 'I will not rest until I find that painting and see for myself how accurate it is. I believe…I should see it for myself.'

She shut her eyes when she answered. 'I don't have any idea where it is.'

'Where would she put it? Or if you were truly going to hide it—where?'

She shrugged. 'If I knew…'

'Fine. Think hard. Imagine you have your mother's resources and servants. How would you conceal something? The print claimed it was rather large.' He paused. 'How large is it?'

'Slightly bigger than the other one.'

He put the glass to his temple. 'The size of Boadicea. It must be.' He shut his eyes and then slammed the glass on to the table.

He leaned closer to her and, even in his anger, the sight of her worried eyes brought out something inside himself he didn't want to feel. And her touch on his arm reminded him of something else he didn't dare explore.

His wish to have the painting in his possession was only matched by his need to embrace Beatrice again and to hold her would be putting him—them—on a path for more devastation in the future. Once children stepped into the muddle, the conflagration of emotions only grew.

'And how well do you think I will sleep? Knowing—*that*—is out there.' He put a palm to his forehead and let his fingers rake back through his hair. 'No flowers in the original?' He looked at her. 'Right?'

'Of course not.' She shook her head. 'That would be ridiculous.'

'Oh, my.' His hands fell to his sides and he

forced the quiet words from his lips. 'One must not make a naked man look ridiculous.'

He thumped a fingertip to the white knot at his neck. 'My cravats. I would never appear in public without one properly tied. I do not take it off in front of others—unless it is in darkness.'

'Andrew. Everyone has a body. But not as fine as yours. You should embrace your perfection.'

He thought of the mark on his chest and shook his head. 'You painted your imagination. Not the truth.'

And then he had another thought. He would be thankful for ever that she'd not known of that mark. For if the scar had appeared in print he would have had no choice but to leave the country. Particularly when Sophia's book was printed. To have the painting on display and then mention in Sophia Swift's book of the odd encounter would bring shame on him from which he could never recover. He could never marry, never have children who would have to deal with the scandal.

'Your mother will have to tell me where the painting is.'

She shook her head. 'Mother has disappeared and not from foul means except her own machinations. The painting is in her possession and no one knows where she is.'

'No.' He felt himself deflate. 'I must clear my head.'

He strode from the room, wanting to shake the knowledge away, but he knew he couldn't. He didn't stop until he'd left the house.

Beatrice rushed behind him.

Outside, he stopped. The cattle stood grazing. They did not seem properly dismayed, except one did raise her head. He hoped she hadn't seen the painting.

'I wish to see your studio,' he said. 'I want to look at your paintings again. All of them.' He moved down the path and into the cottage.

Inside, she saw him sniff and his brows furrowed.

'You may look if you like. But this room always—always—smells of pigment and cleaner.'

He nodded and his eyes travelled the room.

Seeming satisfied, he turned to go to the two bedchambers. She heard the door open.

'...lot of paintings...' She heard through the walls.

She stood and walked to the doorway of the former bedchamber which now was a storeroom of sorts. Excess dining-room chairs sat inside with empty framing boards stacked on them. An ancient desk housed painting supplies. A broken easel. But the main occupants of the room were canvases she'd given up on, or completed and didn't like. And maybe a few pieces she liked, but didn't wish to display. Some framed ones she'd once taken from the house so it would be unlikely Riverton would destroy them when he was in a temper.

Andrew took two steps into the room and, when she walked behind him, he moved to a group of five paintings of various sizes leaning against the wall.

'Can you forgive me?' she asked.

He turned to another painting, studying. 'Ask me in ten years. I will be closer to knowing then. Perhaps fifteen would be better. Best not to rush it.' He put the painting back in place. 'I can't help thinking how much you love attention, Beatrice. And I can't help thinking you might have wanted this to happen. Would Michelangelo create a statue and hide it away? Artists don't hide their creations.'

'I would have hidden this one for ever. It was locked in this room.'

He turned to her. His chin lowered a bit and then another bit. 'For private perusal, Beatrice?'

'Of course.'

Eyes narrowing, he said, 'I'm not even comfortable with that.'

She believed what she said, but he knew the truth of her better than she herself knew. She could not have kept that canvas secret for any length of time even if her mother had not taken it. Beatrice would have thought to display it in France, assuming the betrayal would not get back to him, or done something else on a whim that caused notice of it to flourish.

That was Beatrice. The little bird with wings, who could only feel the air at her face and might never see the ravening cats who hid among the perches.

He shook, as if shaking raindrops away. 'If you would have just put someone else's face. Instead, my head and an imagined body.' He gave a dry laugh. 'I have a new rule. Never trust a woman in mob cap and spectacles who smells like baked goods.'

'Your body wasn't totally imagined, Andrew.'

He didn't speak, but walked around the room. He looked at two of the smaller paintings and commented on them. 'You painted the same thing twice.'

She stood at his side. 'Three times, actually.'

He turned to face her. 'You had better not even consider another one of me, Beatrice.' He saw the speculation in her eyes. 'Never.'

She raised both hands. 'I promise.'

'I cannot quite understand it. The world is full of men other than me.'

'It had to be you. Don't you see? I had to capture you on the canvas. I was pulled by the muse.'

'I see none of it. None,' he said. 'I agree you captured me and then you gutted me.'

She moved forward, putting a hand on his sleeve. 'Your body was made for canvas. You must understand.'

'No. I don't. I saw the engraving and, frankly, I was not impressed.'

'But when you see the real—'

'I will destroy it.'

She would not let him spoil her work. She'd not meant to harm him and she had no intention of compounding the problem by ruining the work itself. Riverton had destroyed her efforts before. She would not let it happen again. Andrew understood art no better than Riverton, which meant he understood her no better.

'I was married and yet not truly,' she said. 'I had a lot of time on my hands. Best to lose myself in my art than to be thinking of what Riverton might be doing.' She bent down, and picked up one of the smaller paintings, a rose, looking at it.

But then she glanced back to the two paintings she'd done of the same thing. 'A footman posed for the highwayman and the victim. But I never really managed the look I wanted—even in the final rendition. I even had the carriage pulled out for a few days and the footman stood by it with an old duelling pistol.' She shook her head and put the art back. 'But I was not trying a fourth one. I was sick of it before I finished the last brush strokes on the third.'

She moved behind him and pushed aside another painting, locating one, and pulling it free with a clatter. 'Agatha Crump refused this one and I could not blame her. It is one of my earlier works and I don't like it. I keep it to remind me never to paint someone if I am not sure I like them. It's so unkind, but I did not mean it to be.'

Holding it where he could see, she frowned. 'Even the flowers in the vase beside her I could not get right. They have a withered look. But if you step back and look at her, you see so much I did not want to know. This is when I discovered the truth of my brush.'

'Not bad, though.' He examined the work. 'I can almost see her breathing.'

'Sometimes I think I truly do not see things until I put them on canvas.' She pointed to the picture of a rose. 'And it's not the examining of my model—then I am looking at bits of pieces, of lines and curves. But the finished art, *that* I study for a while. Because it tells me what I am truly seeing. Seeing in a way my mind doesn't tell me until later.'

Andrew didn't move, except for turning his head. Brown eyes. Very intense, darkened pools stared at her.

He let out a deep breath and didn't take his gaze from her. 'Nude, Beatrice?'

She shrugged and her smile appeared tinged with guilt.

He pressed his lips together and turned back to the art. He took his time, starting at the paintings directly in front of him on the floor, then moving up, looking at the ones hung haphazardly on the wall, and then going to the right, starting again at the lower works and examining each one. He didn't give any a cursory glance, but studied each one.

At one, he gave a snort. 'This must be Riverton. And his clothing may be rumpled, but he is definitely clothed. The shadows you've painted...'

'It was done after we were married for a year. I needed to do it so I could get him from my thoughts.'

He stared at the painting. 'Was he that vacant?'

'To me—at the end, yes. His father died and the man had had some control over him. Perhaps I had had some control as well. I suspect Riverton tried to kill himself once not long after his father died. He went out on a cold, cold night, with no coat. We found him before dawn. He had two empty bottles with him and was no worse for wear once we brought him home and warmed him.'

She took the painting from Andrew's hands and put it as it was before he found it, its back towards the room. 'When Riverton thawed out and woke up, I told him he was in charge of his destiny from that moment on. He cursed me and I didn't care. It was pleasant not to care.'

He turned back to the art. 'How many people have seen this room?'

She thought for a moment. 'I only locked it when I put your painting in it. I suppose the maids. If I have a painting I wish to show someone, I take it to them.'

He picked up another painting. A man from the back on a cold winter's day, withdrawn from the cold and wearing a ragged coat. 'This?' he asked.

'That is my brother Benjamin. He is…gone from us now. He was older. The star I looked up to in the sky and then he plummeted to earth and lost himself. I am not certain he will ever be in our path again. He closed his world to us when his wife died.' She gave a rueful laugh. 'Can you imagine? Benjamin wished to follow his wife into the grave. That is when I realised how much I did not love Riverton. I could have given him a gentle push. Almost did with the scissors.'

He pointed to a stack. 'You've a nearly finished painting of Wilson—and he looks rather a tyrant—majestic, but still human. A miniature of your mother is in the crate with your supplies. It's well done. But hard to decipher.'

'That does not surprise me at all.'

Turning, he stepped to her and grasped her hands. He might as well have grasped her heart. She could not move. She wanted to hold him close and let him take her into a world where nothing existed but the two of them. That world she could live in for ever, but it was no more real than the dreams she'd had before her first marriage.

'Beatrice, to look at these paintings, a person can see more of you than you probably know of yourself.' He released her touch, but he still held her with his eyes.

She shook her head. 'They are not my best works. My finished pieces, the ones I have taken the time on and done well, are on a wall somewhere, except for three that did not survive life. An artist often gives her best children away.'

His shoulder gave a twitch and she didn't know if it was disagreement, but she knew he hadn't changed his mind about what he'd said.

'Andrew, these are little more than scribblings to pass the time between the paintings I am truly working on…' She put her hand on his coat sleeve.

He stilled, his eyes fixed on her hand. He took her fingers and she thought him moving them away. Instead, he clasped the tips and moved her knuckles to brush his cheeks.

She moved closer, longing for him.

She couldn't stop herself and she heard the quiver in her voice. 'Andrew. Your reluctance for lovemaking…I'm sure, if you concentrated and worked on it, you could find true enjoyment.'

He ran the back of her knuckles again over his cheek, the feel of stubble captivating. 'Beatrice, you are lovely. Your body inflames me. I desire you so much…' His palm flattened, taking her chin. 'But your teeth…'

She shook her head. Puzzled.

'You bit me,' he explained.

Bit him? What was he talking about? She frowned. 'What?'

He nodded. 'I was aware when you felt the scar on my chest that you knew I had been marked, but I did not believe you would think it so—inviting that you might wish to add another one.' He angled his head sideways. 'Do you realise that if I acted on my impulse, and you bit me every time, I would— My body would be covered in scars.'

'I did not bite you.'

'Teeth. Yes. You used them.'

'Perhaps your body…' she squinted and frowned and moved her head in puzzlement '…got in the way of a gasp and I may have kissed too strongly.'

He dropped her knuckles. 'I realise this is an extremely personal question and I would not normally ask it, but did you ever bite your husband?'

She shook her head. 'No, I did stab him with scissors and knock him to the bed.' She took a deep breath. 'I may have hit his head against the bedstead, but he was not himself and needed a nudge. The sewing needle I pressed into his hand later was only to see if he was still alive.'

Breath whooshed from his lips. 'But, did you ever bite him?'

'Just gentle love nips. He liked them.'

'And if I were to say that I did not like such a thing?'

'Then I would certainly never, ever do so.'

He took her chin in his hand, pressed his lips to hers, the kiss slowly deepening into an exploration of her mouth. He moved enough so that he could speak, breaths aligned with hers.

His voice rumbled softly. 'I would like to test that.' Just this one last time. He wanted to hold her again before they parted.

His eyes and the soft inhalation of his breath silenced her.

She looked at her painting come to life before her. She didn't need the oils to decipher what her eyes saw. Her mind floated. If she touched his skin now, might she feel the coldness of oils, or would her hand find air?

Unable to stop herself, she moved her hand slightly out and found the bottom of his coat sleeve. Wool. She ran her hand up, receiving sensations of him. Suddenly, she could smell the wool, feel the fibres and the heat from his body underneath.

She moved to his shoulder, across to the cravat, white, always just so, and then she stopped, afraid to touch skin without anything between to dilute the strength of sensation.

'Go ahead, Beatrice.' His voice, strong, baritone and rich, flowing more lushly than perfectly blended pigment on to smooth canvas, took control of her.

She touched his jaw and felt bristled skin, a perfection of natural beauty, and she heard the intake of breath again. His. Not hers. She wasn't sure if she breathed at all.

She touched her painting. The artwork was living in front of her.

And her body responded. Each contact of her hand against his skin seared itself into her, running wild and strong. Everything else fell away but the presence of him before her and the reactions of her body.

Her hand fell to his cravat and slipped among the folds. She half-expected him to tense, to step back, or to push her hands away.

He didn't move.

Her finger slipped into the knot and her other hand moved up, and the cravat fell open into her hands. She slid the fabric down and tossed it on to the empty frames propped against a crate.

His shirt, warmed by the skin beneath it, still felt crisp to her hands. She reached up, braced her feet and carefully slid the coat over his shoulders. And she was lost.

Her mouth was dry and her fingertips unsteady.

Before she could throw his coat to the side, he took it and tossed it over the back of a chair.

The waistcoat followed. Her heart pounded all the way into her stomach.

And she stood perfectly still, mesmerised by the form in front of her. The perfection and the way—with nothing more than his presence—he could make her a captive of his smallest movement. How could she take her eyes away? This sight, Andrew, erupted her insides into the intensity of flames. She couldn't feel past the burn inside of herself and the longing of her hands to explore more of him.

But the moment her hand touched his shirt, he stilled again and she touched the buttons at his collar, undoing each tiny white orb, amazed that any man's fingers could ever manoeuvre the fastenings.

When her hand trailed to pull his shirt free from his trousers, she became aware of the thinness of the garment. More thin than any chemise, yet such firmness beneath.

When she ran her hand along the fabric, she felt the same as if she stoked a fire inside herself. She rubbed the cloth of his shirt, fanning her desire, unable to stop.

After she pulled the garment loose and over his head, she put both palms flat against him, reassuring herself this was Andrew, not a portrait. She shut her eyes and let her cheek rest against his shoulder while she let her fingers savour him, feeling the ridge of a small scar. Women would be giving their men hammer and boards if the tools alone created such masculine form.

She moved her fingers up, feeling the chiselled curve of his chest, the wall of man, the pebbled nipples, and then kept her eyes shut and let the expanse of his shoulders treat her sense of touch, wondering if she might take up sculpting next.

He came alive when she touched his lips. She let her body flutter against his.

His hands grasped her shoulders and he pulled her into an embrace, locked her into his arms and melded her against him, his mouth taking hers.

The moist kiss tasted of Andrew more than anything else. No brandy, wine or essence of anything but the man. He was tenderness and strength all in one.

He pulled her into him, grasping her bottom, reminding her he was flesh and blood, but then she looked at him and decided he wasn't.

She forced herself back, backhanded her paintings from the chair and gave him a nudge on to the now-empty seat.

Her eyes registered the placket of his clothing, the rise behind it, and her fingers made short work of the barrier.

She raised her skirt and sunk on to him, fully clothed. She knew her deepest fantasy was in her arms, her body and her whole being.

To paint the most beautiful being of one's imagination, and then experience him fully, was almost more than she could bear.

He took control, blossoming their passions, creating a wash of sensations.

She forced her face past his shoulder and brought her fist up to her mouth.

And later she didn't remember release, his or hers, or completion, she just awoke to the feel of herself draped over his body and his rhythmic breathing.

'Beatrice?' he asked softly.

She mumbled her answer against his damp shoulder. 'I love art.'

Chapter Twenty-One

Beatrice disentangled herself and stood. Andrew helped hold her upright with two hands at her waist. She felt that, if he dropped his hands, she'd slide right to the floor.

'Beatrice?' he asked again. 'Bea?'

Her eyes focused on him and her voice was little more than a whisper. 'I hate to think what you'd be like with a little more practice.'

He let her go, watching her and making sure she wouldn't tumble. Then he pulled his trousers in place.

He adjusted his shirt, tucking it back into his waistband, but she interrupted him, wrapping herself around him. He leaned down to put a kiss in her hair, but gently, he moved her back.

'Andrew, you are my painting come to life.'

'No. The painting is solely imagination.'

His face. Shuttered. Distance. But this time she could see what he thought. He had taken his mind from her, shut her away and made his decision.

Well, she was no green girl and she had lived with disapproval from all sides. Never again.

True, she had painted the portrait, but it had been stolen. 'I did not tell the scandal sheets of the painting.'

'I am aware.'

'I would never do that.'

'I know.'

His face. No softer than the walls of a crypt. She turned away and pushed her hair, pulling out a pin so she could secure the knot again. She dropped the clasp, but didn't move.

His hand touched her waist, and he leaned beside her, picking up the pin from the floor and putting it in her grasp. Their fingers touched, but only for a moment.

She jabbed at her hair, finishing.

The painting. Her imagination had overtaken her again. It had created something of her dreams, but not the truth. She was no different than Riverton. She'd fogged her mind but it had been with the scent of linseed and varnish and the splash of pigments.

When she painted, hours and hours could pass without hunger, or thought. How different was that than the mixtures of Riverton? How different was the thin, flat surface of the canvas than the haze of the smoke? She'd created her own smoke and her own poison.

She had put her heart in the brushes.

But she would not walk into the haze. She wanted to live life in all its real and glorious colours and emotions.

Inside, her thoughts gnashed against each other, swirling in the same way the smoke from Riverton's pipe had clogged her throat and clung to her skin. The scent of a dying spirit. She moved to the window, but couldn't see past the panes.

If the painting had been before her, she would have slashed it herself.

The knowledge of that rubbish out in the world somewhere with his countenance on it evaporated all the feelings of pleasure he'd just experienced.

'I will find the painting and burn it. It's too notorious to stay hidden for ever and I'm not above whatever means it will take to retrieve it.'

'Do what you must.'

'Are you planning another portrait?'

'Yes. I'll always paint. That is what I must do.' She half-turned to him, the window highlighting her rueful smile. 'It is the way I breathe. It is my weakness—my strength.'

'What are you attempting next?'

'A self-portrait. A true one. Not an imagined warrior for which I use my face merely as a guide. I am going to do a true likeness. I am going to paint myself and see what my brush creates. I wish to know.'

'Clothed?'

She nodded.

He looked back to the window, anger buried so deep he could not feel it. He spoke to himself, but the words carried into the room. 'You stabbed me, Bea. With your paintbrush. More deeply than you did Riverton. I want children and a quiet life for them. I want my home to be a haven for them. You gave me a past I can never erase.'

He thought back to the day he had walked in on his father crying. His father slowly read aloud from the letter he'd received, grasping for each word because he could hardly speak for the tears. His mistress had taken the little boy. She'd sailed for the Americas with her husband. It was too late to stop her. She was gone.

His father had leaned over the letter, both elbows on the table, his face buried in his hands, shoulders shaking.

Andrew's mother had walked by the door, looked in, did not speak, did not flicker so much as an eyebrow and continued on.

That night, Andrew had started the plans for the home he would some day live in. The world he would create for his children and a peaceful place their grandparents could visit and shut the rest of the world away.

He was almost finished with the house, but his father had passed shortly after the letter, and would never see the home.

'I am living my life as I should,' Beatrice's words interrupted his thoughts. 'I cannot lock myself away. I must feel and experience and paint. I do want to be in the scandal sheets now. I want people to see my paintings. I want to stir their spirits.'

Her eyes lowered, but her voice rang true. 'All would have been fine if Tilly hadn't returned.'

He let the silence stand between them for a moment, then he spoke. 'I'm not even sure of that. Things will always happen around you, Beatrice.'

He saw the reflection of his words in her eyes. Her life would never be quiet or calm.

Sunlight haloed her hair and he walked to her. 'You have a speck of paint.'

Softly, he touched the hair where a dot of paint had dried on one of the locks.

He worked it loose and looked at it in the light, rubbing it between his thumb and forefinger.

Vermilion.

He let the flecks fall to the floor and enfolded her close to his heart for one last time, taking in the scents of Beatrice and the studio around her. Her world.

He pulled back, adjusting the sleeves of his coat and pulling his white cravat into place as he left.

Andrew opened the door of his house, closing it in time to see Fawsett on the upper level rush to the top of the stairs, grabbing the banister to stop himself, and almost being carried forward by his momentum.

'I am so pleased you are home.' He stopped and then composed himself, chin high, voice carrying a reverence. 'Welcome back, my lord knight. I am your vassal.'

It was as if a carpenter's saw wove to and fro

against the grain, inside the bones of his skull, and he just wanted to find some relief. 'I assume you have had some time to read the scandal sheets.'

Fawsett nodded, briefly rocking to his toes. 'The engraving in the newsprint did you no justice. No justice at all. You are a valiant knight in truth.'

'No references to the...sword.' He met Fawsett's face, his own commanding.

Fawsett stood taller. 'I cannot help it. I am so proud to have this post. It is worth every hammer, every bent nail, every starched cravat.' He paused. 'I am honoured.'

Andrew felt mollified. For all his faults, Fawsett truly was on his side. He didn't want to see his employer ridiculed either.

'The shoulders. Much too narrow in the print. Much too narrow.' Fawsett stood back as Andrew moved up the stairs.

Andrew wasn't sure that in Fawsett he hadn't hired a replica of his cousin Foxworthy. Andrew ground his teeth.

Fawsett waited until Andrew walked past. 'Indeed an honour,' Fawsett said.

This prattle by Fawsett would have to stop. Andrew could not be reminded of the scandal sheets in his own home. This was his haven, but the day's events had caused such an ache in his head. He just wanted the mess to die away.

As Andrew paused, planning to direct the valet on that topic, Fawsett darted around and opened the door, chin proud, shoulders stiff, face pressed into a perfect servant's gaze. Andrew could not bring himself to admonish the valet.

When Andrew walked into the room. He stopped. Sniffed. Lacquer? Linseed oil?

There, on the wall, replacing his precious landscape painting by Richard Wilson, was something else. In all its glory, he saw the Nude.

The blow to his stomach knocked him back a half-step.

He stood. His mouth opened, but the rest of his body couldn't move.

'It arrived this morning,' Fawsett said, moving beside Andrew. The valet clasped his own hands in front of him and looked up as if he were staring at all the great artworks combined into one. 'The original—and I must say, the shoulders are correct in it. And, I disagree with your having her leave off the scar, but I will concede you your vanity. And the rest—I suppose she did well enough on. Except the hands. I would say she did not quite capture those. Had her mind elsewhere, I'm sure.'

'Get. It. Down.'

'But…'

'Now.'

'But, sir. It's famous. You're famous. And you have the original.' Fawsett fairly hopped on both feet now.

Andrew whirled to Fawsett. 'How did it get here?'

'Came wrapped. A man, claimed to be a solicitor, brought it to the trade entrance. Said an older woman paid him to deliver it here on your birthday. But we all knew it wasn't your birthday. We all thought it some error. So it was unwrapped, by who we cannot recall. An innocent error, I'm sure.'

Most certainly innocent, Andrew knew, what with it reeking of the scent of oils. And the whole of London knowing of the caricature and suspecting the original existed. 'Every servant in this house is sacked. Without reference.'

Fawsett stepped backwards as if a flintlock ball had entered his chest.

He turned to Fawsett. 'Do you still have the wrapping?'

Fawsett nodded, his bottom lip poking too far

forward. His voice was quiet. 'But we all care for you so much, sir.'

'Fine.' He gritted his teeth. 'Then you may all remain.' He took a breath so he could speak normally again. He pointed to the painting. 'Wrap the monstrosity up and bundle it up to the attic. Tell no one it is here.'

'All the staff admired it,' Fawsett whispered, leaning in to Andrew. 'The woman who opened it shrieked and then the ones who ran to see what was the matter called out, and, well, one cannot stem a tide.'

Andrew reacted much in the same way as when he'd hit his thumb with a hammer. 'All?' Andrew heard his voice and didn't recognise it.

'Yes. I thought the cook might have an apoplexy, but her smile was genuine, and I had to spirit it upstairs or the women would not complete any work. I would say, sir, the staff is all quite proud. We are *famous*.'

Fawsett rubbed his hands together, his eyes alight. 'And we have had quite the number of enquiries from young women concerning the possibility of employment here. I suppose the news, whispered by a maid to the rag-and-bone collector must have traversed quite quickly.'

'Attic.' Andrew pointed over his head. 'Lock it and make sure no one knows where it is.'

'If you insist.' Fawsett took small steps towards it, straightened it first, stepped back, then reached forward and lifted it from the hanger to take it from the wall. 'Although, it is quite—' he smiled at Andrew '—invigorating to the maids to view it.' He whispered, 'We could charge coin for people to observe it.'

Andrew's jaw clicked. He glared.

'Just a thought, sir,' Fawsett said, striding sideways, managing the bulky load, but not taking his eyes from his master.

Andrew shook his head. 'I cannot believe the staff has seen it.'

'Of course, your mother has not,' Fawsett reassured him, letting the painting rest on the floor.

Andrew paused, his body tensing. 'She's here?'

Fawsett squinted and bit his bottom lip before answering. 'Not at this very second, but she will possibly return. She doesn't quite seem to understand the honour done you. I considered showing the painting, with a loincloth of sorts, draped over it. But I don't feel she's ready to admire it. Mothers can be so motherish. They never realise their little boys become men. Your mother took the carriage to her sister's after she arrived here, but she was able to calm the duke.' He frowned. 'His Grace is not well. I fear he is destined for an early grave if he doesn't watch himself. Your mother, ah, I am not sure, as it was behind closed doors, but she may have had to box his ears or some such.'

'Attic.' Andrew slammed out the word and pointed overhead. 'Now.'

When Fawsett left, Andrew sat at the edge of the bed and looked at the blank spot on the wall for how long he didn't know.

He had the painting, but he didn't have Beatrice.

A soft rap at his door interrupted his reverie. 'Open,' he called.

Fawsett tipped his head around. 'Your mother's carriage has returned. It is in front of the house now. I saw it from the window.'

Andrew stood. 'You should have been a spy, Fawsett.'

'And miss working for The Naked Knight—I think not.'

Andrew did not change his tone. 'You are sacked. Again. And this time I mean it.'

'I pledge my fealty.' He crossed his fisted arm

over his chest. 'Even if you bodily throw me out, I will crawl back across burning coals to work for you.' He spoke, hardly moving his lips. 'You would not believe how many women have asked for details about you.' His lips puffed. 'My imagination does you proud and I do not mind consoling the women that they cannot be yours.'

'You know the truths of me.'

'I only thought I knew. I was deceptively misled. You even had me convinced.' He pursed his lips before narrowing his eyes. 'I should have known when I saw the scar.'

'It is nothing.'

'Ooh. You are much more adventurous than I thought, to believe that nothing. I bow to you.' And he did, then left.

Andrew went to the sitting room and met his mother at the staircase.

In one hand she had a crumpled handkerchief in her grasp and a folded newspaper clutched in her other.

'Mother. I would have done everything to prevent this from happening. To prevent you from knowing.'

Her face was white and her mouth thin.

'Well…I could not have ever wished for this to

happen. Never. I saw my sister and she is quite aghast. Quite. She said you have set the family name back a century, totally ignoring all her son Foxworthy has done. I was deeply hurt.' She sighed, and if one could put a caustic edge into such a simple sound she did. 'But I was gracious enough to stay for tea—while she told me how my perfect son had finally erred.'

She waved a hand. 'One little indiscretion by my son and she is quite superior.' She turned her head and made a tsking noise, before she met his gaze. 'But I stayed for tea.'

He saw a look in his mother's eyes—one he'd never seen before. One with hard glitter and which might have been better suited to Beatrice. 'While I was listening to the woe she poured out, Agatha Crump dropped by for a morning call and to tell us about Foxworthy's latest conquest. I think he did not take well to you being in the scandal sheets without him. Agatha brought a copy—' she raised her hand '—of this tawdry little tale.'

She thrust the paper towards Andrew and took a step into the room.

'It says Foxworthy proposed marriage to Lady Wilmont, on bended knee, at the Lamshire soirée at the end of a waltz and right in front of the violinist.' She handed the paper to Andrew and leaned to peer at the caricature. 'He looks quite earnest in the engraving—even though he was probably sotted. But do not believe everything you see. Agatha was there and said Lady Wilmont's husband wasn't really restrained by two men, apparently it took three.' She looked up, face placid. 'I suppose they had to omit the third man because they didn't want to devote much space to it. And I think Foxworthy's size looks quite diminished in the drawing. For you, they devoted a whole page.'

She stepped to the door and glanced over her shoulder at Andrew. 'I suppose I should make sure I do not miss a copy of any scandal sheets in the future. I feel it isn't the last time my family will be mentioned.'

'Mother.' He raised a hand to reassure her. 'I am certain—'

She cut him off. 'Andrew. Do not make promises. And besides, you never know when I might decide to go to Drury Lane. There is also a tiny mention of Lady Riverton's cousin, Tilly, and how she confessed to everyone she had painted that rubbish. But the paper scoffs at that. Everyone knows who really painted it. They are all jealous, Andrew. Jealous.'

'I did not mean—'

Andrew stared. His mother's lips turned up into a smile he'd never seen before. 'And your maid informed me your copies sold much quicker than Foxworthy's—not that we are in any kind of competition. She said by teatime the drawings of you had all been bought and were looking tattered from being passed around. But Foxworthy's were available much longer.' She gave a quick double-blink. 'And his were not tattered.'

She walked out the door, still talking. 'And I really do not wish to delve deeper into it, but the maid has also whispered to me that the servants are indeed proud to work in your household.'

Andrew looked at his desk. The sun had risen. The duke had visited. They had both survived, although it had not been a sure thing.

The world continued on. But he missed the vermilion.

He touched the tip of his forefinger to his thumb, set it against the pen, released it and the object skipped across the desk and on to the floor.

No one ever needed to tidy his desk. Not once had it ever been straightened. He never left anything out of place. Never. He always put each item precisely where it belonged when he finished with it. He could not do otherwise.

The chair had been built precisely to his specifications. He'd taken an old chair and put blocks under the legs until it fit his height exactly, and did the same with a desk. He'd spent hours working, readjusted the blocks many times until the heights of the furniture fit perfectly for him. He could work for hours without strain.

He looked at the paper in front of him. The ink. The drying sand. Pencils. The pens. A miniature of his mother.

The duchess had told his father that if Andrew wished for a castle, he should be allowed to have a small one in the garden, and she had hired a carpenter to work with him when he came home on school holiday and even put the stable boy to work for him. And Beatrice had turned him into a knight, of sorts. At least there was a discarded helmet in the background and some chainmail lying about—with the sword.

He kept seeing Beatrice as he'd seen her last. The crown of brown curls and the blue eyes. And this time, the blue eyes didn't sparkle with laughter, but with unshed tears. And the lips weren't quirked up in laughter, but trembling with apology.

He missed her. The wonder who could not quite manage a silent moment, but saw life as a rainbow of colours, and he would bet his life she didn't own a white dress not splotched with paint.

Standing, he made the trek upstairs.

Unlocking the door, he went into the small room, knowing the space would soon become dust covered if he didn't let a maid into it. He supposed he'd dust the room himself.

The chamber housed the simple furnishings of a servant's quarters and two pieces of art.

He pushed back the window curtain, then turned to the parcel. He unwrapped the painting and put it beside the window. The thing took his breath away. He'd never seen so much of himself all at once even in a mirror.

Beatrice. He could see the reflection of her spirit in the canvas. Then he took a deep breath, and just looked at the painting. The last painting Beatrice had added to the room at the cottage. The place where one could look and see what she really thought.

His father had forgotten the most important thing in his life. His family. He'd let the weight of his fascination for the other woman pull him from what mattered most and he'd died, still clinging to his vision of an imagined life with a woman who did not want him, and left behind a woman who had. It was not the impulsiveness of his nature which had destroyed him, but his inability to see what he had in his own home.

Andrew had placed the *Boadicea* painting with the nude. They belonged together.

He turned to look at Boadicea. If only she'd known not to fight the battle uphill. If she'd only had better help in planning her offensive. A knight by her side. Perhaps history would have worked out differently.

Back in his library, Andrew slid the ink bottle closer, took the ink and dipped the pen. But this time he wasn't working on renovations for a house, or plans to increase his holdings. He took a soft breath and began to draw. He entered the state in which his hand and his mind worked as one, and he didn't think, or really feel, but lived the strokes of the pen inside the lines he drew and life outside sped on, but slowed within him. And the dimmed light of the sun setting roused him to light a lamp, but everyone knew not to ask him to eat, or sleep or move.

He could caricature as well as Gillray. The skill

had nearly caused him to be sent down from university, but he'd been saved by it, too. As punishment, Andrew had been instructed to draw every building on the grounds. He'd not minded. Used it as an excuse to stay in his room when his friends wanted him to follow along on a lark.

When he finished the caricature, he smiled. His chuckle was silent and he stood, shaking his head. This would do well as an engraving.

He left the room. If the sun rose in the morning, he would take that as a sign he had done the right thing.

Chapter Twenty-Two

Beatrice looked up to see Andrew standing at the doorway of her sitting room. Something inside herself changed. The world shifted and she could see nuances of colour again. The shadows which had overwhelmed her blossomed into… into the life that was Andrew. She let her eyes fill with the sight of him.

'Beatrice.' He leaned against the door, rolled newsprint in his hand. He tapped it against the facing. 'I would have asked to be announced, but no one answered my knock.'

Andrew's eyes had a smile behind them and she knew, without asking, she'd been forgiven, at least somewhat.

She let herself admire the wide shoulders. The riding pantaloons hugged the long legs and fit well on his narrow hips. The wide and narrow blended together perfectly. Eyes she could paint a thousand times and never grow tired of.

She rushed forward, staring. His cravat still white, but— 'Andrew. Your waistcoat is grey. Not black.'

He smiled. 'I have decided that I might increase the array of colours in my wardrobe. I ordered three new waistcoats.'

'In all colours?'

He shook his head, brows knit. 'Just grey.'

'I somehow expected you to say red,' she said, 'though I wouldn't have believed it.'

'You outshine even that colour, Beatrice.'

She raised both brows, and put her fingers out, aware of the Prussian blue that had dried on her knuckles.

She took the paper, their fingers touching briefly, and she had to bite the inside of her lip to keep from throwing herself at him. She'd missed him. She'd been alone—alone. And the feeling hadn't been the same as before. With Riverton, she'd never minded. Appreciated the chance to paint. And if she'd needed activity, she'd visited her brother's house, or spoken with her mother. But without Andrew around, the colours of her palette became very flat. Her creativity became forced. Nothing seemed the same.

She hadn't even wanted anyone to notice her, or look at her. She'd realised there was only one person in the world whose notice mattered. Whose opinion mattered. He had wanted to transform her, but he also respected her and cared for her. He had sat at her side during the theatre performance and encouraged her to stare in the faces of those who'd tormented her. When she hadn't altered into someone demure, he'd still returned. He'd not faded away or added his voice to the detractors.

Now he stood in front of her. He'd changed from his black waistcoat to grey.

His life wasn't like Riverton's, but the opposite. His life was more than a puff of smoke and an imagined haze. He'd built a world around himself to stand the test of time. Her brother had told her that Andrew never had anything in his home he did not consider of the best quality.

'What do you think of me?' she asked .

'I saw you in the *Boadicea* painting. Brave and exposed and ready to take on the world. Unafraid. You are a woman who is true. Who traversed her own path and did not fall into her husband's mire, but remained true to her promise to him, even when she did not care if he lived or died. A woman who would fight any usurper to her home. A woman who stayed true to herself.

She unrolled the paper, still smelling of fresh newsprint, and saw the drawing titled *Eden*. Adam stood, prudently covered at the waist by garden foliage and wearing a perfectly tied white cravat, and holding out a fruit to Eve. Eve, a rather curvaceous being—with a paintbrush tucked into curling brown hair and an easel in the background—looked hesitant about taking the heart-shaped fruit.

'It's my drawing, Beatrice,' he said.

Beatrice took the copy, examining it. 'Your Beast is different from the others.'

'I find her an appealing creature with big eyes and rather large fig leaves over the bosom—if you've noticed.'

She laughed, holding the paper close to her chest. 'She still has the tufts at the top of her ears. But you drew me as a much nicer Beast than the other engraver did.'

He nodded. 'My life without my Beast is incredibly dull.'

'Isn't that what you prefer?'

'No.' Again the darkness in his eyes. The face which appeared emotionless, but she knew was not.

She looked again at the drawing. 'If you can forgive me the painting…'

'I can't say I am thrilled with it. It is quite astounding, though.'

'You've seen it?' she asked, eyes wide.

'I now have it. A gift from your mother.'

'You have not destroyed it?'

'Absolutely not.' His eyes narrowed. 'It is art. One could not take a hammer to Michelangelo's *David* and, while I do not care to have this on display for anyone else to see, I could never harm it. It would be hurting you.'

He put his hand to her chin and tilted it up, and his own head down. 'A man should not hide away his feelings though, Bea. Not from himself. Not from the people he cares about. I love you, tufts and all.'

She gurgled a gasp.

'I had made certain I could not get close enough to anyone,' he said, 'so I could not be overwhelmed by passion. But for your passion, I would be a knight. I would fight dragons so that I could be in your presence.' He smiled. 'A few words spread about by tattlers are easy to slap aside when one has Boadicea to love.'

Pressing a light kiss to her lips, he stepped back, indicating the man in the drawing. 'He's offering her his heart and wants her to be his. If he had pockets, he'd have a ring in one to offer her, should she accept his marriage proposal.' He ran a lone finger along the side of her waist and trailed her hip. 'I do believe I have pockets, Beatrice.'

His voice flowed into the room, creating shivers in her body and toasting them.

She breathed him in and could smell his own scent, the woodsy one, and realised it might have a dash of spice in it.

'Andrew, I did not know you could draw so well.'

'I'm actually quite good with oils, too.' His breath touched her lips. 'I can pick up any skill I try rather quickly—given a chance to examine it.'

Her mouth formed an O, then her thoughts just stopped and she looked at him.

He smiled. 'I am quite particular, Beatrice. I do not like to fail at any endeavour.'

Epilogue

Fawsett gave a last flip to the cravat knot and Andrew had allowed two loops, just to please the valet. The waistcoat was grey. The colour seemed to inflame Beatrice in quite the nicest way. Blue, oh, he was saving that colour for later. She'd quite purred in pleasure when he'd informed her of his order. He planned vermilion for their first anniversary, but he would not tell her that.

'I am so pleased you have finally hired your own carpenter and decided to forgo such projects yourself for the time,' Fawsett said. He leaned forward and whispered, 'I have taken the liberty to have *two* bell pulls installed in the mistress's chambers.' He held up a hand and gave a brief imitation of a tug. 'And they're very sensitive— so you've only to tug the smallest amount should anyone need to be bandaged or untied.'

He stepped to the door. 'I want you to have the freedom to have a very adventurous wedding night.' Before his hand touched the knob, he paused. 'And as my wedding gift to you, you'll find an advance copy of *The Memoirs of Sophia Swift* in your bedside table. It's quite enlightening. But she did spell your name wrong.'

Andrew blinked, then shrugged.

Fawsett grinned at Andrew. 'You scoundrel.' He touched a hand to his chest and his eyes watered. 'The other valets are begging me for tales of you.' He reached to the points of his waistcoat hem and gave a sharp pull. 'I have the most envied post in town. I am *the* valet, uppermost in all England.'

'Andrew...' The door opened in a rush, almost knocking Fawsett into the wall.

His mother stood there, hand on the latch, eyes distressed. Handkerchief fluttering in her other hand. 'We have lost Beatrice. Knowing her love for scandal, we fear she's...changed her mind.'

Andrew let out a breath. 'I'll find her. Don't worry.'

Sniffling, the older woman walked away. 'I was hoping for *Beatrice the Beautiful Bride* in the scandal sheets, but now I'm concerned they'll put *The Beast Bolts*.' She turned back to Andrew. 'Bring her over your shoulder if you have to and I'll put my stocking in her mouth and we'll have everyone rounded up and get this thing done before she knows what's happened.'

After his mother had seen the portrait, draped with a loincloth, she'd accepted Beatrice. His mother said she could see Beatrice's love for Andrew in every brush stoke because—while Andrew was handsome—he was not quite the perfection Beatrice had created. But very close, she'd amended, and said no other woman would ever do for him but someone who could see him with such love.

Andrew stepped from the room, walked upstairs and opened the door to the small room. *Boadicea* hung on the wall, but Beatrice stood staring at the companion painting, a brush in her one hand and palette in the other.

'Do not worry yourself about it,' he said, shutting the door.

'I just wanted to make another adjustment on the hands.' She looked at him, giving a tiny shrug before she made a few deft strokes on the oils.

'*After* we are married.' He reached, taking her

arm and turning her towards him. 'But we must be married—today. Now.'

She looked up at him. He saw a smudge of fresh paint on her cheek.

'You mustn't keep using your mouth to hold brushes,' he said. He reached up, first taking his thumb to rub away the smear, then the tips of his other fingers followed to wipe her cheek clean.

He looked into her eyes. 'No second thoughts?'

'Yes,' she muttered. 'I've been working on the hands, but you must let me add the little scar. It is a part of you and I love every inch of you.'

'Fine. After we are married.'

'I never realised it before, but we each have had our share of misadventures—and you are in the Swift book.'

'I checked with the publisher when I heard of the *Memoirs* being published to see what would be printed. Miss Swift must have confused me with someone else. Our encounter did not end with applause. She used her imagination to portray me as someone totally unlike myself, possibly because of the fame of the portrait. Nothing she wrote was the truth. It was much the same as the painting. You used my face and an imagined body. She used my name and made up an imagined encounter. In truth, I left before any of the events she remembers occurred, my trousers still on.'

And he'd been inordinately relieved that she'd not told the real story.

Beatrice looked at him and her eyes twinkled. 'If you say so.'

'Between you and Sophia, no one will ever believe the truth of who I am.' He kissed the spot where he had wiped away the paint. 'But notoriety is not all bad, I admit. I'm getting used to it. So be quick and let's get married.' He slipped the brush from her right hand and the palette from the other, and placed them on an old trunk. 'I suggest we get the ceremony over with so we can move on to our future as a very staid, boring, respectable couple.' He leaned towards her, knowing the words would be lost as soon as he said them. 'Staid. Boring. Respectable.'

Then she reached her arms around his neck and he felt her body press against his, and the huskiness of her voice tingled his body. She growled delightfully. He would never tire of the growl.

The tender kiss they shared let him know he'd truly found the woman of his dreams and he reached around her, pulling her against himself.

'You will have ample time to compare skin tones later, after the guests leave, if you wish.'

'Oh, I will,' purred his little beauty.

Andrew spared a glance for the painting of *Boadicea* on the opposing wall, pleased to have them together. Then he took Beatrice by the hand and they stared into each other's eyes before they walked downstairs to begin their vows.

'Blast,' he heard the duke hiss and he saw the quick, puzzled dart of the vicar's eyes. Someone snickered—Foxworthy. Andrew's mother whispered, 'Hold your tongue. Anybody have any doubts about this marriage taking place?'

'Continue with the vows,' Andrew said and the rest of the ceremony went exactly as planned.

He saved the engraving of their wedding, framed it and put it in the double-locked room with the portrait. They had both stood so prim and proper in front of the vicar, their backs to their friends and family. He'd seen the dress himself, afterward, and he knew the paint daubs in the shape of his handprint on Beatrice's bottom were only slightly embellished.

When he'd shown Beatrice the print, he'd called her Blushing Beloved, and thought her adorable.

He'd reached up, removed the amethyst earring from her ear, nuzzled his nose against the tender lobe. And to bring out the screech of laughing surprise he loved so well, put his lips to her ear—and then he bit her.

* * * * *

MILLS & BOON®

Why shop at millsandboon.co.uk?

Each year, thousands of romance readers find their perfect read at millsandboon.co.uk. That's because we're passionate about bringing you the very best romantic fiction. Here are some of the advantages of shopping at www.millsandboon.co.uk:

* **Get new books first**—you'll be able to buy your favourite books one month before they hit the shops

* **Get exclusive discounts**—you'll also be able to buy our specially created monthly collections, with up to 50% off the RRP

* **Find your favourite authors**—latest news, interviews and new releases for all your favourite authors and series on our website, plus ideas for what to try next

* **Join in**—once you've bought your favourite books, don't forget to register with us to rate, review and join in the discussions

Visit **www.millsandboon.co.uk**
for all this and more today!